Freed by Flame and Storm

Books by Becky Allen

Bound by Blood and Sand
Freed by Flame and Storm

Freed
by
Flame
and
Storm

BECKY ALLEN

Delacorte Press

Text copyright © 2017 by Becky Allen
Jacket title typography © 2017 by Pomme Chan
Jacket photo of girl © 2017 by Morgan Norman-Gallery Stock

Visit us on the Web! randomhouseteens.com

Educators and librarians, for a variety of teaching tools,
visit us at RHTeachersLibrarians.com

Library of Congress Cataloging-in-Publication Data
Names: Allen, Becky, author.
Title: Freed by flame and storm / Becky Allen.
Description: First edition. | New York : Delacorte Press, [2017]
Summary: "Jae, a sixteen-year-old former slave girl, has found magic and broken out of
the curse imposed by the ruling class. To free the rest of her people, she may have to lead
a violent revolution" — Provided by publisher.
Identifiers: LCCN 2016049841 (print) | LCCN 2017023187 (ebook) |
ISBN 978-1-101-93220-9 (el) | ISBN 978-1-101-93218-6 (hc) | ISBN 978-1-101-93219-3 (glb)
Subjects: | CYAC: Slavery—Fiction. | Magic—Fiction. | Social classes—Fiction. | Fantasy.
Classification: LCC PZ7.1.A438 (ebook) | LCC PZ7.1.A438 Fre 2017 (print) |
DDC [Fic]—dc23

The text of this book is set in 12-point Electra.
Interior design by Ken Crossland

Printed in the United States of America
10 9 8 7 6 5 4 3 2 1
First Edition

Random House Children's Books supports the First Amendment
and celebrates the right to read.

For Dad

Thanks for always letting
me steal your books.
(You're not getting them back,
but you can have this one.)

Chapter 1

ERRA STEPPED INTO THE SMALL MEETING CHAMBER WITH HER mind already racing. The room was lantern-lit, with lattice-work over the flames casting strange shadows and making the faces of the four Highest look even more serious. She took a breath and tried to match them, grim for grim, and waited to be told what this was about. Two other Highest heirs had already been in, one at a time, and then dismissed just as quickly. Their expressions had betrayed nothing but bafflement, given no sign at all of why they'd been called here, in front of their parents, or what had happened inside.

Now it was her turn.

The four current Highest were waiting for her, seated on cushions around the low table. Her father, Elthis Danardae, was among them. He wore the same dead-eyed expression he'd had since returning home from one of their remote estates weeks ago with the news that her younger brother, Elan, had died. He hadn't spoken about it much, but she'd learned from others that Elan had had an affair with the lady of the estate, even after Elthis had forbidden it, and the two of them had fled into the desert together. There had been an enormous sandstorm, and there was no way anyone could have survived it.

Elthis hadn't mourned outwardly, given Elan's history of defiance, so Erra hadn't been allowed to, either. But the other three members of the Highest had been celebratory—not over Elan's death, but over the rain that had coincided with Elthis's return, ending the drought that had stretched on for years. As the reservoirs overflowed and people danced in the streets, only the Danardaes hadn't celebrated. Now, though, the other three Highest's faces were just as serious as her father's.

"Don't sit," said Gesra Caenn, the oldest of the four. So Erra didn't, just waited, as Gesra nodded at Tarrir Pallara.

Tarrir stood and made his way to the small fireplace at the back of the room. A flame was burning, but it was so low it was barely more than embers, a soft glow in the small room. "Come here."

Erra stepped forward. All four of them watched her—her father, Gesra, Tarrir, and Callad Kavann, the fourth member of the Highest. It was Callad's heir who'd been in here last, though he wouldn't have that title officially until he took his vows in a matter of only a couple of weeks.

Tarrir reached for the handle of a fire iron, which had

been left with its tip pressed into the coals, but as he lifted it out, Erra realized it *wasn't* a fire iron. It was a brand, one she'd seen plenty of times before. The heated end was shaped into a circle, cut into quarters. Every member of the Highest and the Avowed who followed them had had it pressed to their skin when they'd said their vows—Erra included.

"Take this," Tarrir said, shifting to give her the handle. "And shut your eyes."

Baffled, Erra did as he said. He released it into her hand and she tightened her grip and closed her eyes.

"What do you see?" Gesra asked.

"What?" Erra said, but before anyone could answer, she *saw*. Flames appeared behind her eyelids, as if she were staring into an endless fire that flickered and changed colors. The flames were green one moment, then purple and blue, throwing up sparks that seemed to envelop her. The scent of smoke and blood seeped into the world around her, so thick she had to cough, her eyes flying open.

The vision faded, the smell with it. Everything was exactly as it had been, the four Highest watching her expectantly. Gesra even had a smile on her lined face, a sight Erra had almost never witnessed before.

"Flames," Erra said, staring around wildly. "I saw flames."

"Good. That's what I see, too. Put that back, and have a seat," Gesra said.

Erra did as she was told, her hand trembling, the choking feeling of the smoke still in her throat. She folded down onto the cushion between her father and Lady Callad and tried to catch her breath. Callad gave her an approving nod, but her father's expression was blank. It was as if it had gotten stuck that way. He'd rarely smiled or laughed to begin with, but he'd done neither at all since he'd come home without Elan.

Finally, when no one said anything, Erra said, "I don't understand what just happened."

"It's . . . hard to explain," Tarrir said. "And we normally wouldn't tell you any of it until you were ready to inherit, but our hands have been forced." He paused, glancing at Elthis, who only looked back, wordless and expressionless.

"Is this somehow about Elan?" Erra guessed.

Tarrir nodded. "Your brother broke his vows—a fact that we've gone to great pains to conceal. The world doesn't need to know that one of our own betrayed us."

"He . . . Elan . . ." Erra couldn't even form the question. But . . . "He's alive?"

"He did something none of us would have thought possible," Tarrir said, not quite answering her question. "He awoke magic—real magic, the kind they used in the War. But it's not in his control. The mage is a slave girl. We think the two of them together ended the drought."

"But that's *good*," Erra said, struggling to understand. The drought had been growing worse for years; even though the mighty Well that sustained their world was fueled by magic, it hadn't been able to fight the depth of this drought. The rain, when it came, had been desperately needed. "If Elan did that and survived, then he's a *hero*. And a Closest slave with magic? We can do great things with her."

"No," Gesra said, voice sharp. "There's no way to control her. Because the girl—the Closest girl—she used the magic to free herself. Not one of us has power over her or her magic. Think of the disaster she could bring if she strikes against us."

Oh.

Erra reeled, the implications of that almost too much to take in. The Closest were their slaves, held in bondage by a generations-old Curse that forced them to obey any order they were given. If one of the Closest had escaped the Curse, and had real magic, magic strong enough to end a drought . . .

"She can't be allowed to live," Elthis said, finally speaking. "Elan may be alive, but she took him from us. And she'll take more."

Erra sucked in a breath, trying to hold herself steady under the deluge of information. Elan might be alive. She wanted to sag with relief but didn't dare show so much emotion in front of the Highest. They'd see it as a weakness, but her brother might be *alive*.

But if he lived, he'd committed a crime that couldn't be allowed to stand. The last time Closest had freedom and magic, they'd nearly destroyed the world with it—and they'd nearly succeeded in seizing control of the Well. The Highest had vowed to do anything, including give their lives, if needed, to keep the world at peace. Loyalty to a brother or a son was nothing compared to those vows. If Elan lived, he was a vow-breaker.

"I don't understand," Erra said again. Her brother was so good-natured, eternally smiling, always eager to do his duty. He was occasionally foolish, but he was never malicious. She couldn't imagine him breaking his vows.

"We can stop this mage—and Elan, if he lives. We have to," Gesra said. "And we need you to do it."

"Me?" Erra asked. She looked around the room, her gaze finally settling on her father. For just a moment, she thought she could make out a hint of sorrow in his expression, but then he blinked and it was gone.

Maybe Erra could find and reach out to Elan. The Highest all knew she'd practically raised him. No matter what had happened during his banishment, if she could find Elan, she could make him listen to her, and if he'd broken his vows, she'd find a way to make it right. But instead of suggesting that, Gesra continued, "There's much to explain. And it begins with the brand."

Chapter 2

SOMEONE WAS FOLLOWING THEM.

Jae fell into other-vision even as she continued forward, seeing the world half as it was physically and half from above, lit up with the magical energy of all the elements. It was dizzying, though not actually difficult. The muddy ground still squelched under her feet, clouds still blotted out the late-afternoon sun above, it was just all brighter with magic illumination.

By looking at the magical world, she could see that, yes, several people were following her and Elan, their energies bright and swirling, and getting closer. That couldn't be a coincidence anymore, not since she and Elan had ditched the main road and slipped away to the far side of the nearest farm. This wasn't even a real path, just a muddy track that no one but the Closest used. No one else would be out here without reason, so whoever was behind them, they *weren't* the benevolent traders they were dressed as.

She grabbed Elan's elbow and he jumped a little, then stumbled as he continued forward.

"They're still following," Jae said, voice barely audible even to herself. "We need to get out of sight."

Elan nodded, but their choices were limited. Though the land had been growing greener and more cultivated over the last few days of travel, their attempt to lose their pursuers had already taken them out to the edge of the fields. Beyond them on one side was a muddy wasteland, and beyond that, the world gave way to dunes. If they got that far without being caught, it would provide some cover, but not much.

On the other side was the fields. The one they were hurrying past now was flax, with its pale blue flowers and delicate stalks. They weren't the tallest crop in the world, but it would have to do. She jerked around toward it.

"All right—but stay low. There will be an Avowed overseer somewhere, and we can't afford any questions," Elan agreed.

Jae nodded and split from the path, pushing her way into the flax stalks. They were slender and gave way easily, and once she was past the first few, she dropped to her hands and knees. The ground was muddy and within moments she was fully coated in it. It pulled her robe down and squished under her hands as she crawled. Elan grumbled faintly, but even he didn't bother to complain too much anymore.

She shifted her pack a little to make moving forward easier and kept going. There were paths beaten out here, too, where the Closest who tended the fields walked. When she finally tumbled onto one, she stayed low, just as Elan had said, and followed it away from the road.

It wouldn't be hard for pursuers to guess where they'd gone. In their haste, they'd left quite a trail. She glanced back at it and winced. But it was fixable.

Elan caught up to her, gave her a questioning look. She didn't speak out loud, though, just fixed her other-vision gaze on the field they'd trampled. She focused and reached for the energy of the water within the plants, and reshaped it, straightening what they'd knocked askew. Then she reached for the earth within the mud where they'd left hand and knee prints. That was even easier to fix. Earth was the easiest element for Jae to work with, and it only took a moment before the signs of their passing were erased.

"Smart," Elan said.

In other-vision, she saw that their pursuers hadn't left the dirt path. Even though that was a relief, she still held her finger to her lips—there were Closest in the field who might hear, and at least one Avowed watching them. He gave a tense nod. He wasn't as good at communicating silently as she was—after all, she'd been raised one of the quiet Closest, and he hadn't—but he could manage it when he needed to.

Once again, they stayed low as they continued down the muddy path. It was only a few minutes later that they reached the first of the Closest. He was short, with white hair and brown skin that was much lighter than Jae's own, and he did a double take as he saw them—but didn't miss a single stroke with his sickle, cutting down the handful of flax he'd gathered.

He kept working but also kept glancing at them. Jae held up one hand for him to see, then closed her open fingers into a fist. It was one of the most basic Closest signs: the Avowed were too near for them to speak. In other words, danger.

He nodded, and jerked his head just slightly in the direction they were heading. Jae looked up but couldn't see anything. Daring, she mouthed, "Avowed?"

The man gave a terse nod.

Elan inclined his head toward the next section of uncut stalks. With the Avowed supervisor somewhere nearby, they couldn't risk staying on the path. Now they moved more slowly, damaging as few of the plants as possible. Jae tried to right them even as they moved, and finally fell into the rhythm of it: crawl several body-lengths forward, pause to check that they were safe, repair the damage they'd done to the plants, and then move forward again.

Elan hissed a warning and grabbed her ankle. She jerked away, surprised, then went statue-still. Another Closest loomed nearby, not having noticed them yet—and beyond him, just at the edge of their vision, was the Avowed supervisor. He wore a bright blue robe and a sneer of disdain, visible as he gazed around.

Slowly, so slowly they barely moved at all, she and Elan flattened against the mud and crept backward. The stalks around them rippled, so Jae summoned a breeze to make it look more natural. The energy of the air didn't come as easily as water and earth did, and it buzzed in a way that made her feel like she'd swallowed a bee, but it was worth it for the tiny amount of cover the gusts provided.

They hadn't made it far yet when the Closest man saw them. He did a double take, eyes wide, but was midmotion with his sickle. He must have lost focus, because a moment later his lips parted in a silent, pained gasp. Blood soaked his robe, his sickle's blade having caught his thigh. But he didn't cry out—he couldn't. The Curse didn't allow Closest to speak, let alone shout, in front of the Avowed. He couldn't reveal their existence to the Avowed man, even if he wanted to.

But as he limped forward, still working, he also still bled, and that was their fault.

Elan wormed his way up until he was even with Jae, a thin line of stalks separating them. He shot her a questioning look—and then his features contorted with anger as he understood what Jae had immediately. The man couldn't stop working any more than he could shout. With as much rain and flooding as there had been in the last few weeks, crops had begun to rot and spoil. He'd probably been ordered to keep going until the Avowed supervisor said he was done for the day, and it didn't matter how much pain he was in.

Sure enough, he kept at it, though he limped as he made progress, and the bloody spot on his robe and pant leg beneath grew darker and larger. He stole glances at them, and Jae again made the sign for danger. He didn't respond, and his movements grew slower. He dragged his leg with every step, leaving bloody footprints between cut stalks. Jae only knew a little about injuries, but with as much blood as he was losing, the cut had to be deep. She could only imagine how much it hurt. She clenched her jaw against her anger—at the

Avowed, for not realizing or caring that their orders would force an injured man to keep working; at their pursuers, for driving them into hiding like this; and at herself, for startling the man she now didn't dare help.

She didn't even know *how* she'd help him, with the Curse still compelling the man to work, but it didn't matter. They couldn't chance attracting the Avowed overseer's attention. If they did, they'd have to fight, and Jae would have to use magic to escape. That would bring the Highest's wrath down on these Closest, and all of them here would suffer, maybe even be killed. Not just the one man who was limping away from them.

The sun inched forward in the sky as they waited. Elan occasionally shifted next to her, sending the delicate flax stalks waving, but Jae was still as stone.

Her legs were beginning to tingle from the lack of movement when the Closest worker *did* finally make a noise, the slightest groan, and he dropped unconscious. From the sun, or from blood loss, or a deadly combination of both—she had no idea. But the Avowed supervisor swooped into her field of vision.

She braced herself, reaching for the earth's energy, just in case. If he saw them . . .

But he just looked at the fallen Closest, muttered, "Cursed clumsy idiot," and walked off again.

"He'll send someone to help," Elan said, leaning as close to her as possible, keeping his voice as soft as the wind. "He has to."

Jae shook her head. He didn't have to—no one but the Highest could make the Avowed do anything, and the

Avowed didn't care about the Closest at all. If that man died, the only thing the Avowed would mourn would be his ability to work the fields—and even then he'd just insist the rest of the Closest cover more ground to make up for it.

It was maddening to lie there in silence, the unconscious man so nearby but still beyond their help. The longer they lay trapped, the more Jae found herself thinking that *Tal* would have helped. Her brother would have found a way, even if being caught would have risked his life. But Tal was dead. He'd given his life to save the Closest from the drought and to give Jae a chance to free them all, so now Jae couldn't risk getting caught if she wanted to honor what he died for. If the Highest found her before she could break the Curse, it was all for nothing.

Finally the sun started to sink. The supervisor hadn't returned, and Jae couldn't stand it anymore. Hoping dusk was enough of a cover, she rose to her hands and knees, her limbs protesting at the sudden movement, said, "Keep watch," and crawled forward. Elan followed her slowly.

She reached the man and found him still breathing, but the pool of blood around him was thick and it was possible he wouldn't ever wake again. She pulled his robe open, and then the material of his pants.

The wound was as deep as she'd feared. She didn't have any bandages, but she pulled her canteen and an old shirt from her bag. She poured water onto the man's leg, used the shirt to pat the blood away and try to clean out the dirt and mud, then flipped the shirt over and pressed the other side against the wound itself.

Elan let out a ragged breath and held out a small jar to

her. "Here. Shirrad gave it to me before we left. She didn't have much, but . . ." He hesitated. "It's a salve for wounds, to stop infections. She thought we could sell it if we needed money, but I thought we might need it."

Jae nodded, not bothering with words, and twisted it open. She peeled her shirt off the man's legs and spread the salve over it, then pressed the shirt back in place. It was hard to tell, but within a few minutes she thought the bleeding had slowed down, maybe even stopped.

The Avowed supervisor yelled something in the distance, and the Closest straightened up from wherever they were in the fields. They started to walk off, hauling what they'd cut with them. Luckily, only one saw them as they walked by—the same man who'd seen them in the first place. His gaze cut over to them.

Jae gestured at him to keep moving. He frowned but probably had no choice in the matter anyway.

The sky grew darker, and the field grew still. As stars started to come out overhead, Jae decided it was as safe as it was likely to get—hopefully the Avowed had left for the night and they could get the man to safety. She couldn't stand the thought of leaving him when they'd been the ones who'd distracted him. "Let's get him to the enclave. Maybe they can help him more there."

"I'll carry him," Elan said. He was very, very careful as he picked the man up. The man moaned a little but didn't wake. Elan had to straighten up all the way to carry him, cradling him carefully so he didn't jostle the man's leg any more than necessary, but no one else was still waiting around.

Jae kept alert but didn't see the Avowed or any signs of

the fake traders who'd chased them off the path as she led the way toward the Closest's enclave—the gathering of low, stone buildings where they all lived. It was still a little odd to her. She'd grown up in an estate house, constantly anxious about keeping out of the way of her Avowed masters, but most Closest lived like this. Their houses all held several families who lived and dined together, and for the most part, when they weren't working, they were left alone. Doubtless with orders that kept them from running off, or doing anything else the Avowed wouldn't approve of—but unless there was some kind of crisis, no Avowed would ever come to the enclave to bother them. The Avowed considered the whole place dirty and beneath them. It was nothing like freedom, but in its way, it was closer than anything Jae had known.

More Closest noticed them as they drew near, going still, giving them wary looks. She and Elan didn't look at all like Avowed, who always cloaked themselves in splendor, but they also didn't look like Closest—and no Closest would ever trust a stranger.

Jae held up her hand again, this time making the opposite gesture, opening her fist to a wide palm. The signal that meant it was safe to talk. Even so, no one spoke a word. She glanced at Elan, who still held the unconscious man, and kept going forward.

Finally one of the Closest walked toward them—the one who'd seen them in the field. He stopped a good way away, though, sizing them up.

"He injured himself in the field," Jae said, answering the unspoken question. "We saw but couldn't help, not until it was safe."

"We treated the wound with salve," Elan added.

The man frowned, but finally said, "This way."

He led them into one of the houses, and a few other people trailed, curious, now that it was clear they *weren't* Avowed. The house was long, with only a few rooms sectioned off within, and large, gaping windows. The ground inside was dirt—mud, really, especially by the windows—covered in some places with old, stained rugs. There was a cooking area near the center of the main room, where two women were tending a fire in a low stone pit, the smoke wending its way out an opening in the ceiling. Both women jumped up, startled.

Elan laid the man carefully on one of the rugs. "The bleeding stopped, but he did lose quite a bit of blood before we were able to help him. I don't know if we were in time. . . ."

One of the women all but ran to them, crouched next to the man, pressed her hand against his cheek, then stared up at them. "Thank you."

"I'm sorry we couldn't do more," Elan said, and then, with a glance at Jae, added, "I know we're strangers, but I promise we're friends. We aren't Avowed, and we won't ask you any questions. When we leave, we'll be careful that no Avowed see us. You won't be asked about us, I swear it."

The woman let out a large breath. "Thank you. My name is Salla. This is my husband, Badann." She stroked the unconscious man's cheek.

"I'm Elan," he said. "This is Jae."

"We don't have strangers here often—ever," the older man said. "I'd like to know what you're doing here."

Jae hesitated and looked at Elan, and he shrugged a tiny bit. The chances were that no Avowed would ever know they'd been here, so it was safe enough to say. Besides, a part of Jae was still fiercely joyful about this, what she was about to tell them.

"My name is Jae," she repeated. "We're here because . . . I was born Closest, like all of you." That earned her shocked looks, and she nodded, acknowledging them. "But now I'm free."

"Impossible," Salla said.

"Not quite. Watch."

Jae held out her right hand, palm open and up. She shut her eyes for a moment, focused fully on other-vision. It was easier to do when she was surrounded by Closest and could feel the binding that tied all their bloodlines together. She grasped the beautiful shimmering energies and crafted what she wanted in her mind. Then she pushed the energy out, filling the space in her hand with it, shaping what she wanted. She heard the gasp, and opened her eyes.

A beautiful purple flower sat in her palm, grown from thin air. Jae offered it to Salla, who took it, hand trembling, eyes wide.

"I'm a mage," Jae said. "I was born cursed, but I freed myself once I found my power. And I'm going to free us all."

Everyone in the house except Elan stared at her, silent and awed, but before anyone could work up the courage to ask more, there was a clamor outside. Another woman, this one almost as young as Jae herself, skidded in and gasped, "Outsiders. Looking for someone. They—" She broke off, saw Elan and Jae, and stared. "Oh, *no*."

Chapter 3

JAE GLANCED FROM THE FRANTIC NEWCOMER TO ELAN, BUT before she could figure out what to do, a shrill female voice yelled, "All Closest outside—*now! Right now!*" Jae winced as everyone but her and Elan suddenly jerked into motion, compelled, which meant it was an Avowed yelling. Which meant trouble for everyone.

The older man and Salla worked together to pick up the still-unconscious Badann. *All Closest* hadn't meant every Closest who was awake, who could walk, but as they dragged Badann toward the door, Salla said, "Hide, Lady Mage, or run."

Jae swallowed. She understood why Salla urged her to go. There wasn't a Closest alive who wouldn't risk their life for a chance at freedom from the Curse—Jae had taken plenty of risks, and sacrificed so much. But it was bad enough that she'd had to wait so long to help Badann when he'd fallen. Any Avowed who were looking for her and Elan wouldn't care what they did to Closest who'd seen them. Once the Avowed found out they'd been here, they might kill the whole enclave, or at least everyone in this house. Jae didn't know what would happen, but she couldn't leave the Closest to that.

"We can't go," she told Elan.

"I know," he said, despite the fact that if he was caught by the Avowed, he'd be killed right along with her. They were terrified of her, but he was a traitor—if any of them knew what he'd done, they'd despise him the way even his own father did.

Yet he didn't run. He followed Jae as she straightened her spine, kept her head up, and walked out into the lane between Closest dwellings.

There, outsiders were easy to tell from the Closest: while Closest were barefoot, their robes faded under muddy patches, fraying at every seam, the outsiders were in the same fake tradesman garb they'd had on earlier. They had colorful robes, jewelry around their necks and wrists. But they were also all armed, brandishing blades.

The Closest outside were perfectly still. Even so, Jae could tell they were terrified.

"You aren't looking for these people," Jae said, pushing past Salla. "You're looking for me."

"Yes," one of the outsiders said. A woman whose voice was too deep to have been the one who had summoned all the Closest. "And him. Good evening, Lord Elan."

"I'm no lord anymore," Elan said, stepping up even with Jae.

"You, Closest, come here," one of the other outsiders said, and *this* was the Avowed who'd shouted. She pointed at Salla, gestured her forward. Salla had no choice but to obey, walking toward the Avowed as if dragged by an invisible rope.

"Leave her alone," Jae said. "Leave them *all* alone."

The first woman glanced over at her companion and said, "Leave her be. We don't want any trouble." She looked back at Jae. "We truly don't, Lady Mage. If you'll come with us, we'll leave here, and no one needs to be harmed."

Jae hesitated, even as she gathered as much magical energy as she could. It would be easy to get rid of these people — to create an earthquake that would knock them off their feet, to open a chasm to swallow them. Except that any magic that enormous would draw further attention, bring even more Avowed in to investigate. But a single order from the Avowed woman could hurt all of the gathered Closest. Jae couldn't think of a single non-magic way to protect them.

"We aren't your enemies, Lady Mage," the woman said, stepping forward slowly. She paused a few feet from Jae, then pushed her robe and shirtsleeve up her arm, revealing a tattoo.

Jae gaped, recognizing the symbol immediately: four circles, all overlapping in the center. It represented the four elements, an ancient symbol mages had used in much of their artwork.

"In fact, we've been trying to find you before your enemies can. They're searching for you everywhere. But we want to help you. We do," the woman continued.

"I don't believe you," Elan said.

The woman regarded him coolly, and Jae regarded her right back. It was hard to tell how old she was, but certainly older than Jae, with wrinkles on her face from frowning. Her hair was thick, pulled into locs that were starting to gray, but she looked strong and solid, and she was armed. Jae suspected she was extremely skilled with the blade she had at her side.

Finally the older woman pointed at the younger and said, "Push down your hood."

The Avowed woman hesitated, then did so, giving them a clear look at her features. She was young, but before Jae could take in more than that, Elan gasped.

"Palma?"

The woman dipped her head, nodding. "Elan. I . . . didn't expect to see you again."

Jae turned to stare at him, but his wide-eyed shock was fixed on the woman. Someone he *knew*.

"Turning me in won't get you back on my father's good side," Elan said, but his voice was shaking a little. "Nothing can do that."

"I know," the woman said, sour. "If I could get back on your father's good side, I wouldn't be *here*. But I am."

"Enough," the other woman said. "We aren't your enemies, Elan, Lady Mage. In fact, we all want the same thing. I'm just asking you to hear us out."

"And what's that?" Jae asked, letting the question fall blunt and direct between them. "What is it that you think we want?"

The woman slowly looked around, first at Jae and Elan, and then at the gathered, terrified Closest. "You want to topple the Highest's rule. So do I. And if we join forces, we just might be able to do it."

At her side, Elan frowned, but he didn't say anything. She almost wished he would—he knew one of these strangers, and he knew much more about the world of the Avowed than she did. But Jae was the mage, and the one these people were looking for. It was her decision.

She didn't trust the woman who seemed to be in charge, and she trusted the Avowed woman with her even less—no Avowed would ever defy the Highest. Even Elan had needed to hear from his father himself that the Highest were liars and murderers before he'd been willing to give up his title. But Jae didn't want to see any harm come to these Closest, either, and listening had one advantage. "Fine. I'll listen. But not here. Not where you can hurt anyone."

"Of course, Lady Mage. Come with us—that's perfect. We'll leave this place behind, and no one will know we were here. Everyone will be safe."

"They'd better be," Jae said. "Because if I find out that you've harmed anyone . . ."

She trailed off, letting the woman imagine what would happen. The woman nodded quickly, gestured her people away, and hurried back between buildings, toward the same muddy path Jae and Elan had been following earlier. Jae followed, tense, and some of the outsiders circled around her and Elan. Palma, the Avowed woman, walked especially close, and Elan kept stealing glances at her. As they left the Closest enclave behind Jae could only hope Badann would recover, but at least getting this threat away from the enclave would protect Salla and the others.

Eventually they came to a group of horses and wagons. The woman in charge dispatched someone to dig a set of clean robes out of a pack on the wagon. "We'll be traveling into a town, and you look like . . ."

"We've been avoiding towns," Elan said.

"I know, it's a risk," the woman agreed. "But the people looking for you are looking for the *two* of you—not a group— and they *know* you're avoiding towns, so more people are watching for you in fields and farms. The closer to the central cities you get, the safer you are."

Elan still looked skeptical, but Jae accepted the clean robe in place of her own. At least she was able to keep her own boots. She preferred to go barefoot, as she had her whole life until recently, but that simply wasn't practical for traveling— and she'd discovered that breaking in boots was painful.

The woman ushered them up onto one of the carts, sat with them, and motioned everyone else to get going. Palma and the others mounted horses, and one of them got the horses attached to the cart moving, too. Jae's stomach lurched but settled after a moment. She'd never traveled like this before.

"My name is Lenni Talmotta," the woman said at last. "And these people—everyone here—is part of my group, and sworn to end the Highest's rule. We are called the Order of the Elements."

"Palma is Avowed," Elan said. "That's vow breaking. She wouldn't . . ."

"It's only *really* vow breaking if she gets caught," Lenni said. "We're very careful. Most of us are Twill, but she isn't the only Avowed."

Twill were the caste between Avowed and Closest—they

weren't cursed by the Highest but weren't favored by them, either.

"The Order is actually quite ancient," Lenni continued. "We are older than the Highest, older than the Closest. We are older than the Well itself, our members forming an unbroken chain back through history. Here. Look at this, but be careful with it."

She'd pulled something from one of the cart's packs and handed it to Elan. It was a sheaf of papers, ancient and brittle and yellowed, but Jae couldn't read the lines scribbled on them. No one would ever bother to teach a Closest how to read.

Elan could, though, and after a moment he stared up at Lenni. "This is about magecraft!"

"Yes, it is," Lenni said. "We've been keeping it, and many other texts, safe for generations."

Elan shuffled to another page, then another, and stopped. "I've seen writing like this before, but I can't read it."

"I can," Lenni said. "Somewhere in there is a key—to help translate the mage script to something legible. There's another script, too, unfortunately, but it's ancient. From before the time of the Well's founding. If we ever had a key to read it, that was lost long ago."

Elan set the sheaf of papers down in his lap, keeping them safe from the wind as the cart continued to rattle its way down the path, heading toward the main road. "How do you have all this?"

"I told you, the Order is very, very old. Back before the War, it was a group of teachers and historians. It kept records, wrote books on magic . . . there was so much information back then, but it's gone now. All we have left are a few pieces and what knowledge was passed down, person to person. We try to find and teach as many mages as we can, but—"

"There are no other mages," Jae said.

The woman shook her head. "You're incorrect about that, Lady Mage. They're rare. Most of them aren't very powerful, but there are a few in every generation, and I know of one now, other than you. You see, it's . . . well. The Highest did *something*, generations ago, to keep themselves and their Avowed from having any kind of mage power. And the Curse seems to be a fetter for the Closest's power, because there haven't been any Closest mages since the War. Except you, of course."

"Of course," Jae repeated. Lenni wasn't quite right, but she was close. One of the Closest had sealed their power away so the Highest wouldn't gain control of it.

"The Order didn't fight in the War, but I think they were wrong not to get involved. Back then, everyone knew that the Closest crafted the Well. It was theirs by right, and they shared its water with anyone who needed it. Until the Highest tried to seize it."

Jae gasped, and even Elan looked shocked. Lenni knew the *truth*. And from the way she smiled at their reaction, she knew *they* knew it, too.

"After they won, the Highest consolidated their power. They cast the Curse, enslaved their enemies," Lenni continued. "They wouldn't let anyone threaten their power. But the Order's mages *were* a threat."

"Naturally," Elan said. "If they ever did decide to get

involved, they could start another war. The Highest would never let a threat like that go, but . . ."

"And they didn't." Lenni's expression went grim. "There used to be Twill mages, too—a lot of them, actually, before and right after the War. The Order ran magic schools that trained them. Most of its people were found at one of them or another. One night, with no warning, the Highest attacked. In that one night, nearly every member of the Order was killed and much of their knowledge lost—their books, all their records, torched. So no one would find them and learn the truth.

"Those who escaped had to hide, and had to pass down their knowledge in secret. To this day, the Highest know they're out there, and any mage they find, they slaughter."

"You're not a mage, though," Jae said.

"No, but my mother was, and I . . ." She shook her head. "I grew up knowing about the Order, and that there were only a few of us left. So I've been growing it, reaching beyond mages to find more people who are frustrated by the Highest's rule. We have spies, and plans, and we've been preparing for years. Now, with your magic to help us, Lady Mage, we can end this once and for all. End the Highest's rule, and help you break the Curse. If you'll just work with us."

Jae leaned back in the cart, staring at Lenni. Lenni wasn't frowning now, but she looked intense, almost desperate, and she knew the truth. She knew mages, knew about magic, and she knew *history*. Jae and Elan had been on their own, but Lenni had allies and resources and plans. And they wanted the same thing.

Jae caught Lenni's eye and nodded. "I will."

Chapter 4

ELAN INHALED THE SCENT OF COOKED LAMB, RELAXED ON the cushion, and felt a little guilty at enjoying the luxury. Being in a real household again after so long was such a relief. He and Jae had been traveling for weeks—longer, if he counted their trek through the desert—and they'd spent the whole time creeping around, usually camping on the ground. He'd tried not to complain, but it hadn't been a comfortable trip.

They'd traveled for two days, heading toward the central cities with Lenni and her group, and had finally reached the town where Palma lived, now that she'd moved out of Danardae.

"I'm sure this is nothing near what you're used to, Highest,"

Palma said, after handing Elan a plate. She'd told her few servants that she'd take care of the guests herself and banished them to elsewhere in the house or out on errands.

"Elan," he corrected. "I have no title anymore, and this . . . this smells wonderful."

Palma smiled at him.

"I don't understand how you could be involved with the Order without breaking your vows," Jae said.

It took Palma a moment to unravel. Jae almost never came out and asked questions—Elan was used to it, but it was a strange way of speaking.

"Well, it's . . . I . . ." Palma trailed off.

"It's a delicate matter." Lenni strode into the room where they were eating and took up the last cushion. She'd sent the other members of the Order away, too, back to their regular lives. Most of them were Twill, who couldn't afford to vanish from their work for very long or they'd be noticed. "We're careful. Only a very few Avowed know of us, and we certainly wouldn't let just anyone join."

Lenni set a thick stack of papers down on the table, then helped herself to some of the meal.

"But if the Highest discover you, you'll be declared a vowbreaker," Jae said.

Palma gave a tiny, nervous shrug. "It's a messy business, but . . . but the Highest took what was *mine*. My estate, my home! As if it were nothing."

Ah. Elan set his meal aside, guilt gnawing at him, and explained, "Palma's estate, Lanadann, was abandoned before your home was, Jae. All the Avowed were sent elsewhere, given other duties, and . . . they weren't all pleased about it. And when I asked about it . . ."

"You were banished to Aredann, and your cursed sister had me kicked out of Danardae and sent me *here*," Palma said, gesturing around. "I never even got to say goodbye to you. Never got to thank you for . . . for *trying*."

Jae didn't look terribly impressed by her plight.

Palma turned to Jae. "No one else cared about Lanadann at all, and now it's nothing. You can't imagine what that's like."

Jae snorted. Elan said gently, "Actually, she can. Aredann was abandoned, too, and Jae . . . she gave up everything to save the Closest who were still trapped there."

"Oh," Palma said. She examined Jae for the first time.

"I'm sure if it came down to it, Palma *would* defy the Highest," Elan continued, now to Jae. "She questioned them even before I did."

He shot Palma a quick smile and she ducked her head a little, but he could see her smiling, too—an expression that had once made his heart race. With her hazel eyes and hair in long twists that fell past her shoulders, she was one of the most beautiful women Elan had ever seen.

He'd barely thought of her at all after arriving at Aredann, though. The infatuation had faded once he'd been away from her—for all her smile was still beautiful, he didn't feel much of anything at it.

Jae glanced back and forth between him and Palma for a moment, raising her eyebrows just slightly, but didn't ask any questions. She didn't say anything at all, actually, just waited.

It was almost unnerving how good she was at waiting silently for someone to speak.

"Then ... then your father told his Avowed you were dead," Palma finally continued. "I couldn't ..." She took a breath; her voice steadied. "Then Lenni told me the rumors. That it was all false and you were disavowed. I was so relieved. And I'm happy for you to stay here as long as you'd like—both of you, of course."

"Thank you," Elan said.

"We won't be long," Jae said, and took a mouthful of lamb. At Lenni's surprised glance, she said, "We have to reach the central cities. In secret."

"We can help with that," Lenni said. "We'll help you with anything you need."

Jae nodded a little and didn't volunteer more information. Elan wondered if she didn't trust Lenni fully enough to tell her their plan, or if she just didn't realize Lenni wanted to know. Jae wasn't used to dealing with people who weren't Closest yet. The Closest were always honest—they had no choice; the Curse forced them to tell the truth—and so they were straightforward about everything except asking questions. Jae herself was blunt to a fault and often missed the nuances of what people said to her.

Lenni cleared her throat. "Well, here are the rest of the texts that I have on hand, Elan. And here"—she slid the page from the top of the pile—"is the key."

Elan accepted the paper, a brittle page with the alphabet he knew written along one line, and a series of symbols and letters he didn't know underneath it. They felt a little familiar; he'd seen pages full of them before, but he hadn't been able to read any of it. Now he would, though it would be slow going until reading this new script became instinct.

"Thank you," he said, and paged through the rest of the papers—carefully. Some seemed so old they might crumble if he handled them too roughly. Those were the ones with the ancient script Lenni had described. Something about it seemed familiar, just a little, but he couldn't quite place it and he certainly couldn't read it.

"The central cities," Lenni said, as Elan pushed the papers far enough away to eat without risking dripping anything on them. "What is it you need from them?"

Jae glanced up from her food, irritated, and Elan jumped in quickly. "It's actually considered very rude to ask direct questions of a Closest. Because of the compulsion to answer."

"Ah. Forgive me," Lenni said, bowing her head a little. "I didn't know."

"It's fine," Jae said, and then after another moment, she continued, "There's a knife. The Curse is bound to it, so to break the Curse, it must be destroyed. We don't know where it is, but Elan thinks it must be in the central cities."

"I can get you all in," Palma said, voice going high, almost a question. "If . . . I mean, Lord Nallis Kavann, his vow ceremony is in only a week or so. I'm going to attend—all Avowed are invited, even those of us who are out of favor. It wouldn't be out of place for me to bring a few servants with me. And with so many people traveling into the cities for the ceremony, they won't have time to really, thoroughly check everyone."

"That's a good idea," Lenni conceded, and Palma looked relieved at the affirmation.

"I don't know what this vow ceremony is," Jae said.

"Oh," Elan said, surprised. The vows were so ubiquitous that it had never occurred to him that *anyone* might not know about them. But it made sense that a Closest from somewhere as remote as Aredann wouldn't, now that he thought about it. "All Avowed come to the central cities to pledge their loyalty to the Highest when they turn thirteen. There are small ceremonies every other week or so, usually just the new Avowed and their families and the Highest, but when one of the Highest's heirs is ready to pledge, it's a true celebration. Everyone who can travels to the cities to celebrate—all the Avowed possible, and even plenty of Twill. Especially artists. There are buyers for everything."

"And the ceremony itself is more elaborate, too," Palma said. "I remember your sister's. It isn't held in the house, it's in that . . . that pavilion."

For Jae's benefit, he explained, "The four central reservoirs all come together, and there's an island in the middle. There's a pavilion built on it, where the Highest themselves take their vows, and when they do . . ."

He trailed off, stricken, as the pieces all came together in his mind.

"Elan?" Palma asked.

"The Avowed are branded when they pledge their loyalty," Elan said.

"I know that. Shirrad had one, and yours . . ."

Elan raised a hand to his chest, fingers seeking the remnants of the burn under his shirt. When he'd broken his vows, his brand had turned red and raw, once again a fresh burn. "The Highest all take the brand, too, but then there's another step. They take further vows—vows of responsibility to the Well—and then, Jae, they trace the brand with a knife."

"You think that . . ." Jae trailed off, prompting him, still not quite asking a question.

"I don't know," he said, then added, "Yes. It must be, it's . . . I saw the knife when Erra took her vows. I've never seen anything like it before. It's some kind of black stone, not like anything else I can think of."

Jae sucked in a breath. "The knife I saw in my visions was made of black stone."

"I've never seen it anywhere else," Elan said. "I don't know where they kept it, but I *do* know it's ceremonial, some kind of . . . of artifact, from before the Well. All the Highest swear on it, from all four families. It must be the knife from your vision. It *must* be."

"Then we don't need to know where they keep it," Lenni said. "We just need to have eyes on it at the ceremony, and then follow it when the ceremony ends. We'll seize it as quickly as possible. But this means we have to get to the cities, fast. We have to be there before the ceremony, and have as many people ready to follow as possible. We can't afford to lose track of it."

"I'm ready to go now," Jae said.

Elan glanced at the window. It was evening, but it wasn't as if they hadn't traveled through plenty of nights. Still, Lenni said, "In the morning. Palma, prepare what you need to travel. I'll start spreading word among the Closest. If we do it right, so none of the Avowed notice, they can prepare themselves. When the moment comes . . ."

Jae nodded. "They will take up arms."

"And their chances will be much better if they've had time to plan and prepare," Lenni said. "I don't have enough followers to send word to every estate, and we need people in the cities if we're going to find that knife. But I'll do what I can."

"Thank you," Jae said.

Elan's gut twisted and he found he wasn't hungry any longer. There hadn't been war, no more than an occasional skirmish, in generations, not since the Curse had been cast. He couldn't imagine what it would be like, or how many people would be injured or killed. The newly freed Closest would have an advantage in numbers—they far outnumbered the Avowed and Highest—but no training or organization. Or even weapons. The skilled, armed Avowed would be able to tear through them easily.

But the Closest would have Jae on their side. Elan had already seen her cause a massive earthquake and stop a sandstorm at the peak of its rage. She would defend her people, giving them an advantage. But she wouldn't be able to prevent the fighting.

The clash, when it came, would be brutal.

Maybe once they were in the cities he could get a message to Erra. Their father listened to her, at least sometimes. Certainly more than he listened to Elan. Elan didn't know how she'd feel about him, now that he'd broken his vows, but he couldn't imagine her turning him away—or worse, turning him in. If he could talk to her, convince her of the havoc that would happen in a war and bring her to their side, maybe the whole thing could be averted.

Maybe.

Elan reached over to brush a hand against Jae's elbow. She glanced at him, and he didn't know how to give her strength, but she squared her shoulders.

"Once we get to the cities, I want to contact my sister," Elan said.

"What?" Lenni shook her head. "That's a terrible—"

"She'll listen to me," Elan said.

"Yes, and tell your father everything you say," Lenni said. "Which means he'll know we're there. The longer we can keep that secret, the better. If the Highest have warning, they'll hide the knife—or lay a trap."

"Erra wouldn't do that," Elan said. "She'll listen to me."

"You think she'd break her vows for you?" Lenni asked.

Elan hesitated, mouth open to say yes, but then he shut it instead and didn't answer.

Lenni rose from the table as if his nonanswer settled things, and Palma followed her. He didn't argue, but he was still turning it over in his mind. Erra would *want* to listen to him, he was sure of that, but now he was a vow-breaker—she wouldn't trust him, not after that. But she *would* want the best for her people, so maybe she'd still listen to him, maybe he could make her see reason. . . .

Jae glanced at Elan, then said in that barely audible murmur of hers, "I'll destroy it as soon as I have it in my hands— once we take it, the Highest will know what we're doing.

They'll do anything to stop us. But that means the Closest won't have much time to prepare."

"True," he said, and he could understand her concern. "But they'll be free."

The line of worry didn't ease from her forehead, but she nodded. "That's the most important thing. More important than anything."

Chapter 5

Erra paced, restless, and the brand tangled with her robe. She'd belted it to her waist, almost like a blade. It tangled *less* that way, she'd found, especially since she was in trousers instead of a dress for this muddy excursion. But it was still an ever-present annoyance, and she hated having to grab it even just to untangle it from her clothes. When she touched it for a few moments, she saw the world of flame and smoke unfurl around her, and she had to fight not to flinch and yank her hand away. Especially since no one else knew why she carried it with her.

Gesra had warned her to keep it as close as possible—it had been Gesra's duty within her generation. But she was too old to face a potential battle now, though frankly, Erra thought she was still plenty fierce. There was nothing soft about that woman, even if she was a little stooped from age.

Erra regarded the reservoir in front of her and the work that was being done, building a bridge across to the center island. There were only a few days left to get it done—they had to be able to reach the island for Nallis Kavann's vow ceremony, a scant few days away. It should have been done already, but things kept going wrong—ropes that might have frayed, or might have been cut; support stones that had either been stolen or forgotten in a warehouse. Strange things that no one could *prove* were done intentionally but had slowed the process down. In response, Lady Callad Kavann had brought in more guards to keep everyone away from the build site, and the builder in charge had gotten rid of his usual workers and instead brought in a bunch of muddy, wretched Closest.

It would have been easier if the reservoirs weren't still flooded from all the rain. Erra wondered why the Highest didn't simply bring the water level down for a few days—but of course, there probably wasn't anything simple about it. She hadn't been taught the magic that allowed the Highest to control the reservoirs yet, but she would learn someday, when her father was older and she started assisting him more with his duties. All she knew for now was that it was incredibly difficult, which was probably why building the bridge was preferable. But the Well was so important that sometimes that magic was worthwhile. Erra actually looked forward to being trusted with its secrets. It would be a vastly preferable duty to using the brand.

"I don't understand how this is supposed to make things

safer," Erra said, squinting. There were clouds in the distance and the air was thick with water, enough that she felt moist even out on solid land, but for now, the sun was shining through and reflecting back off the water. "They obviously have no idea what they're doing."

Out in the reservoir, the Closest workers were slowly laying down foundations, large stones attached to ropes that had to be spread all the way across the reservoir to keep the bridge steady. The farther out the workers got, the slower the going was. They were all ungainly in the water, barely able to move the stones and keep afloat at the same time. Splashing echoed back to the bank, but no shouts or other noise. Even out in the water, the Closest maintained the silence of the Curse.

"It is slow, Highest," the Twill who'd been hired to build the bridge agreed. "But Lady Callad wanted to make sure there would be no more . . . interference. I swear it was none of *my* crew causing trouble, I'm sure of it, but she insisted. And the Closest, well, they do what they're told. No chance of anything going wrong."

"Ah." That made sense. And it didn't matter. The Closest didn't have to be *good* at the work, they just had to get it done within the next few days, and the Twill could have groups of them here working through the night if need be, though the dark would make this process even more difficult. "Where did they come from?"

"Oh, I borrowed them out from one of Lady Callad's steward's estates, and the steward, too," the Twill said, gesturing down the shore to where a red-robed Avowed was keeping a bored eye on the proceedings. That made sense, too; the Curse only forced the Closest to obey members of the

Avowed and Highest castes, not the Twill. The builder would need someone Avowed around to keep them in line. "She arranged the whole thing—it's cheaper for me than my own crew, anyway. And she needed it done like this. Just in case."

"There won't be any more trouble," Erra assured him. She was here, brand at her side, to make sure of that. Because if it *hadn't* just been incompetence that had caused trouble for the builder, it was probably the mage girl. If she showed up, Erra would be waiting.

Erra had been practicing with the brand, under Lady Gesra's instruction. It was magic, a weapon that could destroy any mage. It had been created generations ago, by the last of the Highest who had wielded true magic, left to his descendants as a gift to protect them—and with them, the world. It would respond to one Highest in every generation, as it did for Erra now and had for Gesra before her, but because of the vividly real images of fire, it was hard to hold on to. If Erra could master that, learn to grip it without being overwhelmed, she'd be more than a match for the mage girl.

Erra hated the visions that happened when she held it, now even with her eyes open. It was as if the world caught fire and no one else noticed it at all. She had to ignore not just what she saw, but what she felt, smelled, even tasted. The smoke and blood. The stench of death. But even though she dreaded holding it steady while she and the guards fought, maybe it would be for the best if that battle happened here and now. If this whole thing was ended quickly.

Assuming Elan wasn't with the attackers, if they showed up . . .

But no, no one except a few gawkers appeared on the

shore. Erra examined those onlookers, but they seemed to be bored Twill and Avowed, no one threatening. She turned her gaze back to the water.

A Closest woman was hauling an enormous stone out toward where the water deepened. The stones all had holes broken into them, with ropes strung through so they could be dragged. Later, the rope would be attached to the main lines of the bridge. For most of the trek out, the woman could drag with one hand and keep her other hand on the main line, but the deeper she got, the more she needed that hand to keep herself afloat.

For a moment she went under entirely, water rippling out from where she'd been before she broke the surface again, coughing, hands empty. The stone was gone. She winced, took a visible breath, and went back under. Erra waited for her to surface, this time with the ropes she'd lost. And kept waiting.

None of the other Closest moved to help, caught up with their own ropes and work. Erra frowned. The water rippled again, and one of the Closest turned toward it, alarmed. But he didn't move to help, just made his own way forward, careful and slow. And still the woman didn't surface.

Finally Erra couldn't stand the carelessness anymore. "Hey!" she shouted, and everyone turned to stare at her. She pointed at where the woman had gone under, caught the eyes of the nearest Closest workers. "Help her!"

The Closest responded immediately, several of them dropping their burdens and ducking under the water. Their movements were all jerky and awkward, no grace but plenty of power. Someone found the woman and pulled her upward, and it took two of them to drag her to the shallows. All three of them collapsed into the mud. The woman was still for a moment, but one of the others rolled her onto her side and she coughed.

Erra let out a relieved breath, but the Twill made an irritated noise. "Those supports are cursed expensive; get back out there! Find them all, get them in place!"

The two Closest who'd dragged the woman ashore moved to go back to work—the woman wasn't conscious. "Wait!" Erra called.

They waited. The Avowed who was supposed to be supervising them watched, too, frowning a little, but he didn't gainsay Erra. No one here would dare. Erra stepped nearer to the Closest, pulling her robe up, even though the hem was already coated in mud. "Why didn't you help her sooner?"

"We . . . we were ordered to keep working, Lady," one of them said, his voice shaking. Water beaded on his skin. The workers were only wearing sodden underclothes, even the women. "Not to stop until we're done."

"But she was drowning!"

The Closest didn't reply—couldn't, since he hadn't been asked a direct question—just swallowed, not looking at her. His gaze went to the woman on the shore for a moment, and he bowed his head.

"Has anyone else died?" Erra asked. "How many?"

"Five, Lady," the Closest said.

She turned to the Twill, and the Avowed who'd joined them. "Did you see? Did you realize?"

"I . . . well, they're only Closest, Highest," the Avowed said with a tiny shrug.

"We don't really have time to pull out the ones who go

under. There's too much to do; we're not even halfway there yet," the Twill added. "Highest."

Erra swallowed her disgust. Yes, they were only Closest. No one would miss them in the long run—well, they probably had families. The woman who'd nearly drowned didn't look like she was much older than Erra, but then again, Erra herself already had two children.

She'd never actually seen any Closest so near before, or thought much about them one way or the other, aside from knowing why they'd been cursed. But for all they carried traitors' blood, it wasn't *their* carelessness that had led to the woman nearly dying, and for all the Closest didn't matter, that wasn't fair. "Well, pay closer attention to them, then," she said. "And you—get her out of the way, make sure she's all right, and then get back to work."

The Closest ducked his head in acknowledgment, then reached for the woman. The other one scurried back into the water to work. Erra frowned, watching them go. Five dead, pointlessly. No wonder the bridge was taking so cursed long to build—maybe it really all had been just the builder's incompetence.

She reached for the brand under her robe, letting her fingers brush it for a moment before yanking them back. If that was the case, she didn't need to be here at all. But as the second Closest hurried back to the water, she thought maybe it was a good thing she was anyway.

Erra made her way through the arched gateway from the beautiful gardens of Danardae into the estate house. The tile mosaics were so vibrant they practically glistened, even in the lantern light at this late hour. Erra stopped in at the nursery, a set of rooms that housed both of her children, always attended by several Avowed. The woman who sat with them now looked up as Erra stepped into the room but held a finger to her lips—the children were sleeping.

Even so, Erra walked toward their mats, just to look. Efenn, the older, had the darker skin and tighter curls of Erra's husband. She was nearly three now, and slept steadily. Jarren wasn't quite a year, and was fussier every time Erra held him. But she smiled anyway, because he was sleeping now, too, and because he resembled his mother's side of the family—Elan more than anyone. That had been obvious from the first moment Elan had held him, smiling and laughing, thrilled to be an uncle for the second time.

Erra had to look away from her child for a moment, hit by something like longing as she thought of Elan, who'd always been so much better with the children than she was. If she hadn't been one of the Highest, it would have been different; she'd have been able to marry Andra and her closest relative would have been her heir. She could have waited as long as she wanted to have children. Instead, her father had wanted Elan out of the line of succession, so he'd selected Halann and she'd married him, and together they'd had Jarren and Efenn. She didn't regret that, or a moment of the scant time she was able to spend with them, but she had no particular interest in their father.

"Are they well?" she asked the nurse, who nodded.

"Yes, Lady, and they've both just fallen asleep. But if

you'd like me to wake them . . ." The reluctance in her voice made it clear that getting them to sleep had been a struggle, so Erra shook her head.

"Let them rest. I'll see them in the morning," Erra promised, and backed out of the nursery.

Halann was waiting for her in the hallway. Her husband. She braced herself.

"Good evening, Highest. You're back late. I hope the day was fruitful."

"It was," she said, voice sharp.

Halann waited for her to say more, so she refused. Which was a little spiteful, but he'd only married her for the power being elevated into the Highest family would give him. He was her father's lackey, not hers, and though she'd done her duty to him, she had no interest in giving him information he'd use to build up more power of his own.

"Well," he said finally. "I'm sure you already know your lover is waiting in your study."

"Yes, so if you don't need anything from me, I'll go see her."

Halann crossed his arms, petulant. "Run off to her, then."

"You knew about Andra when you agreed to marry me," Erra said, already striding past him, but he followed.

"I didn't know she'd still be here, years later."

"I told you I wasn't going to put her aside. You get your power, I get my mistress."

Halann scoffed, but there was no argument for that. Erra loved Andra—and even if she hadn't, she'd only ever been interested in women. Once Halann had realized that, he was the one who'd ceased being more than civil. Part of Erra wished they'd at least been able to be friends, since her position of power meant she had few of those, but the marriage was what it was.

Besides, she had Andra.

The study was small but private, and Andra was waiting for her inside. She was lounging on one of the cushions, helping herself to a mug of Erra's favorite wine. Erra had to catch her breath, overwhelmed for a moment. Andra, with her painted lips and eyes, dripping with jewelry beyond what even most Avowed could afford, was almost unbearably beautiful. Even in the torchlight she glittered and glistened, wearing a deceptively simple dress that hung off her curves, and a smile on her face.

Erra shut the door behind her and took the moment to breathe. Andra stood, walked toward her, and after only a moment's pause took Erra into her arms, kissed her gently. "You look exhausted."

"I feel better now," Erra said.

"Good. Sit with me," Andra instructed her, and folded back down to her cushion. She poured a mug of wine for Erra and as Erra sipped, she said, "Would you rather relax first, or hear the rumors first?"

"Rumors," Erra said, and set the mug down. She fixed her full attention on Andra. Erra was isolated by her position, though she was slowly working on creating a network of informers who would keep her up to date on what was happening in Danardae—things no one wanted anyone official to know about. It was slow going, though, finding people who were trustworthy but willing to talk.

"They aren't good," Andra said carefully. "And there are a lot of them. Especially about Elan."

"What do they say about him?" Erra asked, clutching the mug a little tighter.

"Mostly just repeating what your father said—that he's dead in the desert with the lady of Aredann. But there are other stories . . . *Someone* is spreading word that he lives— and that he broke his vows."

"People like to tell lies about the Highest," Erra said, careful to avoid directly lying. She hated when her position forced her to lie to Andra. "Anything to embarrass us. It's petty."

"I don't think that's what this is," Andra said. "People were so angry during the drought—they said the Highest had no plan to help. That the Highest didn't even care."

"That was never true."

"I know," Andra said quickly, placating. "But it's what people said. It's what they felt. This seems to have grown out of *that*—all the anger."

"But the drought is over."

"Yes, but it lasted so long, and now with all the flooding . . ." Andra shrugged. "People who live near the channels and the rivers lost their homes. They're angry."

That was nothing Erra didn't already know. That anger was the only reason the Highest weren't certain the mage was behind the bridge's sabotage—it was possible, barely, that there were Twill who were lashing out at them. But right now, the mage was a much more important problem, so Erra dismissed that quickly. "When the rainy season ends, we'll handle it."

"But in the meantime, they don't have anywhere to go,"

Andra said. "So they talk. And what they're saying is that Elan broke his vows—and that he had some kind of help from a mage to do it. That the mage is going to strike—"

"No," Erra said, sharp, interrupting. "Listen. That's . . . All you need to know is that you don't need to worry. No one does. The Highest know about those rumors already, and are ready to handle anything that might happen."

"So something *might* happen?" Andra asked. "Erra . . . Erra, is it true? Elan is alive?"

Erra hesitated, but no, she didn't want to lie. Not about this, when it was so vital, and not to Andra, who she trusted. She relied on Andra, not just to report back on what she heard in the city, but to listen to her, to support her, to *understand* her. Andra had known them since Elan had been a gawky child and Erra herself had been only a slightly less gawky adolescent.

Erra and her mother had stepped into what was considered to be the best jewelry store in the cities. Every display had been beautiful, but what had caught her attention was the apprentice standing in the shadow, looking awed by the way the Highest had swooped in. It was before Erra knew her father wanted to marry her off, so there had been no harm in it when she'd flirted with the apprentice, or when she'd invited the apprentice to deliver the earrings she purchased herself, directly to the estate house. . . .

It had been just a flirtation, awkward kisses and giggles and smiles as they'd gotten to know each other. Then it had been something more. Andra had taken over the shop when her instructor had retired, handling the jewelry and the business both, despite the headaches that sometimes plagued her.

Erra had been forced to marry Halann, had become her father's right hand, had had Efenn and Jarren. But somehow, she and Andra hadn't fallen out of each other's lives. Somehow, in fact, Andra had become one of the most important people in Erra's life, one of the only people she really, truly trusted. Her father, Elan, and Andra.

So she nodded. "Yes. Elan is alive—and he's in trouble. I need you to find him for me, Andra. Because if the other Highest find him first, they'll kill him. If I can hide him away, fix whatever he broke . . . you have to help me."

"I will," Andra promised, then reached for the wineskin. "But not tonight."

"No," Erra agreed, smiling despite herself as Andra refilled their mugs. Neither of them picked the mugs up, though, as their eyes locked. "I've got something else in mind for tonight."

Chapter 6

JAE WAS OVERWHELMED BEFORE THEY EVEN REACHED THE CITIES.
It was three more days of travel just to get them close, and
"close" meant surrounded by a sprawling town outside the
city walls. The town held more buildings and more people
than Jae had ever imagined existing before.

The buildings, mostly made of tan bricks, reached so far
out into the horizon Jae couldn't even see the fields beyond
them. They must have been there to keep this many people
fed, but Jae couldn't imagine how much land that would
require—or water. Aredann had been a tiny oasis in the midst
of the vast, endless desert, but she'd barely seen sand in two
days. Instead, the world had been greener and greener, more
and more of it farmable, fed by channels from the reservoirs.

Even the sky was different. She'd almost gotten used to the clouds and storms that had plagued the world since she, Tal, and Elan had restored the Well's magic. Smoke from cookfires blotted the sun, and the closer to the cities they got, the larger and higher the buildings were.

"Jae, you can't gawk like that. You'll be noticed," Elan said, his kind voice softening the rebuke. He put a hand on her elbow to nudge her back in line. They were moving slowly now, as they approached the gate into one of the cities—Kavann, apparently. Palma was mounted on a horse and had a camel laden with supplies. Lenni, Elan, and Jae were walking—slowing their progress down, yes, but they'd explained to Jae that for all Palma was Avowed, she was relatively poor, so no one would expect her to have her servants outfitted with mounts of their own.

Palma wore a beautifully embroidered dress under her travel robe, and earrings and bracelets that glinted in the sunlight. Jae didn't know much, but she knew that Palma's clothes were nicer than anything Lady Shirrad had had at Aredann. But then again, Aredann had been considered laughably remote. Maybe Shirrad had been poor, too. For an Avowed.

"You're the one who should worry about being noticed," Jae replied to Elan, but she tried to make herself look as bored as everyone else did.

Elan stroked his beard self-consciously. He'd been clean-shaven when he'd come to Aredann, but now he had a beard and had grown his hair out, almost down to his shoulders. He'd tucked it up in a knot at the nape of his neck, hidden by the hood he always, always kept pushed up now. He was leaner than he had been, too, starved and honed by their trip into the desert and the trek they'd taken since then.

In a lot of ways, he looked nothing like the arrogant young man who'd arrived at Aredann. That was what they hoped, anyway—there wasn't much else they could do to disguise him. No one would look for a Danardae in the plain robes of a servant.

But Elan still *stood* like one of the Highest, carried himself as if he owned the world. Jae suspected that would be far more easily noticed than her gaping.

"They all think I'm dead," he said, repeating the rumor one of the Order's spies had told them. "No one will be looking for me."

"The *Twill* think you're dead," Lenni said. "But the Highest have spies looking for you. Elthis Danardae is not foolish enough to simply hope you'll never come back, not knowing all you do."

The line to pass through the gate to the city of Kavann seemed endless already, but people kept coming up behind them, lengthening it. They silenced their talk in the crowd, for fear of being overheard. Forward progress was so slow that Jae barely noticed anything changing, and then she looked up, and there it was.

The wall around Kavann was enormous, easily five stories high on its own. Unlike the dull buildings out here, it was obviously mage built: the base was red tile, and bright green vine designs slithered across it, never quite repeating in an obvious pattern. They twisted and met and broke apart again, dotted with red and yellow splotches that had to be flowers, though it was hard to see from this far away. Jae was willing to bet the detail, up close, was astounding.

"Magecraft really was an art form," Lenni explained in a whisper as they shuffled forward. "Meaning they used it to make great art. Just wait until you see the estate houses, Jae. You won't believe it—every inch is like that, stunning."

"But I shouldn't gawk," Jae mumbled, and Elan swallowed a laugh.

"It's just, everyone who comes this close to the cities is used to it," he said. "But I suppose servants like us might not have seen it before."

As if he passed for a servant. Jae didn't say that aloud, though.

"Which reminds me," Lenni said. "Jae, do you know—" She cleared her throat and started again. "I thought you'd be interested to know how the word 'Closest' came about."

"Yes, I would be," Jae said. The Closest were the descendants of the Wellspring Bloodlines, the mages who had worked with Janna Eshara to craft the Well. But that title had been lost to time, and now they were simply called the Closest. She'd heard that the name had come about because they were the closest to the earth; they worked barefoot as they tended the land. But so much of what she'd always known had been a lie, so she wondered if even that simple explanation was untrue.

"'Closest' used to be an honorific," Lenni said. "It was a title for all mages, not just the Wellspring Bloodlines, because they were the closest to the elements."

"Hush now!" Palma's voice came down from above and

in front of them. They'd taken another few steps forward, and now they were close enough that Avowed guards were walking the length of the line, looking at everyone in turn. Jae's skin crawled when she felt their gaze fall on her, and even more so when she recognized the uniform. It was the same guard uniform that Rannith and a few others had worn back at Aredann—newer and better fitting, but the same gray robe over loose pants and shirts, and they were all armed with swords and knives. And they all looked deadly serious.

For just a moment, Jae was back at Aredann, with Rannith's gaze roaming over her body. A single word from him had become a command, because she'd been cursed, and unable to refuse even though she'd hated him, even though she'd been terrified—

Elan's hand on her elbow guided her forward, and the guards passed by. They'd loop back eventually, but for now she was safe.

And she wasn't cursed anymore. True, she could only use magic as a last resort, to save her life if it was threatened—they couldn't afford for her to panic and attract attention. But if it came down to it, she could save herself. Rannith was dead, she was here, and she would never be defenseless again.

They approached the gate at last. A guard, a woman who was nearly as tall as Elan, took Palma's name, noted the number of people in her party, and asked her a few questions. She'd be staying with her parents, who still had a house in one of the cities; she was staying at least through the ceremony, maybe longer. The guard seemed bored by it all, since so many people had the same story, but her voice grew intense as she said, "Just be careful if you find yourself near the channels—the guards there are being very careful to keep people out of trouble."

"Has there *been* trouble?" Palma asked, voice high and nervous. Jae couldn't tell if that was an act or not.

"That's not for me to say," the woman said. "Just—be careful of it, Lady. There's been flooding, though, so some of the bridges are inaccessible. You'd do well to avoid passing between cities if you can."

"I'll try to stay away from the channels," Palma said, and dipped into a curtsey. "Thank you, Lady Guard."

The guard nodded and motioned them onward. Lenni gestured to Elan to take the horse as Lenni herself continued to handle the camel—they'd have to walk through the city, and a lady with servants would hardly lead her own mount.

Jae looked around at the city within the gate for the first time and stumbled as Elan nudged her forward. She caught herself but couldn't stop staring.

The town outside had been enormous, but within the gate, it seemed that buildings were packed together so close that if one came down, its neighbors would fold and topple into the space it left. The only way to tell where one ended and the next began was by following the patterns across the tiles—they would stop abruptly, or change colors. Except in some places, where there were dull, small tan buildings between the mage-built houses. They must have been built up in the generations since the War, with no magic to beautify them.

The buildings were huge—six, eight, even ten stories

high—but for every house, there had to be at least a hundred people. The streets were a cacophony—a sandstorm of noise so loud that Jae might as well have been deaf. There was no way she'd be able to hear Elan or Lenni if they tried to speak to her. Merchants shouted about their wares; people screamed to one another. She could hear singing and chanting. People staggered through the streets, some toward the shops and others dashing across the road. What had been a line outside the gate was a disorganized crowd inside, everyone headed in a different direction, and no one too careful about where they walked.

Elan dropped his grip from her elbow to her hand, still guiding the horse with his other. She shot him a grateful glance. The horse at least kept people off them on one side, and as long as they were linked together she wouldn't be lost. If she got pulled away in the midst of this, she might never find him again.

The smells were as much an assault as the noise: sweat and dung, spices and meat as they pushed through one market, sticky sweet smoke in the next. Urine and mold and damp, everywhere.

Thankfully some of the din died down as they moved to an area with fewer merchants and smaller buildings. Here, there was actual space between the houses, and they were decorated with potted plants in front of the tiled walls, even bushes and small trees. The buildings were smaller, but cleaner, and there were fewer people.

"This is an Avowed neighborhood," Elan explained, though Jae's ears were still ringing. "The markets are always busy, but not usually that mad—but I suppose with everyone coming in for the ceremony things are louder than usual. And Twill neighborhoods tend to be . . . noisy. Or so I've been told." He shrugged a little.

It was evening by the time Palma announced, "Here we are. I . . . I haven't sent word to my parents. I know they'll be happy to see me despite everything, but . . ." She cast a look at Elan.

"I'll keep my hood up and stay out of sight."

"That's the best we can do, I guess," Palma said.

They dropped most of their things in a room in the servants' quarters but left right away to avoid Elan being spotted by anyone in Palma's estate who might recognize him. Elan kept one bag with him, slung over his shoulder—it contained the papers and translation key Lenni had given him. It was, without a doubt, more valuable than everything else they carried combined.

Thankfully Lenni didn't lead them back to that market but instead from this Avowed neighborhood to one where more Twill lived. The houses were lower, crowded against one another, but a little less frantic than the marketplace. Soon, Lenni had turned in to one of the buildings. The door was larger than most of the others—it wasn't a residence, at least not on this floor. It was a drinkhouse, crowded with noisy patrons and that same sweet smoke. Jae's nose tickled and she had to sneeze. It was sweet, yes, but overwhelming.

Lenni wound her way around tables to one of the back corners, and as Jae and Elan settled, she walked up to the bar. When she returned it was with mugs of something Jae had never tasted before, a thick milky drink that made her tongue tingle. "You'll want to go slow with that," Elan warned her. "You're not much of a drinker."

It was the better part of an hour later when someone joined them at the table, with another round of drinks. The man had deep brown skin, short-cropped black hair, a goatee, and a mustache that looked more like a stain across his upper lip. He and Lenni nodded at each other, and then he turned to glance at Jae and examine Elan.

"Well, I see at least one of the rumors is true," he said, inclining his head to Elan. "I wouldn't have noticed if I wasn't looking for you, but—"

"But," Lenni interrupted, "the girl is much more important. No offense, Elan."

Elan looked amused and said, "Of course she is. We can all agree on that."

"Jae, this is Osann—a very respected mason, among other things," Lenni continued. "Osann, this is Jae, of Aredann. The one the Highest have come to fear."

"More than you know," Osann said, and turned his attention to Jae.

She didn't enjoy the scrutiny but refused to stoop under it. New people always made her nervous, but she didn't want the Order to think she was skittish.

Eventually Osann nodded. "Lady Mage."

Jae glanced around the room, but no one was paying much attention to them. The crowd hadn't gotten larger, but it *had* gotten louder as people had more to drink. It was hard to hear over the din, and dark enough that she had to squint to make out people's lips moving. But they were mostly talking about lovers and quarrels and what they'd eaten that day, not about the group in the corner. So she turned her attention back to Osann.

"The guard at the gate warned us about trouble," Lenni said.

"There's been plenty of that," Osann agreed. "The reservoirs are flooded, and so are the channels. Half the stone city was washed away."

Jae glanced at Elan, who translated, "He means the stone buildings by the channels—a slum, basically."

"Well, now it's mostly gone," Osann said. "Lots of people lost their homes, the ones who weren't killed in the collapses, anyway, and they're underfoot everywhere now. The guards haven't had much luck getting them out of the cities, and they say they have nowhere else to go. Most of them probably don't."

"That's awful," Jae said, thinking of Palma's anguish at losing her home.

"It is," Osann agreed. "But more to the point"—he paused, smirking crookedly at Lenni, and affected a high, innocent voice—"that same flooding made it cursed hard to build a bridge to the pavilion for the vow ceremony. As you requested."

Lenni nodded, looking satisfied.

"Is that what the Order does?" Elan asked. "Sabotage?"

"It's what we've been able to do," Lenni said. "More than anything, it gives our people an outlet—a way to strike against the Highest, even if it's barely more than a nuisance for them. Though with what we know now, we won't have to hassle the bridge builders anymore."

"So we won't," Osann agreed. "It seems you have other plans for that."

"I hope not that many people know about the plans," Jae said. Too many people finding out seemed dangerous, but if Lenni trusted them all . . .

"We needed to tell some," Lenni said. "There will be guards at the ceremony, so we'll need our people to keep them busy. But we're being careful about who we trust. I swear."

"And we *will* be ready," Osann said, leaning back, looking pleased with himself. "I don't know exactly what your plan is, Lady Mage, but trust me—the Order has been waiting for you for years. No matter what the Highest do, we're ready."

Jae nodded, unsure what she should say. Now it wasn't just her and Elan against the Highest anymore. It would be the Highest's army against Jae's magic and her new allies. She just had to hope that her magic, and the help from these people who were now counting on her, would be enough.

Chapter 7

ELAN BREATHED A SIGH OF RELIEF AS THEY STEPPED INTO THE misty air the next night. It had been a tense, unpleasant day. They'd spent it holed up in the servants' quarters of Palma's parents' house. He didn't dare show his face — Palma's family might recognize him.

Seeing Palma herself was . . . interesting. It was clear that Palma would be happy to pick up with him where they'd left off, trading kisses and secrets, but he didn't find himself particularly tempted. Erra had warned him, and then been so angry at him, when he'd gotten close to Palma — she hadn't believed Palma was at all genuine with her affection.

Elan could see that now. Something about her rang false.

He didn't doubt she was attracted to him, but looking back with clearer vision, he could see she'd used him, too. Mostly just to increase her social standing, but she certainly hadn't *discouraged* him from speaking out against his father.

He wasn't the same man she'd known anymore. He wondered if Palma realized that, what she saw when she looked at him now.

"I hope you aren't afraid of the mud," Lenni said as they walked. They were heading in toward the reservoirs, which lay at the heart of the cities—and the world. The four cities spilled into one another, separated only by channels that brought water from the reservoirs out to the fields, joined together by plenty of bridges. The four reservoirs were just as linked—they were all roughly circular, or would be, if they didn't overlap at the middle. That was where the pavilion stood, though Elan had only actually been there a few times in his life.

"As if we haven't spent days slogging through it?" Elan asked. "At least it's kept most people inside."

"They think it'll rain again tonight," Jae said. "I bet it will. But not until late—near dawn."

"How . . ." Lenni regrouped. "Is that . . . Do you . . ." She made a frustrated noise. "I don't understand how you can tell all that."

"I can feel the water in the air," Jae said. "I mean, with my . . . other sense. It gathers, and now that I've seen so much rain I can just sort of tell when it's finally too much."

"Useful," Lenni said. "Do you think you could make it— that is, it would be useful if you could make it rain."

"Hm." Jae's noise was noncommittal, and her head

cocked slightly as she walked, as if she was listening. Finally she shrugged. "Maybe. I've never tried."

They couldn't walk directly to the edge of the channel. A full block away, the water was up past their ankles. They had to pick their way through the stone city—or at least, what remained of it. Streets and alleys were blocked off by debris, and mud coated every surface. Vagrants stared out at them from the buildings that still stood, and people were lying among the piles of rubble.

"This is terrible," Jae said. "And the Highest don't help at all."

"There isn't much they could do," Elan said. "I don't think anyone could fix this mess."

"I don't see why not, if they tried," Jae said. "You saw Aredann after the quake. You helped repair it. The Highest could do the same out here, or at least help the people, if they cared at all."

Elan blinked. He *had* helped repair Aredann, now that he thought about it, and he'd insisted all the Avowed help, too. They'd hauled fallen tiles and bricks, making sure every hall was usable again, and that nothing was in danger of collapse. There hadn't been anyone else to do the work, so they'd just . . . done it. But still, that had only been one estate house. This was a whole neighborhood, dozens of buildings, thousands of people.

Jae was right, it was terrible. He wondered if the Highest had even come to see the damage themselves. More likely, they'd sent Avowed stewards to look for them, and the stewards hadn't thought that the homes of a bunch of poor Twill were worth much.

As they drew nearer to the reservoir, the neighborhood improved a bit, eventually opening up into a park. A flooded, muddy, miserable, trampled park, though, trees tilted over at odd angles, actually knocked askew by the water.

Lenni led them to one that was large enough to climb up on. It was slick with rot and mud but got them above the water, which grew deeper with every step.

Lenni pointed off into the distance. "There, you can see the pavilion—I just wish we had a way across," Lenni said. "It would be good to be able to look back at the shore, see where people will be. This park will certainly be overrun. . . ."

Jae slid down from the tree, the knee-deep water splashing as she hit it. Elan called out to her, but she waved him off and walked forward, grabbing soggy, tangled branches to keep herself steady. Then she said, "Follow me."

Lenni frowned, but Elan trusted Jae. He did as she had but found the ground under his feet sloping up, the water getting shallower. Jae was walking slowly, very slowly, forward. Muddy land was rising to meet her feet.

"Oh," Lenni gasped.

Jae said nothing, concentrating on each step. She led the way out, not just of the park but onto the water itself. The bridge they left behind was slippery, nothing more than a tiny sliver of land. Waves washed over it; it would be all but impossible to see from a distance. Assuming the guards who watched the shore didn't look at them.

But the guards were distant, and there wasn't *that* much light. The guards wouldn't expect anyone walking over the reservoir like this. Even if they did glance over, they'd assume it was something strange in the wind. Shadows, or trees floating by. Not people moving inch by inch closer to the island.

The pavilion looked almost as if someone had intended to build a hut but had only gotten as far as the corners and hanging the roof and stopped before building the walls themselves. The corners were covered in white tiles, with mosaic artwork climbing up them and across the ceiling. Waves and flowers at the base, a brilliantly realistic skyscape across the ceiling. It was almost disconcerting to look up and realize that the moon and stars above were only tiles, and if he turned his head he could just make out the *real* moon outside, half blacked out by the ceiling.

The corner supports were decorated, too; above the wave-and-garden pattern there was writing. He stepped closer to the nearest and read the script written ceiling-to-floor on it: *One for each element, joined here. This is the center.*

One for each element—four elements, four reservoirs, four cities, four Highest families. He tapped his fingers against his chest, where he'd been branded with a circle split into four quarters.

He walked to the next corner but couldn't read the text. It was faintly familiar—it wasn't the mage script Lenni had given him the key for, but if he was right, it was the more ancient script. The one no one could translate. And seeing it here, in this mage-built and mosaic-decorated pavilion, he realized why it had looked so familiar in the first place.

"Jae," he called, splitting the silent night. Jae winced from the noise and he mouthed "Sorry," sure she'd read his lips. He hadn't meant to startle her. She rolled her eyes but walked over to join him, Lenni trailing her curiously. "This whole place feels familiar. It reminds me of the mosaic room, by the Well. Especially this." He pressed a hand to the writing.

"Mosaic room?" Lenni asked.

"There was a memorial for Janna Eshara by the Well," Elan explained. "It was a lot like this place." He walked to the next corner. More writing, still not in the common script he was familiar with. *This* one was mage script—he could recognize a few of the symbols, just enough to be sure.

He racked his brain, trying to remember enough to put together some of the letters, and made out the word "element." That had been common in the texts he'd been poring through, so he was sure of it. And while he wasn't as certain, the first word looked almost the same as common script for "one." He studied the rest, trying to remember, and the memory of one of the instructional texts leapt out at him. It had been about mages linking together.

Joined.

Which meant the text in front of him read *One . . . element, joined . . .*

He took a step back, staring. He couldn't be sure without the key to translate, but he would have bet all the water in the reservoir that the wall of mage script said the same thing as the wall of common script.

"They're the same," he said. "The common script and mage script writing, they've got the same message. Why would they do that?"

"To make sure everyone could read it," Lenni said. "It's hard to say for sure, but I think they all used to be more common, and not everyone could read every script. So if the Highest wanted *everyone* to be able to understand this island's importance . . ."

"Then they'd have written it in as many scripts as possible," Elan finished. "Which means that wall is . . . it's a key!"

Jae looked at him like he'd gone mad, but as he dug into his bag for anything he could write on, Lenni understood.

"Not to a door," she said to Jae. "If the older script says the same as the other two, we can use it to put together a key to the script—we'll be able to translate the oldest writings! There's so much we could learn. You're brilliant, Elan."

Elan smiled but didn't say anything, too busy carefully, painstakingly, trying to capture every curve and flourish of the ancient script message in front of him. Then he'd copy the mage script and common script, just to be sure.

"That's good," Jae said. "But we need to make a plan to get the knife. That's why we're here."

"We'll need a way to get close," Lenni said. "Their bridge will be heavily guarded."

"So we'll need a bridge of our own," Jae said, and looked out at the water—back over the slippery, nearly invisible path she'd raised for them. "I can create one. From wherever our people are grouped. And I can sink theirs before they ever cross—they'll be trapped here. With no extra guards, and no way out except through me."

Jae never spoke loudly, but her voice now was like the desert night. Cold, dark, and deadly.

"That's perfect," Lenni said. "We've got what we've come for—and more than we ever could have hoped."

Elan finished his work and checked it one last time. Then

he tucked the paper away, not in his bag but against his skin, under his shirt, protected by his shirt and robe both. Now that they had a plan, there was nothing left to do but go back to Palma's and wait. In a few days, if everything went well, centuries of wrongs done by his family would come to an end. If this worked, then everything was about to change.

Chapter 8

JAE ALWAYS WOKE BEFORE DAWN, SO SHE WAS ALREADY AWAKE THE morning of the vow ceremony when Palma knocked lightly on the servants' door. Palma and Lenni both came in. Palma roused Elan while Jae sat up.

She looked up and met Lenni's eyes. This was the day. By tonight they'd have the knife, and soon her people would be free.

"Come downstairs," Palma said, reaching out to take Elan's hand. "Before my parents rise. You can have some tea and eat and then get going. The streets are going to be awfully crowded today."

They ate quickly and then headed out into the noisy streets. The trek was a lengthy one, since they had to travel to the city on the opposite side of the reservoir, Caenn, where the crowd would hopefully be thinnest.

Traveling through Kavann was the worst of it. It was so crowded that Jae felt crushed by the sheer number of people, all of them buzzing around, pushing, trying to get somewhere that seemed to require crossing in front of her and stopping short. She found herself elbowing angrily, barely able to make it through the thick of things without losing track of Elan and Lenni. But ultimately most people were trying to make their way to the reservoir shore, even picking their way through flooded streets and parks, to get a glimpse of the ceremony on the island.

It wasn't quite as bad when they reached Caenn, though even there it was still crowded and busy—busier even than the streets the day they'd come into the cities through the giant gate. Everyone seemed to want to come out to see the ceremony, or at least get close enough to be able to claim they had. The markets were flooded with people, selling food and drinks and even flags and whistles, turning the whole thing into an enormous, noisy, overwhelming party.

Finally Lenni led them into what remained of Caenn's flooded stone city. Here, too, people had climbed the rubble to get close, but someone jogged up to greet them—Osann, muddy up past his knees, who then led the way through the debris-filled streets to where a low wall still stood. It separated a park—the estate house grounds—from the city around it, and with the channel and reservoir as swollen as they were, the water flowed right up to the wall itself. The crowd here was thinner, held at bay by Avowed guards, there to ensure the peace, that this party wouldn't become a riot.

"Will you be able to work from here?" Lenni asked.

Jae tried to ignore her automatic irritation at being asked a question and nodded.

People began to fill out the area around them. Jae didn't know how many of the people in the gathering crowd were with them, but Lenni had promised it was enough. As the drought had grown worse through the years, she'd found more and more people who secretly raged against or resented the Highest and had grown the Order from a mere half dozen into a secret force only she knew the true size of.

They had offered Jae and Elan masks, as the rest of the Order planned to wear, but Jae had refused. She was going to seize the knife and with it her people's freedom, and she didn't want anyone to question who had done it. She wanted to look Elthis in the eye as she shattered his world. Elan had made the same decision—wanting to prove to the world that he was alive. He was already disavowed, and the more people who learned the truth of why, the more people would be swayed to their side. Or so he hoped. Jae wasn't as optimistic, but spreading the truth could only help them in the long run.

Soon, the ceremony started. A procession marched across the bridge from Kavann to the island, muddy water lapping at their ankles and the hems of their impressive, bejeweled robes and dresses.

Next to her, squinting, Elan said, "Those are guards at the front, and then Lady Callad and Nallis. I can't tell who else is who from this far away, but it looks like the rest of the Highest, then their families . . . Erra should be there somewhere."

Jae blinked into other-vision, let her mind's eye float up above, closer to the procession. She could find Elthis near the center of the parade easily enough. The younger woman at his side had to be Erra. She and Elan both resembled their father, with golden-brown skin and finer hair, looser curls, than most people had. Several Avowed flanked the two of them, some of them holding small children. Elan's niece and nephew.

Lady Callad and Nallis were at the front of the procession, Callad's skin as dark as Jae's own, and she wore a gleaming golden robe. They were surrounded, too, but Jae didn't know who else in the group were the other Highest and who were just Avowed, lackeys lucky enough to be allowed to witness the ceremony up close.

The group reached the island quickly enough. Two servants hurried to set things up, placing a brazier within the pavilion and lighting a fire inside it. Erra stepped forward and placed a brand to heat on the flames. Then the servant produced the knife and laid it out near the brazier.

Jae focused on it in other-vision so she could look more closely. Though the whole pavilion now shone slightly with magic, the shifting energies that surrounded the Highest, the knife was by far the brightest thing on the island—probably in the cities. Jae reached for it with her mind and felt the deadly, deep thrum of the Curse, and pulled away quickly.

"That's it," Jae murmured. "I can feel the Curse in it."

"Wait for it," Lenni advised. "We want them to get started, to think they're safe and start to relax."

Jae nodded but couldn't take her mental gaze from the knife. She knew it had once belonged to Janna Eshara, but it was even older than that. It was maybe the most ancient and magical thing in the realm.

Finally Lady Callad deemed the ceremony ready to begin. No one would really be able to see it from shore, but Jae could observe with magic. And, she realized, she could even hear. It was just a matter of manipulating the energy of the air, which jangled and buzzed as she reached for it. It was easy enough to twist it around, pull it into herself, so anything said on the island would sound in her ears as well.

"Are you ready?" Lady Callad asked, standing next to the brazier.

"Yes, Highest," Nallis said. His voice trembled, but he managed not to shake, despite knowing that the heated brand would be pressed to his skin. He knelt next to the brazier, facing his mother.

"Will you, Nallis of Kavann, vow your loyalty to me, to my line, and to the rest of the Highest families?" Lady Callad asked.

"I will," he said.

"And will you vow to do all you are asked, and all you are able, to uphold the order we Highest have given the world, and to strike down those who seek to overturn it?"

"I will," he repeated.

The magic in the pavilion flared, bright and glowing, almost like a fire in and of itself. Nallis let the robe fall from his shoulders. He was shirtless underneath, dark skin shining in the light of the fire, as Lady Callad wrapped a gloved hand around the brand's handle.

"If you speak the truth, and you vow to uphold these things with your life and all your energy, you will feel this brand for only one heartbeat, and then you will be healed."

"I swear it," Nallis said. "On my life and my energy, I swear."

"I accept your vows," she said.

Nallis went stiff and terrified as his mother pressed the brand to the skin above his heart. The crowd yelled again, the people at the front able to see what was going on enough to know when to cheer. Nallis recoiled in pain, swaying on his knees, and the magic went mad, a frenzy of sparks and light. But after a moment it faded—and Nallis's glow in other-vision had dimmed.

Around the shore, people screamed and cheered. Lady Callad set the brand back in the brazier and now held the knife, which pulsated with magic, as dark and cold as the brand had been hot and bright. Jae shuddered as she listened.

"You are now Avowed, but you are also my first child, and heir to my line," Callad was saying. "Without the Well, we are nothing but dust in the desert. Will you vow, above all else, to protect the Well and its magic—to serve it, guide it, and use it wisely?"

"I will," Nallis said.

"This responsibility may cost you your life. It may take the lives of all you love and hold dear. Will you still swear?"

"I will," Nallis said, yet again. "I vow by my life, all my energy, that I *will* protect the Well and its magic."

Callad held out the knife and Nallis accepted it. The magic swelled, and Jae felt it like pressure gathering in the air, the moments before a cloud burst. Nallis pressed the blade against the newly healed brand on his chest.

"Ready, be ready," Lenni said as Nallis traced the quartered circle and the Curse thrummed. Jae reached for the energy of the world around her, calling on as much of the earth as she could. The Curse was strengthened by the vow and the knife, so Jae held on to the rest of the magical energy in the area, readying it to do her bidding.

Nallis finished and offered the knife back to his mother. The Curse echoed in Jae's ears as Lenni yelled, "*Now!*"

Jae raised an arm, staring at the bridge, then dropped it. As her arm came down, so did the bridge, sinking beneath the water and tearing itself apart. Foam and bubbles rose where it had been. People on the shore and island alike started screaming, as the island group realized they were trapped.

Jae raised both arms this time, the energy curling out from her, and the land obeyed her, mimicking the motion. Two new land bridges unfurled in front of her, from points she and Lenni had picked during their first excursion. The trails of muddy land hadn't even reached the island yet as the members of the Order charged across them. People slid and slipped but hit the island at the same time the bridges did.

"Let's go," Elan said, and took Jae's hand so they could follow the Order's mad dash.

Fighting had broken out by the time they reached the island. There weren't nearly as many guards here as there had been on the Kavann shore, where they were now uselessly staring across the water, but it had only taken moments for them to realize they were under attack. Maybe the magic shocked them, but someone was yelling orders, telling them to concentrate at the jug neck where members of the Order were trying to push away from the bridges and toward the pavilion.

Jae found herself in the middle of a crowd, shoved and jostled. She could still sense the knife in other-vision, but there was too much chaos, even too much magic, for her to keep track of everything. Someone pushed her and she found herself facing a guard armed with a sword, but before she could scream or try to defend herself, Osann was there and stabbed him from behind.

"Go, get the knife!" Lenni shouted from nearby, and Jae struggled to get through, finally breaking past the thick of the fighting, nearly slipping on a spot that was slick with mud and blood.

One of the guards had grabbed the knife as an extra weapon. Jae pinned him with her gaze, then ducked as a guard took a swing at her and Elan shoved him back, trying to keep her safe. He gave her enough time to dodge away from the guard who'd attacked, toward where she'd seen the man with the knife—

The world seemed to spin around her, but it wasn't her magic; nothing really moved except that she collapsed. She found herself on her back, the world around her first blinding white and then black. She screamed, not exactly hurt, but suddenly helpless. The magical energy that should have wrapped around her was gone, vanished, leaving her off balance and defenseless. She tried to find it in other-vision, but couldn't see anything at all, and someone collided with her, breaking what little concentration she had.

A guard was kicking her, and raising a sword—

"Jae!" Elan slammed into the guard, knocking both of them over. "Jae, *go!*"

"Elan!"

The voice that screamed it was female. Jae looked up and saw Erra Danardae staring at the two of them, almost close enough to touch them. Elan whirled to face her, his jaw open.

"Erra, look out!" he yelled, as someone from the Order attacked Erra from behind. She whirled, holding a blade in one hand and the brand in her other. She dropped the brand to fight and Elan grabbed Jae's hand again.

The world lurched again, sputtering as Jae scrambled forward, the bright energies blinking back to life. "Do you have the knife yet?" Elan shouted to Jae, pushing her toward the edge of the fray, leaving Erra behind.

Instead of being helpful, Jae's magical senses returning felt like opening her eyes after too long in the dark. The pulsating magic overwhelmed everything else, but at least she could feel the knife. Its magic was unmistakably dark, horrible, and twisted, as it tied together her people and the Avowed, knotting pain with honesty and obedience. All of that bound into the ancient blade, and when she forced herself to focus, she could see that a guard still held it.

She lurched forward and the ground in front of her trembled, the whole island shaking. People toppled and flailed and fell, off balance, shouting, and she didn't know whether the Order or the guards had the upper hand. All she knew was that when the guard with the knife tried to catch himself, he had to drop the blade to do it. Jae ran, feet barely touching the ground, and her hands closed around the knife's hilt at last.

She straightened up, shouting, "I've got it, go, *go!*" But before she could take a step herself, someone crashed into the backs of her legs, her knees buckled, and her head slammed against the ground. She kept her fingers clenched around the knife, refusing to let it go, even as someone grabbed her and raised a bloodied blade.

Recognition sparked. It was Elthis Danardae himself, and he knew her, too. She struggled, trying to shove him away as he took a swipe at her. Pain exploded in her arm; she heard herself scream and raised the knife to try to stab him or shove him or do anything to keep him from ending everything right now.

Someone grabbed Elthis from above, dragging him back. He struggled and freed himself, falling and hitting the ground as Jae rolled away, leaving a trail of blood behind her. It was Elan again, facing down his father, who snarled, "Traitor!"

"Liar!" Elan shouted back.

"Elan," Jae tried to say, even as she limped to her feet. She had the knife; they had to get away, get to safety. Elthis let out a bellowed scream, already back on his feet and rushing forward to try to stab Elan. But Elan dodged, and Jae threw magic in their direction, the ground buckling under Elthis's feet. He slammed into the dirt and Jae grabbed Elan's hand, pulling him away. She hurt so much she could barely breathe but somehow found the strength to run anyway, back toward the bridges she'd raised. It was even harder to reach them now than it had been to get off them, with so many bodies — injured, dying, dead — on the ground.

Jae looked up beyond them and could see that guards had gathered at the distant shore, waiting for anyone who tried to escape back across the bridge. There weren't many of them, but she didn't know how many members of the Order had survived to face them.

She gathered energy and looked at the teeming, struggling mass on the island. "Follow me! Everyone follow!"

She took off headlong down one of the two bridges she'd raised but threw out an arm as she did it. A branch split off, leading to another spot, farther down the shore. She turned abruptly and the remaining members of the Order followed, once again leaving the guards stunned and useless, in the wrong position, allowing the Order to retreat into the streets, to the hiding places and safe houses they'd prepared.

She, Elan, and Lenni slipped into an alley, into a basement, up a staircase and into another house, then out and around. They kept moving until they were sure no one had followed them, and they were hidden away under a mage-built house, where no one had seen them enter, where no one would expect them or look for them. They were, for the moment, safe.

And somehow, not only safe, but successful. Because Jae was bloodied and exhausted, and she had no idea why her magic had disappeared for those few awful moments, but they'd done it. She had Janna's knife.

Chapter 9

"You. Inside. Now." Lady Callad stood in the doorway, fury in her gaze. Erra unfolded herself from the cushion where she'd sat, her body protesting the movement. She dutifully stepped inside Callad's study and faced the four Highest. All of them were frowning.

She didn't say anything. She'd learned from her father that making apologies first thing was a sign of weakness—and she wasn't weak. But she *had* dropped the brand in the midst of the fight on the island. The whole world had seemed to be flame and smoke, screams of agony echoing back at her, louder than the sound of the very real battle around her. The only thing she had been able to see clearly was Elan.

Elan, alive. And on the side of the traitors.

As distracted as she'd been, one of the traitors had snuck up on her, and yes, she'd dropped the brand. Gesra had said that the longer she held it, the more it would affect the mage—it would suck out her power, and the longer Erra held it, the longer it would be before the girl's power came back. All they had to do was kill her while she was still helpless. Erra was bruised and cut from having been in the thick of things, but she hadn't bought them enough time.

"This is your fault," Callad hissed, seating herself on one of the cushions. Erra sat at her father's side, but his expression was just as irate as Callad's. Which really showed just how awful this was—usually her father cloaked his emotions carefully. Either now he was too angry to do it, or he wanted her to know just how angry he was.

But he still turned that expression on Callad. "*Your* guards were the ones who couldn't even—"

"And *you*," Callad cut him off, turning on Gesra, whose expression soured like milk curdling. "You said that brand would—"

"Callad, calm down!" Tarrir interrupted. "Screaming won't help anything. Erra, what happened?"

Erra suppressed the urge to shudder as she remembered the field of flame. "I . . . dropped the brand," she confessed. "When one of the traitors hit me. Keeping a grip on it was so hard to begin with, you don't know what it's like—"

"I know," Gesra said. "And Callad is right, this *is* your fault, girl. There's no room for mistakes, not now. And when people talk about this—which they will, they already are—

that's what it looks like. But the Highest don't make mistakes. We can't afford for people to think otherwise. So next time, hold your breath and keep a hold on the cursed thing!"

Erra bowed her head, chastened. Keeping the faith of the people, especially the Twill, was one of the most important duties of the Highest. People needed to know that they were safe under the Highest's rule, and chaos like this . . . Gesra was right. It looked bad, and if people now doubted their rule, it was her fault.

"I . . . I'll be more prepared next time," she promised.

"As if that was the only issue," Callad said. "Elan was there—"

"Don't—" Elthis started to say, but Callad actually shouted over him.

"—and people will talk about *that*! You know they will, Elthis, curse you. You couldn't even keep your own son in line—"

"Listen here, you—"

"Callad! Elthis!" Again, Tarrir broke through their fight, his voice booming in the room. He was usually so soft-spoken and pleasant, always the peacemaker. But apparently he could yell, too, when he had to. "Shouting won't solve the problem— and Elthis, it *is* a problem. You have to tell the world he's disavowed—"

"Don't tell me what to do, you child," Elthis snapped.

Erra blinked, silent, still. She definitely didn't want to get involved in this, especially not if the other Highest thought of Tarrir as a child. Yes, he was the youngest of the four of them, but he was nearly a decade older than Erra, who, as she glanced from face to face, felt very, very young, and very, very inexperienced. She'd grown up mimicking her father, learning from him, and she could handle almost any matter that the Avowed brought to her—but this, her brother's disavowal, and this brewing rebellion, was beyond her.

For the first time, she wished she wasn't heir to the Highest, because someday she wouldn't just be sitting by silently. She'd be in a room just like this one, with the burdens they now faced on her shoulders. Her failure with the brand was a heavy enough weight, but someday it would be worse. When she inherited and keeping order for the whole world fell to her . . .

Elthis held up his hand, his neutral expression conquering his anger at last. His voice was calmer when he spoke again.

"I'll tell my Avowed that Elan survived his ordeal in the desert—that's true, anyway. And that he returned like this, a traitor and a vow-breaker. Who I will find, and see executed for his crimes."

"But—" Erra started, but fell silent, swallowing her protest as all four of the Highest turned to her. Elan *was* a vow-breaker and a traitor. She'd seen it herself, seen him helping the mage, fighting against the Avowed guards. Even so, something in her rebelled. Elan was her *brother*.

"Do not argue about this," Elthis said, as if following her thoughts. "He was a Danardae—*was*. When Twill gossip, it'll be about *us*. The chaos that will bring—handling that is my responsibility. We will maintain order—we *will*." His voice rang with certainty, and the other Highest all nodded.

"Now that he's been recognized among our enemies, there's no choice. The world needs to know we will stop at nothing to maintain peace, and we can't have any mercy, any pity, for those who challenge us. Do you understand that?"

"Yes, Father," Erra said, her voice small. He was right—but the idea of signing her own brother's death order was too much.

"Good. And there's no need to resume yelling." He shot Callad a quick glower. "Because I know how to draw him out—him and the mage girl both. And this time, we will be ready for them."

❖·❖·❖

Elan stared down at the papers in front of him and tried to ignore the noise of the drinkhouse below. Which was nearly impossible: after the disrupted vow ceremony, all four cities seemed to be in an uproar. It had been hours before he, Jae, and Lenni had dared to crawl out of their hiding place and head for one of the safe places arranged by the Order. This one was a set of rooms above a boisterous drinkhouse. It was certainly more spacious than the servants' quarters at Palma's parents' house, but even more distracting.

He wondered if Palma was all right, if she'd made it home after the ceremony safely. She hadn't been among the attackers who'd charged onto the island with them—she wasn't a fighter. But she must have been there somewhere, watching, and the cities were now chaos and disarray. Though she was on her way out now. Lenni had gotten word to her, a message that sent her on her way home. Except she'd be making as many detours as she could, stopping at Closest enclaves to warn them to be prepared for the Curse to break.

He looked up from his translation. He'd finished as much of the key as the text from the mosaics had allowed. Mage script was confusing enough, but at least those letters had been similar to the ones he was familiar with—albeit with different vowels, marked by symbols at the end of words and lines. It had taken him a while to become familiar enough with that to read it without having to check the key every few words.

The ancient script was even stranger. It used the same vowel-marking system, but the letters were mostly different, too. Judging by the one sample he had, sentences were arranged entirely differently than he was used to. He was working on one of the journals, painstakingly trying to shift the letters into ones he was more familiar with reading, and then move words around until they made sense, but it was very, very slow going.

Meanwhile, Jae sat with her back straight, eyes shut, the knife resting in her lap. Elan was no mage, but it was obvious even to his eye that the knife was odd. He'd never seen anything like the material it was made of before, a deep black stone that gleamed in the light. Jae hadn't relinquished it to anyone else to examine, but something about it made him nervous, like he could sense the magic that Jae said dripped from it.

Lenni was there, too, cross-legged, sewing up a hole that had been torn in her robe. None of them had come through the fight uninjured. The worst Elan had was bruises, but Lenni was pretty well cut up, and Jae's head had bled nastily where it had been slammed into the ground, and so had her arm where it had been cut. At least a bandage had stopped that, but Lenni had needed to sew up the gash on her thigh.

Reports had been coming to the drinkhouse slowly, members of the Order drifting in and out. It was a popular enough place that no one would notice who came and went—their allies were a few among the many, many patrons. Their reports all said the same thing: only a few of their number had been killed, but many had been injured. Worse, a couple had been taken prisoner. Lenni had bowed her head in sorrow at that. Prisoners of the Highest would be forced to give up what little information they had, tortured until they spoke if they didn't answer willingly.

They wouldn't answer by choice, Lenni was sure, and none of them had vital information; no one person knew the extent of the Order or its members except her. Which made sense—of course she had to keep those things secret— but it also meant she was the only one in the Order who could reach their allies, make decisions, give out orders. It was a lot of power, and she hadn't been forthcoming about any of it.

"How's the translation going?" Lenni asked, looking up from her sewing.

"I'm working on one of the letters," Elan said. "From Serra Pallara to Janna Eshara—Serra was one of the founders of the Well, supposedly. She's Tarrir Pallara's ancestor."

"Saize Pallara crafted the Curse," Jae said, her eyes opening. It took another moment for them to focus on the world around her instead of whatever she saw in her mage's vision.

"Serra was his grandmother," Elan said. "It was two generations from the Well's founding to the War. But this seems to have been written *before* the Well, even, if I've got any of this right at all." Jae didn't ask, but he cleared his throat and read aloud anyway. *"Closest Janna, there is more at stake here than just another generation. We have a responsibility beyond them, to the whole world. Not just our children."*

"Interesting," Lenni said. "A lot of the writings we've preserved have been about magic and responsibility—but none from so far back."

Jae looked over at her, and finally her posture relaxed a little. "I'd like to know more about how you came to the Order, Lenni, if you don't mind."

Elan didn't know where that question had come from, but now that Jae had asked—without coming out and making it a question, of course—he was curious, too. Lenni had told them about the Order's history, but nothing about her own.

"Oh," Lenni said, and went quiet. Then finally she said, "Of course, it's just . . . difficult. I told you that my mother was a member—a mage. She taught me to read mage script, taught me as much about the Order as she could.

"We hid for most of my childhood. Moving around, careful that we were never followed. But we were, somehow. The Highest . . . they sent someone after her," Lenni said. "I didn't know who, or how, or what . . . what was happening until it was too late. I'd been out fetching water, but when I got back, the house where we were staying was on fire, there were Avowed guards all around, and my mother . . ."

Elan watched her, the papers almost forgotten in front of

him. Lenni hesitated again, and Elan already knew what had happened, but finally she confirmed it.

"The Highest always kill mages when they find them—I don't know how they manage it. My mother yelled to me to run, and I . . . I ran. She wasn't able to follow me. She . . . She was gone a minute later. The fire was . . ." She trailed off, choked, then took a deep breath.

"I promised myself I'd find a way to do *something,* to get back at them for killing her. Back then, there were only a couple other mages, barely any Order to speak of, but when I was finally brave enough to contact them, I told them I was going to change everything. The Highest have ruled for too long, and too cruelly. I won't let them continue. I won't."

"So you built the Order into what it is now," Jae said.

"Yes." Lenni's expression was grim. "I built my network of spies and soldiers, other Twill who have grievances against them. With the lucky timing of the drought, I was even able to convince some Avowed, like Lady Palma."

"Lucky timing?" Elan repeated.

"A bad way to describe it," Lenni said. "There was nothing lucky about the drought, it cost too many lives . . . but the ranks of the Order have swollen like the channels. Without it, I don't know if we'd ever have enough people to strike, but now . . . now we can, and we can win."

"If I can figure out this cursed knife," Jae said.

"I'm sure you will," Lenni said. "And once your people are freed, there will be even greater numbers against the Highest. We'll win, all of us together. We can lead the Closest against the Avowed who've abused them, and rebuild the whole world. Move forward, finally."

Elan glanced down at the text, not sure what to say to that—and the word "forward" jumped out at him, even with the strange lettering. He examined it, concentrating, trying to make sense of the wispy words and garbled sentences.

Closest Janna,

You are too much like our ancestors. You claim you look forward, but you have never thought of the consequences. Remember the Rise. Our ancestors believed they were gifting us with a paradise and cursed us instead. Your gift could well do the same.

I don't naysay your plan because it's impossible. I know you too well, friend. You believe you can craft this Well; I am certain you can. You are more clever with magic than any Closest I have known. But this is folly.

If we must raise this much magic, let us undo our ancestors' mistakes, not make mistakes of our own. Our descendants will thank us for that.

I cannot help you, and I will not influence my friends toward a cause I believe is folly.

By my hand,
Serra Pallara

Elan sat back and reread it all. Serra Pallara and Janna Eshara had been friends, that was clear, but they had disagreed about the Well. This was the letter where Serra had refused to join the Wellspring Bloodlines, a decision that would lead her grandson to join *against* those mages, to seize the Well. But Serra had believed the Well was a mistake from the beginning.

That was madness. Without the Well, the world was nothing and would never survive another drought. Surely Serra must have seen that. But whatever their ancestors had done must have been more terrifying than drought. Elan couldn't imagine what that could be, and he had never heard of anything called the Rise—he couldn't even be sure he was translating it correctly.

Someone knocked on the door and entered a moment later. A young man, twitchy, who pushed down the hood of his robe and revealed bruises on his face and neck—he'd been in a fight recently. And since he bowed to Lenni and then Jae, that fight was probably the vow ceremony.

"Lenni, I saw this in Danardae, I came as fast as I could," he said in a rush as he pulled a sheet of paper from his robe. He offered it to Lenni, whose expression went grim. She set it down where Elan could read it. He did so aloud, for Jae's benefit.

"The traitorous rebel girl calling herself Jae Aredann is commanded to turn herself in to Highest Lord Elthis Danardae by dawn, two days from now." He paused for a heavy breath, realizing what this notice was—a threat. *"For every day she does not surrender, a hundred Closest will be led into the Danardae gardens and executed for her crimes.*

"Then there's . . . there's information about a reward, if anyone knows anything about her . . . you," Elan finished. "Jae . . ."

"A hundred Closest," Jae repeated. "Every day. Because I—"

"Jae," Elan said again, but his throat felt almost too tight to talk. The Closest his father would kill were innocent and wouldn't even be able to resist—or to protest, beg for their lives. But Jae couldn't turn herself in, not when her magic was their only chance at freedom.

"We won't let it happen," Lenni said.

"*I* won't," Jae said. "Because I'm going to destroy this cursed knife first. And then . . . then I won't turn myself in. But I will go looking for Elthis. And when I find him . . ."

She didn't finish the sentence, but she didn't have to. Elan bowed his head, wondering if his father had any idea what he'd just unleashed. Jae had promised Tal that she'd have mercy on her enemies—but if her enemies had no mercy for her people, if the Highest really killed any Closest just to harass Jae, she wouldn't hesitate to strike them down, and she wouldn't regret it after.

Chapter 10

THE NOISE OF THE DRINKHOUSE FADED TO THE BACKGROUND AS Jae stared at the knife. It was just as cold, and just as powerful, as it had been when she'd first grasped it—despite the fact that she was certain the Curse was bound with fire. The problem was that fire was the one element she couldn't touch, and she had no idea how to get started breaking the Curse without it.

It also kept gnawing at her that she had no idea what had caused her magic to suddenly vanish on the island, leaving her dizzy and defenseless. The knife had been the most powerful object she could sense, though, and she knew just how vast and awful the Curse was. It was entirely possible the knife itself had done it somehow, its magic clashing with hers, and it winning out as stronger.

Not that she'd confessed that fear to Elan or Lenni. She'd told them about what had happened, yes, because they needed to know that—in case Lenni knew something about it, or Elan found anything about it in the texts he was translating. But saying that she worried it was somehow linked to the Curse seemed like it would lend the whole notion credence.

She'd never lied in her life. Saying it, even if she wasn't sure, would make it feel too true. She couldn't afford it.

"What elements can you sense in it?" Lenni asked.

Jae looked up at her in silent irritation. She wasn't compelled to answer anymore, so she didn't.

Finally Lenni rolled her eyes. "I don't think we have time for pleasantries, Jae. I can't help you if I don't know what you can sense."

That stung a little but was probably true. Jae glanced over at Elan, who looked up from his papers. He gave her a tiny, apologetic shrug, and for a moment she missed being on the road with him. It had been just the two of them for weeks, and Elan almost never forgot and asked her questions. He liked to chatter, but he didn't really expect her to answer. And he always seemed to be able to sense when she couldn't take it, and though he fidgeted, he'd fall quiet.

The city was never quiet.

"It's fire, mostly," Jae said. "Which I can't touch. But it's got air bound into it—which I *can* touch, but it's my weakest element. It doesn't hurt, precisely, but it . . . buzzes."

"I'm surprised you can't touch all four," Lenni said. "The stronger the mage, the more elements she can use—and you must be a hundred times stronger than the other mage in the Order."

"I don't think it's really my magic," Jae said. "It should belong to all the Closest. Taesann sort of . . . stole everyone's magic when he hid it away."

"Hmm," Elan said, tapping a finger against his papers. "It must still be rooted in your abilities, then, if you can't use all four elements. And fire may have been the weakest point for a lot of the Wellspring mages—they were focused on water and land. Lenni, does your other mage have an affinity for fire?"

"Yes, but she's weak," Lenni said. "And she doesn't know any more about magic than I do—I had to teach her. She wouldn't be any help at all."

Which meant Jae was on her own, and it was time to get to work. "All right. I'm going to try now. I need to concentrate."

She was sitting cross-legged on the bare floor, rather than a cushion—sometimes other-vision was disorienting, and she didn't want to sway and fall. The knife lay on the tiled floor in front of her, and as she brought herself into other-vision it was blinding. She had to look away, to concentrate on the steady glow of the earth beneath them and in the walls, the pockets of water and how it floated in the air outside, ready to rain yet again. The bright, twisting energy of people, everywhere.

Then back to the knife.

She brushed a mental hand against it, felt the thrum of the Curse in the base of her skull, and yanked herself back so hard she *did* jolt physically. It had felt like the very first stages of the Curse, its lightest touch—when an order had been given but she hadn't yet begun to obey. Or when someone had asked her a question but she hadn't yet answered.

It wasn't even painful, more of a tingle, a reminder that it would *become* painful if she didn't obey quickly.

"What happened?" Lenni asked.

"Nothing. And *don't* ask me questions. I need to concentrate."

Lenni didn't respond, and Jae didn't open her eyes to see how Lenni had reacted. She just braced herself and used her magic to reach for the knife again. This time she knew what to expect, and it wasn't awful. Not like it had been when she'd still been cursed. The thrum didn't grow stronger, transforming into a pounding pain. It stayed just as it was, something trying to reach Jae, but from outside instead of within.

She took a breath, then another. If the sensation continued like this, she would be fine. Even if it got worse—she'd lived with the Curse for seventeen years. She could handle pain. Pain would be worth it, if it led to breaking the Curse once and for all.

Now that she'd adjusted, she tried to find the individual energies within the knife. Oddly, it was the knife itself—the physical blade—that was so cold to her mental touch. It was the magic that burned, as if it was a real, physical flame, one she could pass her fingers through and feel the heat but not grab or change. If she tried for too long, it really did burn, a pain that was as physical as mental.

Trying to manipulate the fire energy wouldn't do her any good. She grabbed for the air instead, felt its strange jangling buzz, as if she were covered in a full hive's worth of bees. The harder she tugged at it, trying to loosen one of the strands of magic, the more it buzzed under her skin, until finally it was so much that her teeth began chattering and she had to clench her jaw shut.

Slowly, she adjusted to it. It was annoying, distracting, but she could work past it.

The knife held all its magic tightly bound together. Usually, Jae could reach out and grab any energy she could sense, pull it into herself, and make it do her bidding. She could manipulate earth without a thought, and water nearly as easily. But this didn't come to her. She tried to pull at it, to draw the air's energy away from the knife and into herself, but the knife sucked it right back. It was stronger than she was—and powered, she realized, almost the same way the Well had been.

But where the Well had pulled energy from the blood of the mages who'd built it—and now their descendants, the Closest—this pulled it from the Highest and Avowed. That was what the vow ceremony really did: their pledge turned the very air into a binding, linking them all together, strengthening the Curse within this knife.

Maybe she couldn't undo the fire or the air, but she was powerful, and as she'd told Lenni, she had the power of *all* the Closest. That had to be worth something, and she had at least one more way to attack before she was out of ideas.

She'd never seen anything like the material that made up the knife before, but it was some kind of stone, cold and foreign though it was. That meant it was earth, somewhere underneath the Curse. She couldn't break the binding directly, but if she broke the knife itself, that would do just as well.

The binding energy wrapped around the knife, encasing it, with no cracks she could pull apart. Instead, she had to push through it, as if she was trying to trample her way through a dune with sand shifting under her feet, searching for the familiar feeling of the earth. The binding energy resisted, but as long as she didn't try to break it, she could slowly push through it. It just needed patience and perseverance. While Jae wasn't precisely patient, she *was* stubborn.

She found it eventually, the steady glow that she knew so well, but when she reached for it, it was cold, tainted, not like any earth energy she'd felt before. She grabbed for it, curling her mental fingers around it—

Something awful slammed into her mind and threw her back, knocking her over, noise exploding like a thunderclap around her, dissipating into people shouting. The feeling was gone just as suddenly as it had been there, leaving only a shadow behind, a sense in her mind of something ancient and terrible, twisted and unnatural. Not purely painful the way the Curse was, but—but *wrong*.

"Jae!"

Jae opened her eyes and found the room in disarray: every tile had been knocked off the walls, and the ones on the floor had shattered and been thrown outward from the knife. Lenni had scrambled backward, covered in dust and cut in a few places from the fallen tiles. Elan was in the same shape but moving toward Jae, shedding fallen tiles as he went.

Jae stared, eyes wide. "I . . . I didn't do that." She looked down at the knife. The chaos circled out from it, as if it had been trying to throw her and everything else away from it. But it hadn't changed at all, except the disturbed tiles under it were singed black.

"You did something," Elan said. "We'd best get out of here. I don't know how far that blast went, but . . ."

Judging by the yells downstairs, it had affected at least the whole drinkhouse. Jae grabbed the knife and her bag but had a hard time forcing herself to move. She wanted to curl up and close her eyes, exhausted after using so much magic. But they had to go.

Elan took her hand, and Lenni had them out the door without even taking the time to dab the blood from her face. They scrambled down a back staircase and out into an alley. People were coming out from the buildings around, shouting and confused, and it would have been so easy to get lost in the crowd. Elan's hand closed around her wrist and he pulled her after Lenni, escaping from that side street into another, and another, all the way into another section of town where buildings were larger, lower, and darker. Lenni hustled them through an alley and into the back of one of the buildings. She pushed them into a small, dark room, with noise coming from nearby. Jae heaved a breath, and Elan helped her down onto a cushion.

"This is Osann's place," Lenni said. "His workers are all out there. I'll slip out and let him know we're here, but first, Jae, what happened?"

"Whatever was at the heart of the knife's energy was powerful and ancient," Jae said. "I was trying to shatter the blade, but there's something strange about it. It's earth energy, but different, *changed*, I don't know how. It's very old and very . . . wrong."

"I don't understand," Lenni said.

Jae shook her head again, helpless. She didn't know how to explain it, just that it felt like someone had taken the energy of a stone and tried to turn it into something else. It was unnatural.

"I wish we knew more about what happened before the

Well," Elan said. "You said the knife is from even before Janna's time, and some of the papers I was reading . . . Something bad happened, I think maybe a long time before Janna. Serra Pallara's letter said their ancestors had made some kind of massive mistake with their magic—she called it the Rise, if that means anything to you."

"I wish it did," Jae said, but it didn't sound familiar at all, not even from the flashes of memories she had of Janna and Taesann. "I don't know what else to do. The Curse is more powerful than I am, I couldn't even touch it through fire or air, and . . . and when I tried to reach the earth in the knife . . ."

"You probably shouldn't do that again," Elan said. "At least, not without giving us some warning."

"I'll try the air again," Jae decided, though she was so drained already she felt like she could barely move. But she needed to break the Curse within two days, before Elthis's deadline.

"Sleep first," Elan told her. "You look like you're going to collapse, and you can't do magic when you're that tired."

"Is that so?" Lenni asked him.

He nodded. "She was totally drained in the desert after a day or so—maybe that's what happened to your magic on the island, Jae."

"Maybe . . . ," she said, but what happened on the island had felt different. *This* felt like the desert—her other-vision was blurry, hard to make sense of, and she couldn't manipulate any of the energy she saw. But she *could* see it, and she knew that once she'd had some rest she'd be able to use the energy again. On the island, it had been as if other-vision had just blinked out of existence.

"Are you sure Osann won't mind us staying here?" Elan asked.

"I'm sure," Lenni said. "This is one of our safe houses, but we're stuck in this room until the rest of his workers leave. I'm sure he can sneak us some lunch, though."

"And this gives you time to rest," Elan said.

Jae nodded and slid forward off the cushion. She pulled off her robe and lay down on it, her head on the sitting cushion. Lenni slipped out of the room, leaving her and Elan alone. She shut her eyes, and sleep came almost immediately.

❁ ❁ ❁

As Jae slept, Elan rifled through the collection of papers Lenni had given him. They were all copies—she said in some cases, the originals had been destroyed; for others, they were kept safe, hidden somewhere. She'd had a random collection with her and that was what he had now. It was mostly letters to and from Janna Eshara, akin to the first one he'd translated.

He examined the first one closely. There *were* a few lines written in mage script, crammed into the edge of the page. Those few notes said *Copied 20 years after the War* and *Unknown reference—disaster?* A few other scattered notes explained where the original had been torn or faded and was unable to be copied over—that text was missing entirely.

Slowly, Elan began to translate what he could, writing it down on another sheet.

I do not want cause another Rise, but I will not be ruled by fear. The other Closest keep trying to have it both ways. They say this is natural. They say it will end. But they also say to remember the Rise.

Father gave me the knife to remind me of what great works can do. But if the Rise was so wrong, why can't they admit it caused this drought? That this isn't natural? This land was a paradise when our ancestors came to it, but it gets drier and drier every year. We've lost so much land already, and the rivers have slowed to a trickle. We used to have lakes; now we can only call them oases.

I wish I had the power to fix this on my own. I know there is a way—I dream of it every night. I would do anything to see those dreams realized. But no mage can do great works alone, and if none of the Closest will risk another great work, then I fear we are lost for good.

It was late by the time Elan had finished translating those scant few paragraphs. His back ached from hunching over and his eyes were blurry from staring too long. He stretched and glanced down again.

He was as sure of the translation as he could be. He was growing more familiar with the script and its syntax now, but he had no way to be sure he was right. But if he was . . .

This was a journal entry someone had saved from before the War. This whole collection seemed to be about Janna Eshara, so it probably came from her journal. He blinked, letting that settle into his mind. If that was so, then this single paper might be the journal entry where she had first conceived of the Well. It was definitely from before she'd gathered any allies to assist with it.

And there was the Rise again, some kind of disaster. Now he understood a little more. The world before the Rise, whatever that was, had been a paradise, according to Janna. Then the mages had done ... *something*, a great work—"great" meaning large, he realized, not brilliant or celebrated. The Rise had changed the world, turned fertile land dry. He couldn't imagine a world with natural lakes and rivers; all he had ever known was the Well and its reservoirs and channels.

The knife was connected to it, too. Jae would need to know that, though he doubted it would help. Not without more information.

He sighed. He was starting to think that information—truth—was more important than water. The Highest had destroyed as much truth as they could and replaced it with lies the world now thought were history. Janna Eshara had once been revered and was now forgotten; and before she'd been revered, he was learning, she'd been frustrated and desperate.

That reminded him of Jae. He wondered what people would think of her, generations from now. If they'd remember her name, or if she'd be lost to time, too, with a few people desperately trying to prove she'd been right.

Jae hadn't stirred and Lenni was out meeting with members of the Order. That made him think about information, too, in that Lenni seemed to have it all. He understood why she had to keep so many secrets, not sharing the name of her other mage, or telling anyone how to contact anyone else within the Order. It was dangerous for too many people to know too much. Someone might be caught, or might turn against them. That would be a disaster, if the person knew anything vital.

He wished there was another way . . . but the only other way he could think of was to contact Erra. She must have seen the notices their father had been put out by now, but he couldn't imagine she'd agreed to them. Elan had learned at Aredann that his father had been willing to slaughter every Closest on the estate. He wouldn't think anything of killing a hundred more—even a hundred a day. Not if their deaths would give him power over Jae, a way to confront and kill her.

But Erra wasn't like their father. Yes, she took after him in a few ways—she could be calculating and manipulative when it suited her. But she wasn't a liar the way their father was. If she knew the truth about the War and the Well and the Closest, she'd never stand for it. But just like Elan—just like everyone—she'd been lied to since birth.

He had to find her and tell her the truth. If he could make her listen, she could help them. Maybe she could keep their father from following through on this threat. If Elthis didn't harm any Closest, then Jae could keep her vow to be merciful. It was still possible.

Elan understood why Lenni had dismissed the idea out of hand. But Lenni didn't know Erra, and Elan did—and Lenni ran the Order, but it wasn't as if Elan had taken any vows to her. The only person whose opinion he really cared about now was Jae's.

Jae trusted him. He could convince her. Then it was just a matter of convincing Erra, but he knew he could do that, too. Because he had one advantage his father never would— the truth.

Chapter 11

"Absolutely not," Lenni said, squaring her shoulders.

Elan mimicked her posture, though not intentionally, bracing himself for this fight. He'd known she wouldn't like the idea—she'd already dismissed it once. But now he was willing to fight for it, if that was what it took. They were both on their feet in the back room of Osann's warehouse. Jae had been asleep on the floor before Lenni had come in, but now she'd pushed up to stand, watching the two of them warily.

"Erra can help us," Elan said. "If I can arrange a meeting with her, she'll come talk to me, and she'll *listen*. Which is more than you're doing."

"I'm not listening because you're being an idiot," Lenni said.

Elan didn't let himself respond to the insult, instead turning to Jae. "Once I tell Erra the truth about the Highest—"

"No Highest is going to care about the truth," Lenni interrupted. "If they did, they wouldn't have continued lying. For centuries."

"*I* cared," Elan said. "And I never knew the truth—I don't think they tell anyone who doesn't need to know. Their heirs, even, until they have to. Because Erra *doesn't* know, I'm sure. Jae, I'm *sure*. Erra isn't like my father, she actually cares about people. And having her on our side can only help."

Lenni didn't look at all convinced, but she also turned to Jae, waiting. Jae was the one the Highest really wanted—the one who had the power to unseat them, to free the Closest. Her focus needed to be on breaking the Curse before the deadline, but this was important, too.

At last, Jae said to Elan, "I don't know Erra. I don't trust any of the Highest. But I do trust you."

Jae's trust was more precious than water in a drought, and knowing he'd earned it gave him a tiny thrill. "I'm sure of her."

"Then go," Jae said, and stretched. "But I can't go with you. I have to break the Curse."

"I'll go, too," Lenni said quickly. "For all the good this will do. You really shouldn't be wandering around on your own, *Lord* Elan. You don't exactly fit in, and if you're recognized . . ."

"Thank you," he said, though he wasn't exactly thrilled at the idea of Lenni following him around. But he'd gotten his way, and that was enough—he could handle her now. Plus, she wasn't exactly wrong. Being recognized had been enough of a worry even before the vow ceremony. Now, people had seen him. They'd be looking for him. Especially in Danardae.

"Be careful," Jae said, as Elan pulled on his robe.

"Stay here," Lenni told Jae. "Osann knows what you're working on—if there's a problem, he'll help you find a new safe house and get word to me so we can meet you."

Jae nodded, but she only glanced at Lenni. Instead, her gaze lingered on Elan, and he couldn't quite bring himself to walk away from her. Not yet. "I *will* be careful," he promised.

She nodded again, and finally looked away. She didn't say anything else, but then, she wasn't one to waste words. So he didn't, either. But he did pause in the doorway, trying to remember another Closest gesture. He knew the Closest signal for safety—the open-handed wave—and the gesture for caution—pulling fingers closed into a fist. Eye contact and a scant nod for a greeting, but for a parting . . .

The gesture Jae had made as they'd left Aredann came back to him. A wave with her hand held low, by her waist, instead of up where it was obvious. Open-handed, like for safety, now meaning *good luck*. Closest did it without looking back, since they were usually in such a rush to obey orders, get their work done, afraid that anyone might see them take the time. He made that gesture and forced himself to leave quickly, hoping he'd done it right.

He followed Lenni out into the early morning. Osann's workshop was in the outskirts of Danardae, near the wall, a lengthy walk from where he needed to go, but in the right city. At least no one was out at this early hour. Even the drink-houses were mostly closed and quiet, and he barely saw anyone else on the street.

"We'll be safest if we stay near the channel," Lenni said.

"The whole bank is in total disarray. There'll be fewer guards there."

"Good. We should follow it toward the reservoirs—into the city."

Lenni sighed. "Where you're more likely to be recognized."

"Where I can get a message to Erra," he said. "Which I can't do without getting nearer to her."

He let Lenni lead the way toward the channel, as the large warehouses gave way to smaller buildings, almost none of them mage built. Soon they'd made their way into another neighborhood—this one still awake, or awake already. It was hard to tell the difference as people staggered in and out of the drinkhouses, across the streets. It wasn't crowded yet, but the buildings were built so close together the alleys between them were practically nonexistent. It was a Twill neighborhood—a poor one.

The mud underfoot and coating the walls showed there'd been flooding here, too. Judging by the water marks on the buildings, it had been over knee deep in some places. That had taken its toll—there were missing stones in plenty of the buildings, and as they drew nearer to the still-flooded channel, there were more and more piles of rubble in place of the houses. But the people were still there, dirty and too thin, their clothing in tatters.

"They don't have anywhere to go," Elan realized, watching as a girl who couldn't be any older than ten pulled a younger child to her side, trying to cover him with her own scanty, torn robe. He instinctively reached for his belt purse, but it wasn't there—he'd left his things in the workshop with Jae, and he didn't have much money to spare anyway. And there were so many people here, shivering among the overturned stones.

"Their lives were hard enough before the flood," Lenni said. "This is just . . . awful."

"They couldn't always have been *this* poor," Elan said.

"They were. You wouldn't have noticed them." There was an edge of bitterness in her voice. They reached the last walkable street as she spoke, and began following it deeper into Danardae. "The stone city out here was already where people went when they had nowhere else to go."

Elan frowned a little. He'd known it was a slum but couldn't imagine anything this bad. "At least they had shelter."

"Sure. But no food, and for so many years, no water." She said it like a challenge, but he didn't rise to it. Because she was right.

Even though the channel was right there—they'd have been able to see it from their stone hovels—only the most daring or desperate Twill would have tried to steal even a mug's worth of it. During the drought, water had been more precious than gold or money, and Avowed guards had patrolled constantly, driving off anyone who came too near, punishing anyone who dared try to steal any.

Elan knew that, because, as his father's Water Warden, he'd been responsible for overseeing the use and safety of all the water in the reservoirs. The penalty for dipping into the channel without permission or payment was ten lashes, and the payments had gotten steeper and steeper with time.

He made himself take a good long look at the people they passed. He'd always hated carrying out people's punishments as part of his job—he'd had guards handle it for him. Guilt gnawed at him as he realized how even the small act of letting someone else oversee that had separated him from these people. The poorest denizens of his city. The ones who'd needed help the most.

Lenni froze, grabbing Elan's arm so he'd wait with her. She let out a muttered curse and pulled him into a drinkhouse.

"Guard?" he asked.

She nodded. "Yes, but maybe it's just as well. You can learn a lot by sitting and listening."

He did as she said, as she went to fetch them drinks— coffee, this time of the morning. Judging by the middling quality of their robes, Elan assumed the people who wandered in were Twill on their way to places like Osann's warehouse, or who worked with the giant looms to produce fabric. Not artists, or even metalworkers—none of the Twill who were skilled enough to make a name for themselves, or much money. But these people were getting by, in a way the ones outside by the channel bank weren't.

"Spectacle's tomorrow," one said, digging into a bowl of grainy breakfast.

"I'm going to watch it," another replied. "See what happens."

"It'll be nothing," a third said, joining them.

"Not nothing, no matter which way it goes," the second said. "And I bet it doesn't go well for Lord Elthis. I went down to the reservoirs, you know? Saw for myself—the land bridge is right there. She pulled it up out of the water. Right in front of them all. Not even the Highest can stand against *that*."

"The Highest can stand against anything," the first said. "When the girl shows herself . . ."

"She'll show them up, just you wait," the second said. "And I'll be there cheering her on. It's about time someone stood up to them."

"Don't say that too loud," the third cautioned.

"The Highest have more to worry about than what *I* say—and I've got plenty to say." The man's voice took on a bitter edge. "All those years of drought and not a single mug went to help us—and now the water knocked down my sister's house. There's not room for her in my place, but where's she going to go? Her, her kids, everyone—the Highest don't care at all. I hope that girl knocks them on their asses."

Elan looked up, and Lenni caught his eye. "That's how I built up the Order. I'd have talked to him," she said softly, mostly into her coffee. "If I'd heard that, just a month or two ago. Asked if he wanted to talk to someone else who thought like he did."

"Are there really that many people who feel this way?" Elan asked, but he already knew the answer before Lenni nodded. Yes, there were—and the ones who'd joined with Lenni were only the ones who were so angry they were willing to act, not scared by the Highest's might. There were probably plenty more who agreed with Lenni and her Order but were too afraid to join.

For these people, the Closest probably didn't even matter. They wouldn't care about freeing the Closest at all. They had concerns of their own, which the Highest had never addressed—which even Elan had never even been aware of. Their outrage was like gathering clouds, looming larger and larger as a storm built. He wondered, if Jae hadn't come along, if the clouds would have burst anyway. What that storm would have looked like.

But Jae *was* going to confront the Highest. On behalf of the Closest, yes—but it would affect these people, too.

"We should go before it gets later," Elan said. "There'll only be more guards out."

"And where precisely are we going?" Lenni said. "You can't just walk up to the estate house."

"No, but . . ." He followed her back onto the street, which was only getting busier as the sun climbed higher. "Her lover's shop. Andra won't turn us in, and she'll be able to get Erra a message."

"That's *not* a good idea," Lenni said quickly, emphatic.

"You don't think any of this is a good idea."

"Because it's pointless, even if . . ." Lenni trailed off, making an irritated noise in the back of her throat. "But what if that shop is watched?"

"Why would it be?" Elan asked. "No one thinks I'd try to contact Erra. Not after the vow ceremony."

"Yet here we are." Lenni shook her head. "Let's try somewhere else—a different shop, one less obvious. Where does she buy her dresses?"

"She has stewards handle that for her. She only goes to the jeweler because, well, it's Andra," Elan said. "There's no one better to talk to."

"There must be—"

"There's not. Why are you so set against this?" Elan asked. He peered at Lenni, but she just kept walking.

"Because, as I said, it's pointless and dangerous. And I don't want to see your Andra. It's *not* a good idea."

But the more she protested, the more Elan wondered why. Her voice had gone from determined to desperate, and soon he was the one leading the way while she lagged behind. He was half-tempted to leave her entirely, slip into the crowd and lose her, but she knew where he was going. Besides, he'd promised Jae he'd be careful, and an extra set of eyes was a good idea.

She tried one last time as they crossed into the brighter, cleaner area of town where the upscale Twill shops were. "I'm sure I can get someone into the estate house to leave her a message—"

"This is *definitely* less risky than *that*," he said. Besides, after the long trek, they were nearly there. He turned onto the familiar square and made his way to Andra's shop. She wasn't out this early, but she lived in the same building where she worked. If she wasn't at Danardae, then . . .

He ducked into the alley and knocked on her door. Lenni's gaze cut around, taking in everyone who was near enough to see them, and Elan's heartbeat sped up a little. Andra would recognize him, she'd help him, he was sure of it. Because if she didn't, he and Lenni were about to be in trouble—

The door opened, and Andra stared out at them. Her eyes widened and she hissed, "Inside, quick, quick! What are you *doing* here?"

But she wasn't talking to Elan. She was talking to Lenni. Who shut the door firmly behind them. "Elan has a very foolish idea."

"It's *not* foolish," Elan said. "How do you two . . . how do you know each other?"

They exchanged glances, and finally Lenni said, "That's why I didn't want you to come here. Because the fewer people who know the truth, the better. Andra is one of my spies."

Elan stared. Andra wouldn't meet his eyes, and she turned away entirely after a moment. It didn't make sense. Andra had been with Erra for years. "You . . . but . . . was it always a lie? You and Erra—"

"No!" Andra said. "No, it's not a lie. It's never been . . . it isn't like that. Here, sit. Please."

Elan let her steer him onto a cushion. Lenni and Andra sat, too, and Elan waited for someone to explain, because it was impossible.

Andra wasn't dressed for the day yet, her hair a curly mass around her face, wearing only the light clothes she slept in and no makeup. She was usually clad in robes so expensive that most Avowed even envied them—she always presented herself in a way that made it very clear why even one of the Highest desired her. Seeing her like this was somehow almost stranger than seeing her naked would have been.

Finally she said, "I don't know how to explain it. I love Erra. That came first. But then I . . . I needed help, and Lenni was the only one who could help me. I owed her. So I agreed to . . . to keep an eye on Erra. But not to hurt her—nothing that will hurt her!"

"Yes, yes, I know." Lenni rolled her eyes a little. "Just information about her comings and goings. Nothing intimate. Barely anything *useful*."

Anything Lenni found useful would definitely hurt Erra. "I don't understand. Lenni helped you how? What could you possibly need that Erra couldn't help you with?"

"It's private," Lenni said, firm.

"But . . ." Elan couldn't imagine anything Andra could possibly need from Lenni—unless it hadn't been help at all. If it had been blackmail, that was another story entirely.

"And it doesn't matter," Lenni continued. "Because *you* haven't exactly been loyal to her, have you? We're all on the same side here. Andra, he wants to send a message to Erra."

"But you didn't want . . ." Andra swallowed. "All right."

"You didn't want what?" Elan said, pivoting to look at Lenni. "You didn't want . . ."

"She didn't want you and Erra in touch," Andra said, when Lenni only stared back at Elan. "Erra asked me to find you days ago, but Lenni said it was too dangerous to—"

"Because it was, and it is!" Lenni interrupted. "Because this is foolishness, madness—"

"No," Elan said, realizing it, anger growing in his chest. "That's not it, is it? You knew Erra and I wanted to talk to each other—you were afraid it would work out, that she'd listen to me and help me. Help *us.*"

"What possible reason would I have not to want that?"

"Because you want a war." Elan stared her down, realizing it was true as his heart thudded in his chest. "If Erra joined us and was able to stop my father from posting that notice, able to bring him or, or *any* of the Highest to their senses, we could settle things peacefully. You aren't on Jae's side—you don't care about the Closest at all. You just want a war."

Chapter 12

BY THE TIME THE SUN WAS ABOVE THE WORKSHOP IN THE SKY, sunlight pouring in the small window, Jae had worked herself nearly back to exhaustion. She was drenched with sweat, starved, and longed to shut her eyes and rest. The magical energies were blurry around her again, hard to differentiate from one another. It was as if her mind trembled the way her body did, her mental hands too clumsy to grab and manipulate the energies she saw.

The door crashed open. Jae almost fell off her cushion, startled out of other-vision, too tired to keep upright. She caught herself on one hand as Elan thundered into the room and said, "We should go. Lenni's been lying to us. She—"

"I have not!" Lenni was right behind him, and she

slammed the door shut. "Elan won't listen to me, but we want the same thing."

"No," Elan said, and rounded on her. Jae made herself stand, her legs tingling after sitting in the same position for too long. "No, we don't. We want to free the Closest. You want war—it's what you've wanted all along."

"Something happened," Jae said, before Lenni could yell back at him.

"Yes," Elan said, his whole body tense. He was almost spitting as he explained, "Erra has wanted to contact me all along. Lenni had her spy make sure that wouldn't happen—even though it could have changed everything! We could have talked to Erra days ago—"

"And what good would that have done?" Lenni demanded.

"If we'd convinced her soon enough, we might not have had to fight at the vow ceremony—she might have just delivered the knife to us. Your own people would have been safer," Elan said. "And—and she might have been able to stop my father from posting those notices, from trying to blackmail Jae. But you're a blackmailer yourself, aren't you?"

"I am *not* blackmailing Andra," Lenni said.

Elan made a noise like a snort and said, "She somehow turned my sister's lover against her—the lover who has been my sister's closest friend for five years. And Andra didn't exactly sound thrilled about it."

"Elan," Jae said, but fell silent. She didn't know what else to say, how to pacify him. Though if he was right—about Erra and Lenni both—then yes, Lenni's interference had cost them plenty. But it wasn't as if Lenni had stopped Jae from getting the knife once she said she needed it. In fact, she'd helped. If Lenni had really believed Erra wouldn't see reason, then she'd probably believed it was the *only* way to help.

That didn't make her right, but it didn't exactly make her wrong, either.

"I don't want war," Lenni said after a moment. "And I never would have put my own people in danger, risked exposing them to the Highest, if I didn't have to. But it doesn't matter what I want, because this was never going to end peacefully. Freeing the Closest is no simple matter, and it *will* bring about violence. You're naïve if you think otherwise."

Elan frowned, but he had no comeback to that. Because Lenni was right. Jae knew it, and she was sure Elan did, somewhere in his heart. He just didn't want to admit it—didn't want to admit that not everyone would be able to see reason like he could. The truth wouldn't matter to people who were scared enough or angry enough.

"We did send her a message, for all the good it'll do," Lenni said, which was obviously a concession. "Maybe something will come of it, after all."

"Maybe," Elan said. "If I can talk Erra around, and she can talk to the other Highest . . ."

"If she can talk them into surrender, then it'll be worth it," Jae said. "I don't want to fight them. I promised Tal I'd have mercy. But if I have to . . ."

"It won't come to that," Elan said. "You'll break the Curse before tomorrow's deadline."

Jae nodded, but Lenni said, "We need to talk about what happens if she can't. And if we don't hear back from Erra, of course. We need a plan."

Jae didn't want to stop to talk and plan or anything else that would take her away from the knife for very long, but she needed to rest before she regrouped and tried again. She didn't have any new thoughts on how to break the Curse—she just had to keep at it, throw all her energy at it until, hopefully, it cracked.

The best method she'd come up with was to try to wrest the air out of the binding—she couldn't handle the fire, but fire needed air to exist. If she could get the air's energy out of the binding, then the fire might fade, too. But the fire and air were bound together just as tightly as they were bound to the knife, and so far, she hadn't been able to pry enough energy away to make a difference.

"You can't turn yourself in," Lenni said, and Jae tried to focus back on her and not on the knife for a minute.

"I agree," Elan said, and gave a sideways glare at Lenni. "Much as I hate to. It's horrible, but it's a hundred lives to save thousands."

"I know," Jae said. But it just didn't feel right.

"There is another option," Lenni said. "Elthis can't give the execution order if he's dead."

Jae stared at her sharply. *That* was a possibility.

"But any of the other Highest could," Elan said. "And so could any Avowed. Even if you assassinate him, it won't save their lives."

"Do you really care? Or are you just concerned that your family will be among the fallen?" Lenni said. "Erra will be there. She'd carry out the order in his stead."

"She wouldn't," Elan said, but he didn't sound as sure as he had.

"Jae, listen." Lenni's voice was calm, clear, like the open sky Jae missed so much. "If we can't save those hundred, we can at least weaken the Highest. Get rid of Elthis, and any of the others we can. You can't turn yourself in—not for anything. But if we can make the world think you will, they'll all show up. If we can't save the Closest, we can make the Highest pay for each and every life they take."

Jae looked at Elan, waiting for him to object. Because Erra probably *would* be there with their father, and no matter which side she was on, she mattered to Elan. Jae had promised she'd have mercy, if she could—though not even Tal would ask her to have mercy on Elthis, if he slaughtered their people just to hurt her. Tal was forgiving, but not *that* forgiving, and before she'd promised mercy, she'd promised to free the Closest. That was more important than anything else. Anything at all.

But Elan didn't say anything. He looked miserable, but he didn't disagree.

Jae shut her eyes and breathed, trying to think it through. A hundred Closest lives in exchange for at least one of the Highest. A hundred Closest lives to buy every other Closest's freedom. A hundred Closest lives so *she* could live on. It was that last one that was the hardest to accept. But the truth was that she had no choice, and she wouldn't exactly weep if Elthis fell to Lenni's blade.

Finally she found her voice. "If they hurt my people, I want to cost them everything we can."

❖·❖·❖

Erra made her way down the hall quickly, long legs carrying her on equally long strides toward her study. She threw open the door, and—

Her father was seated inside. He looked up at her, amused, and said, "I sent Andra away for the night."

"Oh." Erra tried to pretend it didn't matter, that she had only been waiting for an evening assignation and not desperately hoping that Andra's return to the estate house meant she had word of Elan. She hadn't seen Andra since telling Andra he was alive—the whole world knew that now, though. Maybe that had driven him further into hiding, but she'd still held out hope. If Andra could find him and somehow get him away from the mage, Erra could protect him. Yes, he'd been at the vow ceremony among their enemies. She should have given up on him for that. But he'd also saved her life, warned her in time to avoid a killing blow. He wasn't a lost cause yet.

"You have more important things to focus on tonight," Elthis said, and gestured at one of the cushions across the table from him. "Sit. We should talk."

His voice was soft, almost pleasant. That, more than anything, made her suspicious. He'd been snapping at everyone, constantly tense, since returning from Aredann, and outright angry since the disaster at the vow ceremony. But he was her father, and more importantly, he was the Highest, so she did as he told her and sat.

He let the silence wrap around them for a long moment, then said, "Tomorrow is going to be difficult."

"I know," Erra said. "But I've been working with the

brand. I can hold it for much longer now without letting go. I won't lose my concentration again."

"Not even when Elan shows up?"

If her father knew she'd been looking for him . . . She caught herself before she could give anything away, making sure her face was perfectly neutral — the mask she'd learned from him. But something must have given her away, because he spread his hands on the table in front of him, shaking his head a little.

"As I thought. And it's natural that you don't want to see this happen — I don't, either."

That got her attention. She stared, but he looked completely sincere.

"You need to know, I didn't disavow him lightly," Elthis continued. "I had no choice in the matter. None."

"You never wanted him in the line of succession," Erra said, though it walked a line that came close to arguing with him. But her whole life of the last few years had been shaped around making sure that Elan would never become Highest — her frustrating marriage to Halann, and how much her father had pressured her to have not just one, but two children. To be certain that nothing short of a disaster would give Elan that position.

"True," Elthis conceded. "Because Elan could never be Highest — he isn't suited to it, the way you and I are. He's far too concerned about kindness, for one thing."

"Being kind is admirable," Erra said, but even as she spoke, she knew her father was right. Yes, it was admirable — in people who didn't have to rule. The Highest couldn't afford kindness if it conflicted with keeping the peace, and there were times that it did. When they'd had to abandon estates, or deny water to Twill during the drought. There had been places that had needed it more, and it didn't matter that shifting the water allocation was unkind. It had to be done.

Her father didn't bother to point out what she already knew. "He's also far too easy to manipulate. He was easy prey for that—that filthy Closest girl. And I *will* make her pay for taking him from us. But she did. And he's gone."

"But . . ." Erra swallowed her objection.

"No," Elthis said, firm. "Because it isn't the Curse that keeps the world in order. And it's not the Well, either. It's us— the Highest. *We* are what stands between the world and chaos."

"I know that. But—"

"If the Twill were to start to question us, if they ever rose up—if our own followers broke their vows . . ." He shook his head. "We are what protects the peace. We protect our people, all of them. Even the Closest—we could have killed them after the War, after all, but we had mercy."

Erra nodded, though it didn't feel quite right. She remembered the Closest woman who'd gone under the water and hadn't surfaced, how the others had kept working . . .

"The mage girl is challenging us. The longer she keeps it up, the more people will follow her. The more Twill will make demands it's unwise for us to meet, and question our decisions. They'll believe what the cursed mage says, if not now, then soon. We have to make an example of her, and we can't have mercy. We can't afford to let *anyone* believe they can question us. Not even one of our own may do that."

That was why he'd sent Elan to Aredann in the first place. At the time, Erra had thought he was much angrier than Elan's transgression had deserved. He'd even considered disavowing Elan back then—just for asking questions. Now she understood. Elthis couldn't afford to let anyone think he would change his judgments, just because someone he cared about asked him to. He had to be harsher on his own son than anyone else, to make it clear to *everyone* else what would happen if they followed suit.

And now . . . now the whole world had seen Elan not just question him but fight against him. Elan had sided with the Highest's enemies, which meant that when the Highest put those enemies down, he had to be among them. The world had to know it. That was what would restore order and remind everyone, of all castes, that the Highest were to be obeyed, for the good of everyone.

"There's no other way?" Erra asked, her voice small.

"I wish there were," Elthis said. "I truly do. I know the task we've given you is hard to begin with—and made all the harder because of Elan. But we have no choice. So I need you to promise me that you'll do your part. That girl *will* show up tomorrow morning, and we need this to end swiftly. Promise me you'll do everything in your power to make that happen."

Erra needed a moment to just breathe, to fight against the lump in her throat and the tears that wanted to fall. Because Highest didn't cry, and they didn't have mercy. Their vows to protect the world left no room for forgiveness or kindness. As her father had made clear, not even for their own loved ones. No matter what.

So she hated herself, but her voice didn't shake when she said, "I will. I promise, Father. I will."

Chapter 13

It was fully dark when Jae woke. She was still tired, but hours of striving to break the Curse had gone nowhere, and finally Elan had persuaded her to stop and sleep. Her efforts were getting weaker, not stronger, and dawn loomed ever closer. If she couldn't break the Curse—which it was obvious she couldn't, much as she hated to admit it—then they'd need her rested and ready with magic when they clashed with the Highest.

Breakfast was a silent, quick, worried affair. Elan cleared his throat as they walked out, heading to Danardae's gardens, as Elthis's notice had demanded. "I hope getting some sleep refreshed you."

She glanced at him, appreciating that he hadn't asked a question. "I can do magic, if nothing else."

"Good. We'll need it." He drew closer, murmuring in a tone so hushed it was almost Closest quiet, "Stay close, if you can. Things are going to get violent."

Jae nodded. After their decision the previous day, Lenni had gone scurrying out with messages for the Order, getting in touch with as many people as she could so they could strike today. The Highest would have as large a force of guards as they could muster at the ready today, and the Order hadn't recovered from their losses at the vow ceremony. It was Jae's magic that they hoped would make the difference. The Order would still strike as hard as they could, but no one knew how the day would turn out.

The air was thick and moist, and it was impossible to see the creeping rays of dawn—too many clouds had gathered overhead. It would storm soon, again. It felt as if all the rain that hadn't fallen during the drought was trying to get out at once, and Jae wondered if the weather would ever even out again.

The streets weren't as busy as they had been the day of the vow ceremony but teemed with people nonetheless. Jae couldn't think of a reason why so many people were out so early, all heading in the same direction, until Lenni said, "They're coming to watch the execution."

"They're calling it a spectacle," Elan said, sounding disgusted.

Jae made herself keep moving forward. People wanted to see an execution—she wondered if they cared if it was hers or the Closest's. If Elthis dared touch any of her people, then this would be his execution, too. Whatever happened today, it was going to end with deaths, and there would be Highest heads among that count. She just couldn't see any other way.

They hadn't heard back from Erra. If she'd gotten Elan's message and tried to respond, Andra hadn't reached them in time. Not knowing if she was trying to find them or if Erra hadn't responded at all was maddening, but they had no choice except to go forward as if they were on their own and Erra was their enemy.

The twisting, muddy streets of the stone city gave way to the wider streets of a market, lined by Twill shops, and then the Avowed neighborhood, and finally to a crowd that was gathered on the outskirts of Danardae's walled-off garden, the gate opened to the public. The ground was soggy, the greenery wilted—there was now, simply, too *much* water. What little grass there was had been trampled, and the bushes looked sickly. Tree branches hung limp, with bare spaces in the bark where some of their limbs had been ripped clear off by storm winds.

So much for the fabled beauty of the central cities' gardens. Maybe the Highest had kept them carefully tended for generations, even during the drought, but even they couldn't stand up to the chaos of storms and floods.

The crowd wasn't nearly as thick as it had been for the vow ceremony—that was something, at least. There also weren't as many guards as Jae had expected. Probably Elthis thought she'd come to him on her knees, despairing, to give in. The crowd's mood was curious, almost jovial, and still sleepy. A hint of light finally broke through the clouds, a sliver of pink behind the gray and black. As they pushed their way forward, Jae wondered if any of these people were members of the Order, ready to strike when Lenni commanded.

They waited, surrounded by people, as close as they could get. A barricade had been set up, rope tied between trees, keeping everyone back. Jae could spot a pavilion a little way beyond it—and at the side, all kneeling on the ground, a group of silent men and women. Closest.

Fury pumped through her veins, ran up and down her spine, filled her lungs. She slid into other-vision and made herself examine them, forced herself to look closely. These were the people who'd be giving up their lives for her, with no choice in the matter. They were strangers, dragged into this against their will, but they didn't *feel* like strangers. She sensed the connection between them all, and between them and her. They were all descended from the Wellspring Bloodlines. They were bound together by the magic in their blood, which gave the Well its power, and bound again by the Curse.

Yes, they were strangers. But they were also her kin, bound by magic.

Jae blinked. She groped for the knife, tucked into a sheath against her hip. As her fingers grasped it, the energy she saw in other-vision surged.

There was *so much* magic around them. It followed patterns she was familiar with now: the steady glow of land, the glistening shine of water, but now there was more. Something seemed to pull at the energy of the Avowed, both within the crowd and on the other side of the barrier, as if the Highest were sucking it in. Then it simply . . . vanished. There was a strange, empty area around the Highest in a world that was otherwise teeming with energy.

Jae shuddered, remembering the feeling of her magic vanishing. It had left her defenseless in the midst of the battle. She hadn't realized how much she relied on other-vision and her magic until it was suddenly gone.

More than anything, Jae felt the presence of the Closest. When she took her hand off the knife's hilt, the energy around her dimmed, but when she put it back, it surged, brightening. It had never done that before—but she hadn't been so near any other Closest since she'd acquired the blade.

She understood as soon as she saw it happen. The Closest's energy was all tied to the knife. Their ancestors had all used it to cut their skin, to bind their blood together, to bind the Well. That was why the Curse had been bound to the knife: it already had a tie to every Closest's blood.

Jae pulled the knife out. The magic surged again, and when she reached out to the rest of the Closest, that connection rang with strength and intensity. She'd felt it before, the very first time she'd tried to break the Curse, but she hadn't had enough power then. She'd been at the Well, isolated from everyone else. Here, though—there were Closest *right here*. The connection Jae had to them was closer, and the magic kept brightening because it was *stronger*. When she embraced the connection she had to the rest of the Closest, she could access more energy.

It might be enough to break the Curse.

"Attention!" The voice sounded over the crowd and everyone went quiet. She broke away from other-vision to look up at the pavilion, and saw that the gathered Highest, led by

Elthis, had stepped forward to address the crowd. A steward had spoken, but Elthis was the one who was standing at the front. Erra wasn't at his side—but there she was, under the pavilion roof, with some of the others. She kept gazing out at the crowd as if searching them, then looking back at her father.

"I demanded the surrender of the traitorous girl called Jae. Has she come?"

Jae took a hesitant step forward, then stopped. She grabbed Elan's elbow and he startled. "I have an idea, but I need time."

"Step back," he answered immediately, as he himself walked forward. Jae let herself be swallowed up by the crowd, ignored Lenni's confused questions as she retreated a few steps. She only half-listened as she reached for the magical connection to the Closest.

"I'm not Jae, but will I do, Father?" Elan demanded, ducking under the barrier rope. The crowd gasped. Elan half-turned back to the crowd, pushing his hood down. "You all know who I am. Disavowed, disgraced. But unafraid." He turned back to his father. "I'm here on Jae's behalf. She calls you, Elthis Danardae, a liar—you and your whole cursed caste."

There wasn't enough room for this. Jae shoved her way farther back until she broke free of the throng of people. She could still hear Elan, who was shouting so everyone could make out his words, but he felt distant now. She forced herself to focus as she stuck the knife into one of the tree trunks. The wood of the tree accepted it easily, soggy and swollen as it was.

"He has been lying to you—the Highest have been lying for generations!" Elan continued. "The truth is that the Well was crafted by Closest mages, that it belonged to them, that the Highest started the War—"

"Traitor!" Elthis screamed back. "Seize him!"

The crowd roared at that. Jae craned her neck, wanting to help, but she couldn't. It was almost impossible to concentrate with all the shouting around her, knowing Elan was in danger, but she only had a few minutes—if that.

There were shouts and screams and grunts. Something happened but Elan kept yelling: "I have been to the Well, I've seen it, I've seen how it responds to Jae's magic! The Highest have lied, they're *liars*—"

"Silence him! He's a traitor, a madman! And if that girl does not come forward now . . ."

Jae centered herself, ignored the screaming match and the mass of people, the crowd roiling with confused, intrigued, amused energy. As if it was only a fight between father and son, as if none of it mattered.

She pulled on the connection to the Closest, felt the power she had gathered surge. She'd been tired that morning, but now, sustained by magic, she felt like she could fly. When she reached out for the knife's energy, she could sense it all: the fire and air, bound together; the Closest, tangled with them; the strange, pulsating, twisted earth at its core.

When she'd tried to finesse the fire and air away from each other, it hadn't worked. Now there was no time for finesse, and no need. She braced herself and *grabbed*, seizing the first wisp of air energy she could sense, and with all the power of the Closest backing her, she yanked. The response was physical, a rush of wind that almost knocked her off her feet, but that was already a bigger success than she'd had before. Now she could see the binding fraying: the air pulling free, the knife getting hotter as the fire fought to stay tied to the air.

She reached again, gathered as many wisps of energy as she could, pulled and pulled. The knife fought back, trying to hold its binding steady, and the air around Jae grew hotter. She had to brace herself, to endure the feeling of the Curse at the base of her skull, the air energy buzzing so hard she felt like her teeth might fall out, the air so hot she could barely breathe—

Behind her, Elthis yelled, "Enough! Every Closest *will* slit their throats, now—"

She grabbed from the Closest, feeling their terror and the compulsion they had to obey, and even as some of them flooded with pain, others were consumed by rage, which made their energy brighter, stronger. Jae yanked it all, everything she could sense, the Closest and the energy of the earth under her feet and the water in the reservoirs, every last bit of it, and threw it like a spear at the tie between the fire and air she saw in other-vision.

The energies split.

The knife shattered, and a wave of magic, the twisted earth at its core, seized the world, shaking it, upending and quaking as people screamed. The tree went up in flames, and Jae couldn't control any of it. Her power, her connection to the Closest, flared so bright and hot that she couldn't move or see or think or breathe, overwhelmed and amazed, because the Curse had always held Closest magic in check, dampened it and made it hard to sense. Now, that fetter was gone.

The Curse was broken.

Chaos erupted around her.

❖ ❖ ❖

Two guards had tackled Elan when his father yelled to seize him, tackling him to the ground, but they hadn't knocked him out and he wouldn't be silent. He had no idea what Jae was doing, but if she had a plan that needed time, he would make sure she got it. He struggled, not to throw the guards off, just to get his breath back so he could shout the truth he'd been dying to tell since he'd discovered it: "I have been to the Well, I've seen it, I've seen how it responds to Jae's magic! The Highest have lied, they're *liars*—"

"Silence him! He's a traitor, a madman! And if that girl does not come forward now . . ."

Elan struggled again, kicking one of his captors hard enough to break free. He rolled and sprang to his feet, staring around in panic. He couldn't see Jae or Lenni in the crowd, could only barely make out Erra in the pavilion as she gaped at him, but everyone was buzzing with shock now.

He retreated a few steps before wheeling around to yell at his father, and to Erra behind him, "I know the truth and now so does everyone else. You disavowed me because I won't lie, and you can kill me but you can't make all these people forget. Now all these people know, too—"

The guard grabbed him again, this time dealing him a blow to his skull that left him dazed and silent. Just coherent enough to realize he'd failed, that Erra must not have understood what he'd been shouting, as his father ordered the Closest to their deaths.

He could see it. They hadn't all been given knives, but enough had, and those who held them raised them to their own throats. He let out a useless shout of "*No—*"

The world upended.

The blast knocked him off his feet and all he could hear was screaming. The guards who'd been dispatched to deal with him were stunned, too, and he managed to scurry away from them, but now there was nowhere to go. In the panic and confusion, the crowd had broken past the barrier. He craned his neck and could see thick black smoke rising from somewhere within the mass of people, could see ripples in the mud from the shock that emanated out from it—from what had to be Jae's doing.

Someone slammed into him; he staggered, turned, and saw the Closest. Several had fallen, but others were now on their feet. The ones standing still held the very knives they'd been told to dispatch themselves with. An order they were no longer following. Hope built in Elan. If they were disobeying, that meant Jae had done it. They were *free.*

Realization hit the crowd, a ripple of screams and panic as thick as the smoke. Someone else ran into him, elbowing him as he passed, and the barrier between the Highest's pavilion, the crowd of Avowed and Twill, and the Closest, was gone. Everyone was everywhere, brawling as if it was a crowded drinkhouse. He saw a Twill woman fall and ran toward her, but it was too late. She'd already been stepped on, and anyone who leaned in to help got knocked off their feet, too.

Guards seemed to come out of nowhere—they'd been hidden in the crowd, not wearing their gray uniform robes. He spotted several of them trying to corral a group into order, toward the garden's exit, but another stranger broke in, armed and screaming. A member of the Order. *They* were in the crowd, too. The Order and the guards and the Twill, no one sure where to go, what to do.

He shoved his way toward the pavilion, sure of one thing. The Closest who'd survived that last, brutal order would need help.

❖ ❖ ❖

The world was an endless field of fire—Erra had only gripped the brand for a moment and the world seemed to be consumed.

"Erra! Careful!" Tarrir Pallara grabbed her, yanking her back, distracting her. She didn't drop the brand but couldn't focus on it, either, and with her attention on the real world she saw that the smoke was *real*. Not some horrific nightmare. The screams, the panic—it was all unfurling in front of her.

"What happened?" she shouted above the din.

"The Closest—free—the mage is near, you have to . . ."

His voice was lost in the noise and chaos now. Erra touched the brand and the vision came back, her grip so light it only flickered at the edge of her gaze. She stared around, looking for the root of the panic, and saw real fire in the garden. She made herself run toward the line of flame, not away from it, because that was where the mage would be.

Sure enough, she hit the wall of very real heat. She wrapped her hand more tightly around the brand, so hard she thought she might crush it, and looked for what Gesra had described—the brightest area in the terrifying vision in front of her. There it was, the mage girl, trying to fight her way toward Elan.

Elan. Who'd screamed something mad about lies. It took all her willpower to ignore him and focus on the mage instead. To concentrate and feel the strange sensation of magic around her, to feel it and *pull*.

The girl staggered. Erra pulled harder, even as her vision grew stronger. She couldn't tell how much of the world was really aflame, how many of the screams were real, how many people were dying around her. All she could do was stand still in the center of it and concentrate.

"It's working!"

She barely heard the voice, her father, no more than a few people away in the midst of the madness. She couldn't acknowledge him, or the fight he was caught up in, his blade clashing with a dark-skinned, bleeding man's knife. The Closest man was hopelessly outmatched, with guards surrounding them who'd help her father—guards, but rebels, too. And the rest of the Closest, lashing out with their anger and agony. And there, in the midst of it, was the mage girl, Elan wrapping an arm around her to support her—

One of the rebels rammed into her father from behind.

Erra whirled, concentration broken, as her father staggered. The man he'd been fighting seized the opportunity, knife raised, slashed at him—he couldn't move to fend the man off—the knife drew blood again and then again—

Erra screamed as her father fell. She raised the brand like a cudgel, drove it into the nearest Closest's back, sending the woman sprawling. The rebel who'd slammed into her father appeared in front of her, sword raised. Erra met it with the brand, the metal ringing loud in her ears, the impact jarring her whole arm. Her hand opened against her will as the woman got in close enough to bash her other hand into Erra's face.

Erra tumbled backward, couldn't regain her balance. She hit the ground and someone's boot smashed into her skull. She didn't know if it was intentional or accidental, but for a moment her vision blacked out.

Even before it came back, she tried to move, to get up, to find the brand amid the chaos. When she could see, she was staring upward, her limbs too heavy. For a moment she glimpsed Elan staring down at her. Then he moved away. She followed him with her gaze as she clawed her way to her knees, saw Elan mouth a single word—*Father.* Saw their father sprawled on the ground at his feet, unmoving.

She tried to shout Elan's name, but though he turned to stare at her, she wasn't sure she'd even managed to form the word. He started to say something, but the mage girl grabbed him and pulled him away.

He looked back, but someone else crashed into Erra and sent her back to the mud. As Elan and the girl retreated, the world went black again.

Jae pulled Elan away, her stomach roiling. She wanted to bend over and vomit, her whole body off balance from the way her magic had vanished and returned, terrified it might evaporate again at any moment. The whole world was acrid smoke now, making it harder and harder to breathe, and Elan was barely moving. He'd caught her when she'd collapsed, helpless without her magic, and now she had to do the same for him.

He followed her, but there was nowhere to go. The fire had spread, blocking off the exit to the park. The walls were too high for most people to scale. The crowd was panicked, still fighting, and the Closest were free but they were going to be killed anyway. The only way out of the park that wasn't impassable was the channel, but she couldn't swim. None of her people could, either. But she couldn't let them die.

She couldn't control fire with her magic, but she could control water. When she shouted, she used the air to amplify her voice a hundred times, until it echoed above everything else: "Closest, the shore—*now!*"

Elan finally seemed to break out of his shocked, dazed state and took her hand. They raced to the water together, the surviving Closest following them—bloody and battered, only half as many as had been led into the garden in the first place. She hadn't been able to save them all, and they weren't out of danger yet.

But they were free.

They hit the edge of the channel and Jae raised her arm, sending the water away in a vast wave. It seemed to hover above the city for a moment, all the water of the channel suspended in midair, before she released it. It crashed against the far shore, the ground shuddering from the impact, and she raised her other arm. An enormous wall of mud and rock grew from the edge of the channel, keeping the water from draining back in. The bottom of the channel was muddy, a few inches of water still dragging at the hem of her pants as she ran, but it was an escape.

"They're following!" Elan yelled in her ear. Not just meaning the Closest who'd come with them, but guards and panicked Twill and Avowed, too. Jae sprinted faster, coming up toward one of the bridges between cities, overhead from this vantage. She stopped short on the other side but gestured everyone on past her, even Elan, then whirled around to see the bridge—and, grabbing for the land in its base and the stones across it, she dropped it.

The world rumbled, dust rising from the mud, smoke, and screams above them in the distance. She turned away from it all, running again, her people separated from the others by the fallen bridge.

After that, it was just moving forward, getting one foot in front of the other. She could see the ruined stone city in glimpses above her. Most of the buildings had toppled already, but now they were nothing but piles of rocks. The houses that still stood beyond them would be flooded again, whole neighborhoods practically impassible from water that had nowhere to drain, thousands of people's possessions and livelihoods destroyed. But Jae had no time to mourn or regret what it would do to the Twill who lived there—she had to get her people out.

Finally they reached the city wall, with a gap where the channel carried its water out to the countryside. They burst through it, leaving the cities behind, flooded and burning, rioting, caught up in chaos.

Jae caught Elan's eye and they slowed their pace, let everyone with them stop to catch their breath. His expression was serious, but she couldn't hold back a smile, something dark and joyful unfurling inside her. She'd done it. The Curse was broken, and her people were free.

"It's over," Elan said, looking back at the column of smoke that rose above Danardae.

"No," Jae said. "It's just beginning."

Chapter 14

THOUGH THE CENTRAL CITIES WERE RINGED BY A WALL, THE TOWN that sprawled outward from them was nearly as enormous. Not as built up, and there weren't many mage houses, but it was full of people. Some of whom screamed at the site of a contingent of bloodied, battered Closest and their Order allies pushing their way through the channel and up onto the street.

"We have to keep moving," Lenni said. "Get out of this town, get as much distance from the cities as we can."

Jae nodded, letting Lenni take the lead through the winding roads as people shouted in alarm. But no one moved to block them—not yet. No one knew what had happened in Danardae yet.

Then, like a headache that had begun slowly and built to agony, Jae *felt* it. The connection she had with all the other Closest, not just around her but across the world, flared, going white hot. Not with the Curse—that would never happen again. The Curse was gone. This was just pain, violence. Death.

She stared into the distance, but the town seemed unchanged. It was somewhere else, farther outside the cities, not just at one estate but at dozens, maybe *every* estate. The Closest had felt their freedom the moment the Curse had broken. Few of them would have known the why or how of it, though, or if it would last. They'd seized the moment, taken their chances. The Avowed they struck against wouldn't have known it was happening, either, would have no way of sensing the impending storm. The first few would have been easy prey.

After that initial fight, nothing would have been easy. Jae pushed herself forward, the heavy weight of other people's pain slowing her down. She knew what had happened: the Avowed, at least in some cases, had regrouped, grabbed their weapons, and moved to put down the rebellion. Out there in the world, Closest were being slaughtered.

Yet flowing within the agony was a river of triumph, of fierce joy. Despite the pain, there were Closest celebrating. Even as they died, they laughed. They were free.

In some cases, they were even *winning*.

"Look!" one of the members of the Order said, stopping short to point at the horizon. A column of smoke was clawing its way into the sky somewhere in the distance, mingling with the dark clouds that hovered above them. Jae glanced back.

Fire still raged at Danardae, too. Jae used other-vision to fling her mind forward, toward the smoke on the horizon, and saw people fleeing toward them—bodies left in their wake, people trampled in terror, dozens of Twill and a very few Avowed all running directly to this sprawling town.

No, to the central cities. For safety.

"We shouldn't go any closer to that than we have to," Lenni said. "We can circle around toward Kavann—"

"No," Jae said. "We head for the fire. It's a Closest victory. We'll be safe there."

"I don't know if that's . . . ," Lenni said, trailing off. "There are places where the Order can hide us—"

"There are survivors coming toward town," Jae said, walking again. She didn't miss that the Closest followed her, leaving Lenni to hurry for a few steps to catch up.

"They'll spread word of what's happening," Elan realized. "People will panic. We'll want to be out of town by then, and find somewhere for Jae to rest. Using that much magic exhausts her."

She nodded absently. It was the strangest feeling. Her body was tired, but her mind and her power were sharp. Yes, she had to push through the bloodstained pain of her connection to the Closest to really *do* anything, but she'd lived with pain for most of her life. She could focus, she could act. As long as she had this much connection, she could do anything.

But the more people died, the weaker that connection would be. And if she couldn't figure out what the Highest had done in the midst of the fight to suddenly rob her of magic entirely, they'd be left even more defenseless.

Her magic was all that had protected them, gotten them out of Danardae. It commanded the Well, saving the world from the desert. It was what would win the war that was just now beginning. If she was ever left without it, they had no hope.

They moved forward, and sure enough, they hit the wall of incoming people. It was unavoidable: the panic rippled outward from the Twill as they saw the Closest with Jae, and they roared.

Jae gathered her magic, and next to her, Elan held a sword he'd taken from one of the guards at Danardae. Nearly everyone in their group was armed, and absolutely everyone was *ready*, still jangling from the fight in Danardae. Jae couldn't even tell which side struck first.

It was all noise and violence, almost too much to follow. Jae was ready with her magic, but everyone was too closely intertwined. She couldn't think of a way to attack that wouldn't affect the Closest just as much as their enemies, so instead she pushed back, out of the way. She didn't know anything about fighting, and neither did the rest of the Closest.

But they were strong, and angry, and armed. It seemed like there was blood everywhere she looked, bodies hitting the ground, people screaming. Elan grabbed her hand and she almost kicked him in the knee before she realized who it was.

"Run!" he shouted at her. "If you go, the Closest will follow!"

Jae took off. He was right. The fight had actually been a nearly even match, and she didn't want her people to take any more damage, to get hurt any further. As she sped off down one of the streets, still heading in the direction of the rising smoke, others *did* follow. The Closest first, and then the Order.

That was how it was until they finally broke onto the main road and out of the town: skirmishes, some more deadly than others, depending on how well armed the people who attacked them were. They couldn't afford to stand and fight, just flee. Especially since they didn't know how long it would take the surviving Highest to regain control in Danardae and the cities. Once they did, they'd send all their Avowed guards after Jae, and she had to be prepared for that.

She was relieved to still have Elan at her side after everything. The way he'd gone into shock when he'd seen his father fall . . . She glanced at him, brushed a hand across his elbow to get his attention. He startled, faltering as he stepped.

"I know that must have been . . . hard," she said, hesitant, not wanting to ask.

Elan nodded. "It wasn't—I knew we were going to try to get to him, but—" He swallowed. "I didn't expect Erra to be there. I knew she would be, but somehow I thought . . . I hoped she'd get my message or . . . that she'd hear me. When I said it was all lies. That she'd believe me."

"Maybe, if you'd been able to talk to her alone," Jae said.

"Maybe." Elan glanced at Jae, then away. "If he's really dead, then . . . then she's the Highest now. If she didn't get the message, we'll never be able to reach her."

"I'm sorry."

"It wasn't your fault," Elan said.

But it was, in a way. Jae didn't speak up with that thought, but she couldn't let go of it, either, especially not as she looked around at her wounded followers, at the smoke that marked chaos on the horizon. The world was burning; her people were fighting for their lives. All because of what she'd done.

She'd broken the Curse. It needed to happen, and she didn't regret that. But if only there'd been some other way . . .

It didn't matter, now. It was done. But just because she didn't want to dwell on the past didn't mean she could ignore it, either.

They hit the main road at last, as the sun was climbing, light streaming through the few breaks in the clouds, and the view that rolled outward was terrifying.

The fields were on fire. The moisture in the air wasn't enough to dampen it, and the fire would rage until the clouds burst. The air seemed to waver in the distance. This wasn't the dry, steady heat of sun and drought, but something fiercer and more alive, a terrifying heat that Jae wasn't at all used to and couldn't control.

The road itself was still passable, the nearest fields not ablaze yet, but the whole area had been trampled. The people who'd come this way had been in such a hurry that anything dropped had been left, run over in the fierce rush toward the town. Bags of clothes, hastily thrown together; jewelry, a doll, a single boot that had stuck in the mud.

It was only as they got closer to the nearest estate house that they saw the bodies. Some had just been trampled, but as they came nearer to the fires and the town and estate house, there were more. There had been fighting here, and the dead they passed by had been injured first. Blood stained their bodies, their clothes, puddled and pooled on the ground.

Jae made herself look at them for long enough to get

a sense of what had happened. The Closest, when they'd sensed their freedom, had banded together and attacked. They'd come through the fields, killing anyone they found, and the Avowed in the estate house had put together a force and struck back. That fight had happened here. It seemed that more than half of the bodies were Avowed, but there were plenty of fallen Closest, too.

Soon, they spotted a group of people standing in the distance, blocking the road. Elan's hand caught Jae's elbow and she nodded. She saw them, and with other-vision, she could see detail from this distance.

"Closest," she reported. They were barefoot, still in muddied robes, and most of them showed the wear of battle. They were all armed, either with weapons taken from the fallen Avowed or with the same sickles they'd used to work the fields. Those blades were meant for harvesting but were deadly even so.

"Be ready," Lenni said to her people, as one of the Closest opposing them stepped forward.

Jae stepped up to meet her, holding up a hand with her palm open, gesturing that it was safe. The woman hesitated, staring at her, taking in the sight of not just Jae but the whole exhausted, bloodied crowd, in tattered clothes and bare feet. Recognizing them as their kindred, not enemies.

The woman returned Jae's gesture, and Jae let out a breath of relief. "It's safe. We'll be fine."

"Talk to them," Elan urged Jae.

Jae hesitated, but everyone who'd followed her was looking to her now. Even Lenni and the Order. So she stepped closer to the others, meeting the Closest woman between their groups, and said, "We're friends. Closest. We're with you."

"We fled the city," said a Closest man, stepping up even with Jae. "When she freed us. She did it. She's our mage."

He was looking at Jae as he spoke it, and now the woman—and the Closest behind her—stared at Jae. Jae swallowed, and remembered how she'd proved it in the past. She held her hand out, palm up, and concentrated. It was so much easier now that the Closest magic was unfettered, that her connection to them was so strong, and it only took a moment for the flower to shimmer to life in her palm.

The expressions on everyone's faces changed, from wariness or fear to shock to something joyful. Jae smiled back. It was still strangely thrilling that she could create like this. Yes, it was the same magic she used to shake the land, to control the Well, stir the air. But it *felt* different to create something rather than just moving pieces around.

She handed the flower to the woman and said, "My name is Jae. I was born Closest, and became a mage. And yes, I broke the Curse."

"Lady Mage," the woman gasped, and took a step back—then fell to her knees, the flower held gently in her hand. The rest followed suit a moment later, and so did the Closest man who'd stepped up to join Jae.

Jae stared, shocked, out of her element. She looked back at Elan, who gestured upward with his hand. He didn't say anything, but they rose anyway, and she let out a relieved breath.

"I don't need that," she told them. "I'm not . . . not one of *them*."

"The cities are in chaos," Elan said, joining them. "It looks like there was plenty of that here, too. If there's anywhere safe, we'd like to rest. We've been on the run for hours."

"Yes. We took the house," one of the Closest said. "Please follow us, Lady Mage. All your people can follow."

The Closest woman gestured to the others, and they all started forward, two groups mingling and becoming one. Jae glanced at the man who'd stepped up to help her and said, "I'd like to know your name."

"Karr, Lady," he said. "At your service, for the rest of my days."

As they walked, the woman who led them toward the house explained, "We'd heard . . . someone had slipped into our enclave. Told us to be ready for freedom."

"The Order's doing," Lenni said.

"We didn't believe it," the woman continued. "But then at dawn, we all felt it. First it was pain, like being ripped in half, but then . . ."

Jae nodded. She knew what the release was like: it was flying, after a lifetime of being weighed down. It was a drink of water after a day of working in the sun. It was breathing for the very first time.

"We'd just gotten to the fields. The fight wasn't hard," the woman said. "At first. When we felt it, we all fell in together, and . . ." She brandished her sickle. "There weren't many Avowed in the field. They fell fast, and we rushed the house before anyone could realize."

"What about the fighting on the road?" Lenni asked.

Almost as one, Jae and the other Closest shot her a glare.

She held her hands up and grimaced. "I'm sorry. I'm still getting used to that."

"We didn't have as easy a time taking the estate house," another man chimed in. "There weren't many guards—most of them had been called in to the cities, I think. But the ones who were left . . . it was a real fight. We couldn't get in, had to retreat, to regroup. They came after us, wanted to kill us, I suppose. It was a mistake. There were more of us outside— who hadn't been in that first rush. We outnumbered them. Simple as that."

"They were scared," another of the Closest put in. "Terrified. But not us—we had nothing to lose. We fought harder. Any of them who didn't run, we killed. And we put guards up all around. We didn't know who'd come for us, try to put us back in our places, but we wanted to be ready."

Jae nodded. "Wise."

"I'd be interested to know about the fires," Elan said, as they headed through a small town and toward an estate house.

"We didn't know what was happening," the Closest who seemed to be their leader explained. "But we know the central cities depend on these fields. We thought Highest would come for us, try to take back the house, enslave us again, bring enough guards that we could never win. So we decided to be ready—if we can't live free, we'll weaken them when we die. I don't know how much food they've got saved in the cities, but they won't be getting any more. Not from us. Not ever.

"But now . . ." She peered at Jae. "We've got a chance to

stay free, to *live*. We've got *you*, and your magic . . . I never even dreamed the Curse could break. I never dared. I'd've died for that, and—and I'll follow you anywhere, Lady Mage. Swear vows to you."

Her voice was joyful. Despite the battle, despite the blood and fire, despite the dead—and that surely some of her friends were among the fallen. Maybe she'd mourn later, but Jae knew with certainty that even that mourning would be a celebration. The Closest who'd died had helped win the day, and today . . . today would be celebrated by their descendants for generations. Maybe forever.

Jae bowed her head as she walked, awed by all of it, by her place in it. She didn't feel as if she deserved the looks she was getting, the way even the quiet Closest leaned in to speak to one another, gazes fixed on her. Talking about her, what she could do, what she'd done. She didn't deserve the way they'd knelt for her, or offered such unquestioning loyalty.

She'd done what she'd had to, because she'd been able to. Because it was the right thing, and because she'd promised Tal. That was all.

But it wasn't *all* to anyone else. Now they saw her as their leader—their savior. She held their hope and their futures in her hands, and they would listen to her, follow her. Die for her, if they had to.

It wasn't like being cursed, but Jae didn't feel free at all.

Chapter 15

THE FIRST THING ERRA WAS AWARE OF WAS A THROBBING ACHE IN her head—then, eventually, the rest of her aches and pains. Her whole body seemed to be bruised and cut up. She opened her eyes slowly, trying to remember what had happened, where she was . . .

In a resting room. She'd been laid out on a sleeping mat. It wasn't hers, and she didn't recognize the mage-crafted patterns on the walls immediately, which meant she wasn't in Danardae. She struggled for breath, her chest aching, panic welling up inside her. She'd been in the garden; the whole world had been on fire. It hadn't been the awful visions she had when she held the brand, it had been *real*. She'd been in the middle of the fight, and her father—

Her father—

"Highest, are you awake?"

Someone stepped close to her. She nodded, which sent the world spinning, but it settled after a moment. She didn't know the man, but he was an Avowed steward, judging by his embroidered purple robe. He crouched down next to her and handed her a mug of blessedly cool water.

"Thank you," she managed. "Where . . ."

"You're in Kavann, Highest, in Lady Callad's care," the steward said. "She asked to be notified as soon as you woke."

"Yes," Erra agreed. "Yes, of course. I should speak to her immediately, and the other Highest as quickly as they can get here—"

"They're already here, Highest, waiting for you to wake," the steward said. "I'll let them know."

He left her alone. She forced herself upright, first just leaning back against the wall. But that wouldn't do. This wasn't a proper meeting room, but it was spacious, with open windows and plenty of sitting cushions. She hauled herself to one of those.

Someone had cleaned most of the mud and soot off her, though a few places on her skin itched with dirt. She'd been dressed in simple clothes with a golden robe over them. It pulled across her shoulders, a little too small. It was probably Callad's, too.

A minute later, Callad came in, flanked by Tarrir and Gesra. Aside from a nasty bruise on Tarrir's face, they didn't look too badly hurt. They hadn't been in the thick of things, though. Not like she had, at her father's side.

"What happened?" Erra demanded, even as they found

seats. This was more comfortable than a formal study, though she had to concentrate to keep herself upright. She longed to sprawl back out on the sleeping mat but couldn't afford to yet.

"Things did not go as planned," Callad said, a note of dark amusement in her voice. "Are you all right now?"

"I'm conscious," Erra said. That was all she could really say for sure. She had all her limbs, but when she brought a hand up to where the worst of the pain in her head was, there was a sizable lump. "I'll live. But my father, did he, is he . . ."

"Gone," Tarrir said. "I'm so sorry, Erra. But we don't have time to mourn him properly."

"I know," she said.

"Danardae is a disaster," Gesra put in. "The fire spread, and so did the panic—the riot. The marketplaces were completely ruined, overrun with violence and theft and—the whole city is a disaster. We've got guards stationed at all the bridges and walls just to contain it."

Erra shut her eyes for a moment. Her home was in ruins—the city itself might not have been toppled, but the peace within it was gone.

"The cursed mage flooded half of Kavann, too, on her way out," Callad added. "I've had my guards stomping out pockets of panicked Twill all day, just to keep the fear from spreading."

"That's not the worst part," Tarrir said. "The Curse is broken—the world, the whole world, is in chaos. We've shut all the gates, but we don't know what's happening at most of the estates yet, except those we can see from the wall. And all we see is smoke. The world we knew is gone."

Erra swallowed a wave of nausea. The Curse was all that had kept the Closest contained. They'd been traitors, so many generations ago; they still carried traitors' blood. The Curse kept them in check, forced them to obey, obliterated any attempt at rebellion they might wish to start. The Curse was the only reason their ancestors had been allowed to live—the only way to ensure the world's safety with them still in it. Now . . .

"Then we're at war. The brand! Is it—where—"

"I have it," Gesra said. "No thanks to you. We were so close—"

"She was nearly killed," Tarrir interrupted.

"Next time," Erra said. "When I face that mage girl, I'll do it with an army. She won't escape again, and once she's gone, the Closest . . . we can't let them live."

"No, we can't," Gesra said, grim. "They have to pay for this. Especially the mage."

"And Elan," Erra said, and waited for the guilt and the sorrow to hit her. But they didn't come—they'd been driven out by rage. Her father was dead. *Dead.* And Elan had been there, stood over his body, held his arm out to the girl who was responsible. The two of them were on the brink of toppling centuries of Highest rule, of unbroken peace, and the world Erra had always known was *gone*.

They all had to be made into examples.

"We need to take back Danardae first," Erra said. "Restore order in our cities, to show that we will restore order to the world. Take as many guards as it needs. Get it done."

"Good. Yes," Gesra said. "You're thinking like your father."

That sent a shock of sorrow down her spine. Her father

should have been there, been the one who would march triumphantly back into Danardae and rally his Avowed. Erra wasn't ready to do it. She was injured, and she had no idea what she'd say to the people who looked to her for leadership.

But her father was gone and Danardae needed a strong leader, so she'd figure it out. Once Danardae was hers again, and all four of the central cities subdued, she'd follow wherever the cursed mage girl had gone, track her down, and end this. Erra had endured enough images of the world burning. Next time the flames rose, it would be at her behest.

"There's a lot we have to tell you about being Highest," Callad said.

"About how to control the Well?" Erra guessed.

"Yes . . . kind of," Callad said. "I wish we had the time to do this properly. Right now, everything is—"

"There's a lot no one knows," Tarrir interrupted, but then he, too, faltered.

It was fierce, elderly Gesra who finally managed it. "The Well wasn't crafted by the Highest." Before Erra could even gasp, she continued, "The Closest created it. Which means we don't have as clear control as you've been led to believe. But the Closest who made the Well—they were maniacs. Tyrants! They had all the water in the world and denied it to anyone who displeased them. Or for no reason at all. There was nothing fair about it. No order. The War, when it happened, was to wrest its power away from them—so that our ancestors could *give* the world order. There. It's said."

Erra reeled and had to slam a hand against the ground to catch herself. Her wrist jarred, but at least she stayed upright. Knowing the Curse was broken had tilted her world sideways;

now it felt upside down. The Closest had been the rebels. Everyone *knew* the Closest had been the rebels. But Gesra was saying . . .

"We do control it, in a way," Tarrir said. "When we abandon an estate, more water comes to the other places it's needed. We're careful. We're fair. The Closest never were. But if the Twill—even the Avowed—knew we don't have finer control . . . our ancestors couldn't allow that. So they let the world believe they crafted it. Only we four in this room know the full truth. It must stay that way. Do you understand?"

"But . . ." Erra swallowed. She *did* understand. If her ancestors had seized the Well, not crafted it, they must have had a reason; they must have been protecting themselves. If they'd decided it was too dangerous for their descendants to know that, there must have been a reason for that, too. Now Erra understood why their enemies had been cursed to be silent—to make sure that only the Highest's victory would be remembered, not the way the War had started. That was what the world needed, if there was going to be peace. Her father had all but told her that.

It wasn't the Well that held the world together. It wasn't the Curse that kept the world in order. It was the Highest.

"I understand," Erra said finally. "The Highest have to be respected—revered."

"Exactly. Good," Gesra said, nodding as if it was finalized.

"Things will be all right, Erra," Tarrir said, his voice a lot more sympathetic than Gesra's. "Right now you must feel . . . I can't imagine. But we will honor your father by putting down this rebellion. His killers will pay. Now you need to rest so you can look presentable at Danardae when it's time."

"And *we* need to see to the prisoners," Gesra said.

"We took prisoners?" Erra asked.

"Yes—a few. And I'm sure at least one of them will know something useful. Tarrir, help me up."

Tarrir stood and offered his arms, helped Gesra stand, and led her out. Callad stood, too, but before leaving, she said, "Your mistress is here—she was the one who dressed you while you were unconscious. She's desperate to see you."

Andra. The world was out of order, but she still had Andra. "Yes, send her in, thank you."

"Don't let her distract you—you do need the rest," Callad warned, but she followed the others out, and a moment later, Andra came in.

Somehow, seeing Andra made everything seem all the more real. Her usually painted face was plain, scrubbed clean. Her hair was frizzy, wild around her face, instead of held back by one of her beautifully crafted headbands. She wore no jewelry and only plain Twill clothing. Her eyes widened when she saw Erra, but a moment later, she knelt at Erra's side and wrapped an arm around her. Helped her back to the sleeping mat.

"Are you all right?" Erra asked her, even as she lay down. She wanted to shut her eyes, but she wanted to pull Andra into her arms first.

"Yes, I—mostly. My shop is . . ." Andra shook her head a little and sat cross-legged next to Erra. "I only glanced at it for a moment. It's been smashed, everything inside it is destroyed—stolen. All my jewelry . . ."

"I'll take care of it. We'll catch the thieves responsible,"

Erra said. "As soon as everything else is settled, I'll make sure they're caught and punished."

"Erra . . ."

"In the meantime, come to Danardae with me," Erra continued. "You'll be safe there, with the babies. I won't let anyone harm you. I won't."

"Thank you," Andra said, but her voice was thick with choked-back emotion. "But Erra, I—I had to see you—"

"I'm all right."

"I have a message." Andra reached up to scrub at her eyes, as if that would clear the tears out of them. "I got it last night, from Elan. I found him, I was trying to get to you, but your father, he . . . he had guards escort me home, I couldn't even wait for you. Erra, I tried—"

"A message." Erra made herself focus. A message from Elan. "Show me."

Andra had carried it between her dress and her skin, keeping it hidden. A smart move. She handed the scrap of paper over now, and Erra felt a tiny pang as she recognized Elan's writing. But she pushed that aside, let her rage and loss and terror beat it back. She unfolded it and read:

Erra,

> *We need to speak, face to face. As soon as*
> *possible. Do not let Father carry through on his threat*
> *tomorrow—Jae will not sit by and allow her people*
> *to be slaughtered. I fear if he carries through with his*
> *threats, it will mean his death. You must stop him.*

Her hand shook with fury. His death—Elan had known. And had stood at the mage's side anyway.

He is a liar. All the Highest are liars. I have learned the truth, I have been to the Well. It does not belong to us. It was crafted by the Closest—it was Aredann who was the traitor, not Taesann. Our whole world is nothing but a lie.

A lie. Elan might have thought he knew, but he didn't understand anything. Whatever half-truth the girl had told him, he hadn't bothered to learn the rest of it. Her father had been right after all. Elan was too easily manipulated, too willing to be swayed. He could never have been one of the Highest. He would never understand how to maintain peace—but Erra did.

I can explain it in person, and Jae can prove it to you. You must believe me. You must come meet with us, as soon as possible. I know you aren't like Father, I know you will listen. You must.

> *By my hand,*
> *Elan*

He hadn't signed it with a last name—he was no longer entitled to use Danardae as his surname. Not now that he'd been disowned and disavowed. He was no one anymore, nothing but a traitor and a madman.

"I don't know how to reach him anymore, he fled the city with the mage," Andra said. "But there must be some way . . . Erra, you can still stop all this—"

"Stop what?" Erra demanded. "They declared war when they killed my father. When that girl broke the peace."

"Broke the Curse, you mean."

"I *will* find Elan, and I will bring him to justice."

"You don't mean that," Andra said. "You can't."

Erra didn't say anything.

"*Erra*, he's your brother! And if you can reach him, maybe he can help you broker a peace, without having to slaughter—"

"We're at war," Erra interrupted. "There can only be peace once we restore order—once our enemies are dead. Including that traitor."

Andra recoiled, pulling her hand away from Erra's on the sleeping mat. She was silent, her features twisted into an expression of fear, but she didn't argue any more. She didn't question Erra—no one questioned the Highest.

There was no room for kindness or mercy now that they were at war. The last of the sorrow Erra had felt faded away, ebbed like the waters of a receding flood. The world Erra had known was gone; she and the other Highest would have to build a new one from its ashes. And that world would have no place in it for traitors.

Chapter 16

THE CLOSEST HAD STARTED CALLING IT THE BREAK, AND BY THE fourth day after, the immediate violence had ended. In other-vision, Jae soared above the estate town that had turned into their camp, widening her gaze until she could see it all. It was several hours of marching removed from the wall and the central cities—close enough that it was a large town, with its own reservoir and mage house; removed enough to give them a buffer. They'd sent word out in all directions, hoping to bring as many Closest here as they could, and now there were hundreds upon hundreds, from at least a dozen differ-ent estates.

The Twill who'd lived in the town had fled for the safety of the cities—assuming the cities were safe. No one knew what was happening behind the city walls. The Avowed had mostly fled, too; those who had stayed had been killed, or taken captive. As soon as Lenni had realized that, she'd pulled Jae aside to ensure the captives would be kept alive, guarded by the Order. Not executed, the way some of the Closest wanted.

Jae couldn't blame any of the Closest for that, when back at Aredann she had killed the Avowed guard who'd raped her, and hadn't felt a single heartbeat of sorrow over it.

It was possible—maybe even likely—that Elthis Danardae had been killed at the Break. Elthis, who had threatened Tal's life to try to control her; who had left thousands of Closest to die at outlying estates; who had thought nothing of slaughtering masses of Closest to punish her.

She hoped he *was* dead. When she thought about it, all she felt was satisfaction.

But Tal wouldn't have felt that way. Even after what Elthis had done to him personally. He wouldn't forgive, but he wouldn't kill, either, not if he could find a way around it. He'd be disappointed if he knew how Jae felt.

She'd promised him that if it was possible, she'd have mercy on their enemies. Now that the Closest were free, she had to keep that promise when she could. Besides, Elan agreed with Lenni that hostages could be valuable, that they might be able to trade them for food or supplies.

So Jae let them live, and hoped the Closest who had suffered under them would understand. She wasn't sure she would, in their place.

As Jae watched in other-vision, Closest were training with the weapons they'd found or stolen, drilled by a few members of the Order. It was a large force, strikingly silent for a group that size, determined and working hard. They seemed to learn quickly, with a fierce intensity.

They had no choice but to practice as much as they could, as quickly as possible. No one knew when or how, but everyone was certain that the Highest were going to strike back at them. Preparation would hopefully save their lives, though it was mostly Elan and Lenni who were laying out plans for what to do. For all the Closest looked to Jae as a leader, she'd grown up a groundskeeper, and cursed. She understood plants, not people. She had no idea what to do now that she'd broken the Curse, seeing through the one plan she'd been clear on.

"Lady Mage!" It wasn't a shout—Closest never shouted—but it was urgent nonetheless. Karr hurried toward her. Jae stood before he had a chance to bow. "There's a group approaching, I saw it from the rooftop. More Closest, but they're frantic."

"They might be followed," Jae said, striding with him toward where Elan and a few Closest were talking, waiting for her.

"I didn't see anyone after them, but they could be," Karr said.

Jae glanced at Elan. He'd already heard. She nodded toward the hallway, the exit. "Let's meet them, then."

"You can stay," Elan said. "It's safest here. Just in case."

Jae sighed. She'd heard that a few times in the last four days. Yes, her magic made her the single most powerful person among the army—but also the biggest target. She didn't want protection, and she was as safe in the town as she would be anywhere, but even so she nodded.

"I'll handle it," Elan promised her. "Eat something—replenish. You never know when we'll need you."

She nodded again. She hadn't used as much magic in the last few days as she had during the Break, but she'd been dangerously depleted by the time she'd finally been able to rest, despite how her power had increased near the freed Closest. So she ate and drank, a meal prepared by Closest but flavored with the spices the Avowed had kept in their kitchen. Then she sat, rather than paced, until a quiet burst of commotion reached the estate house. She greeted Elan and the others almost at the door, and saw why Elan was frantic immediately.

Yes, this was another group of Closest. But with them, hands tied in front of her, was Palma. She was gaunt and covered in mud, in only a dress with no robe, with frizzy wisps of hair pulled free of their usual twists. Her wrists were tied and her eyes were red and puffy, though she wasn't crying at the moment.

Elan was arguing with the nearby Closest holding her. He turned to Jae. "I tried to explain she's our ally."

"She's Avowed," one of the Closest said, then did a double take at Jae and bowed. Apparently her description had already spread to them somehow. The Closest were quiet, but they did share secrets with one another.

"Jae," Elan implored.

Jae reached for Palma, placed a hand on the rope, and pulled at its energy. It crumbled under her grip, and Palma burst into tears. She turned to Elan and all but collapsed against him as he put his arms around him.

"Palma, what happened?" Lenni asked. Then, to Jae and

Elan, she said, "I sent her home after the vow ceremony—she's not a fighter. She was supposed to spread word among the Closest at as many estates as she could to be prepared."

"I did!" Palma wailed. "I stopped at as many as I could see between the cities and my home. But after the Curse broke, the Closest rose up—against all of us, the Avowed, even *me*. They were going to kill me!"

"But they didn't," Karr said, voice even.

Palma gave a little sob at that, and one of the Closest who'd come in with Palma said, "She did tell our enclave to prepare for something. She never said what." The woman's skin was almost as light as Elan's, but a less golden shade of brown, and her dark eyes sought out Palma for a moment, glaring. "If we'd known, we would have been *ready*. So many were killed . . ."

"So were the Avowed when you attacked!"

The woman looked away but said, "She didn't explain anything—"

"You didn't *ask*—"

"They couldn't," Jae said, an edge in her voice as she reminded Palma. She wondered if Palma's warnings at the other estates had done any good at all, or if they'd been just as thoughtless and confusing.

"She surrendered to us, so we held her, just in case . . . in case she was telling the truth. That she was on our side," the Closest woman continued.

"She was," Elan said, wrapping an arm around Palma again. "She was trying to help."

The woman didn't look impressed by that.

"She was," Jae confirmed. "She's a member of the

Order—our allies. They helped us achieve the Break. Even the Avowed among them."

That finally seemed to mollify the woman. "I see, Lady Mage. Then I'm glad we didn't harm her."

Jae couldn't quite identify the expression on Palma's face at that. But Elan cleared his throat. "I'll find a room for her to rest in."

He led Palma out, and as they went, Jae remembered that Palma and Elan had been close, before Elan's exile. In fact, he'd risked his father's wrath on Palma's behalf. It made sense that he was protecting her now, just as he'd tried to then.

She turned back to the Closest woman. "I'd like to know your name."

"Minn, Lady Mage."

"Minn," Jae repeated. "You and your enclave are welcome here, with my thanks." She glanced at Karr. "There was plenty in the kitchen earlier."

"Yes, Lady Mage," Karr agreed. "If you'd like to follow me, friends, I can show you the way. You can eat and then rest, and tomorrow, join us in training—if you choose."

As if there was a doubt. Every Closest old enough to fight wanted to train. They would defend themselves and their newfound freedom. Jae felt an ember of pride at that, glowing inside her. Even if something happened to her, it would be hard for the Avowed to end this rebellion. Every Closest would fight to the death for their freedom.

If *that* happened, then the Avowed were doomed anyway. It was the Closest's bloodlines that bound the Well— which was weakened, even now. Jae could sense the edge of the binding fraying already. Many, many Closest had been slaughtered in the last four days, and each death endangered the realm's water supply. With every skirmish, with every death she witnessed or caused, the promise she'd made Tal to be merciful grew more distant, more impossible. Closest were still being killed every day, and the Highest were preparing something behind the city walls. Until they were out of power for good, there was no room for mercy at all.

She hadn't meant to follow Elan and Palma, but she heard their voices echoing down the hall and stepped closer.

"It was *horrible*," Palma sobbed. "They were brutal. I saw them kill two Avowed in cold blood. If that woman hadn't recognized me, I would have been next!"

"It's all right now, you're safe," Elan said, soothing her.

Jae reached the end of the hall but hesitated outside the room they'd found. She didn't want to interrupt. She glanced inside and saw them sitting on cushions next to each other, Palma still in Elan's arms. Jae turned away sharply but couldn't bring herself to stop listening, even though this didn't concern her.

"I didn't know it would be like this. Lenni said it would be difficult if we freed them, but I didn't know it would be so awful."

"What did you expect?" Elan asked, a curious lilt in his voice.

"I don't know, not . . . not that they'd be so . . . you'd think they'd be grateful. But they're brutal."

Elan sighed. "They've been through so much. Each and every one of them, Palma, they've survived things I can't even imagine. They can't just forget about all that."

"*I* never hurt them!"

"We all did, every one of us who took the brand," Elan said. "Even if we didn't mean to. But you're safe now." There was the soft sound of movement, and his footsteps heading toward the door. "You'll feel better once you've had some rest. You're safe, I promise."

He stepped out of the room and started down the hall, not even noticing Jae. She hurried to catch up with him, placed a hand on his elbow.

He half-jumped, turning quickly, then let out a bleat of laughter. "Blood and bones, you scared me! I didn't know anyone was there."

"Sorry," Jae said. She hadn't meant to startle him.

But he smiled. "It's fine, you'd think I'd be used to how quietly you can move by now. I should pay more attention. You must have heard that, then—don't worry about Palma. She'll be fine, she just isn't used to people who aren't impressed by her."

"Like you were, before Aredann," Jae said.

Elan gave her a sidelong glance and said, "Yes, I suppose I was. She was beautiful and she needed my help and . . . it feels like a lifetime ago. Not a few months."

"But you still are," Jae said, and felt her cheeks heat up. "Still . . . still feel like . . . you protect her."

"She needs someone to," Elan said, but he stopped walking and looked at Jae. He reached out to put a hand on her elbow, then changed his mind and slid his hand down her arm to take her hand instead. "But I don't feel the way I used to. Not about her, anyway."

Jae stared down at their joined hands and didn't know what to say, didn't know why her heart was beating so fast.

Elan smiled gently and let her hand go, then cleared his throat.

"We need to know what's happening in the cities," he said.

Jae felt as if she'd just experienced an earthquake and only now was the world stable under her feet again. She made herself focus on what Elan was saying and nodded at him to continue.

"We need to know how the cities are faring, what the Highest are doing. If they've managed to contact any of the other Avowed."

"They must have," Jae said. The Closest army had done its best to keep watch on all the roads and stop anyone who tried to get by, but there was too much ground to cover and most of it was too far removed from the town they now controlled. They had to assume the Highest had gotten word out to their followers across the world, made contact, and made demands. There would be Avowed coming to help them soon.

At least, there would be unless the Closest had seized those estates. In which case, the messengers would have been killed on arrival, most likely.

Jae and the Closest had sent out messengers, too, and so far only a few had returned, bringing more Closest with them. There might be more on their way back, more followers to help them keep their freedom, but . . . maybe not. Maybe the rest had all been discovered by Avowed and killed for the messages they carried. It was so hard to say. There were so many crisscrossed roads to the future, she didn't know which path was the most likely.

"I need to get into the city and find out what's happening," Elan said.

Jae felt as if her stomach had hiccupped at the idea of Elan going back to the cities, where his death warrant had been signed. "Someone from the Order can do it."

"Forgive the question, but do you really trust the Order?"

Jae considered that. She knew Elan *didn't* trust them—he hadn't since finding out that Lenni had blocked Erra's attempts to contact him. Even though the Order was on their side, its members having fought with them at the vow ceremony and again at the Break. They were helping to train the Closest now. There was no question that they wanted the Highest out of power.

But Elan thought Lenni saw the Closest only as tools. She wanted the Highest gone, and freeing the Closest had been the best way to strike against them. Plus, he was sure she had done something terrible to force Andra to spy for her.

Jae could see both sides, the way the Order had helped *and* the way Lenni had kept secrets. But for all she wanted to trust Lenni, she *definitely* trusted Elan. In her blood and her bones, she trusted him.

So she said, "All right. It's just . . . I wish you didn't have to go. There's so much to figure out here, and . . . and everyone here is relying on you."

"No, they're relying on *you*," Elan said. "I'm just trying to help you."

"*I'm* relying on you. I wish . . . I'm not good at this. Tal would have been so much better at all of it," Jae said, looking away. She hadn't said Tal's name out loud in a long time.

"Maybe," Elan said. "But he told me, once, he was glad

you were the one who'd discovered the magic. Because you'll always be brave enough to do what needs to be done. And I think he was right, Jae. For whatever that's worth."

Jae found she couldn't quite look at Elan. She didn't feel particularly brave, and she definitely didn't feel like a leader. So much of the time, she didn't know what to do or how to be the person the Closest seemed to *need* her to be. They needed someone who understood them, was one of them, but could lead them to victory. Ensure that their freedom would last forever. Someone who would win this war for them.

She wasn't much of a warrior, but Elan was right. The next step had to be getting information—finding out what the Highest were up to so the Closest could prepare. So she nodded again.

"Getting into the city won't be easy. There are still whole camps outside the walls, they aren't letting *anyone* in. But . . ." She thought. "I think we can manage it. If you really have to get into the city, then I have an idea."

Chapter 17

ELAN STARED AT THE SLOPE THAT HADN'T BEEN THERE FIVE MIN-
utes ago. Jae's shoulders heaved and there was sweat gathering on her forehead, but that was the only outward sign of
what she'd just done—an act of magic that went even further
than opening the entrance to this tunnel.

"I'll keep the water out of this branch until you return,"
she promised him. "It'll be muddy, though."

He nodded. He was wearing boots but had a bag with
sandals and a clean robe he could pull on once he got to the
city to hide that he was obviously an outsider. "I'll be careful."

"Good. I raised the exit in a park by the channel. No one
was around, so hopefully no one will find it and explore in
the meantime."

"All right." He hesitated. It was just the two of them now, out by the reservoir. She'd asked for privacy, and a handful of Closest had fallen in to keep others from approaching them, including members of the Order. He had no doubt his absence would be noticed, but the information he brought back would be vital. And he didn't care that much what Lenni thought about his coming and going. Maybe it would be a good reminder that he didn't quite trust her. That even though the Order had been vital, *Jae* was the one in charge now.

At least, Elan hoped the Order would realize that—and that Jae would. She hadn't exactly embraced the role.

He hesitated, looking at the steep slope of the tunnel, then back at her. "You be careful, too. I'll be back as soon as I can."

He held out a hand and she took it, not hesitating. Her skin was rough with calluses. He stepped close, and her eyes opened wide, but she didn't move. "Jae . . ."

She didn't say anything but looked from their joined hands back up to him, so, heartbeat racing, he leaned in and kissed her. Just for the briefest moment, his lips barely meeting hers, awkward with both of their mouths closed.

Her hand clenched his so tight it hurt and her whole body went stiff with tension. He pulled away quickly, wanting to curse himself. He'd thought . . . He knew how he felt, he'd cared about her for so long, and when she'd started talking about Palma he'd thought maybe . . .

But she didn't look excited or intrigued or any of the ways girls usually looked when he kissed them.

"I'm sorry," he said, stumbling back a step. "I shouldn't have done that. I'm sorry."

"I . . ." She was blinking, breathing hard. "I don't know what . . . don't know . . ."

He hesitated, and it was awful, because she looked lost and he wanted to reach out to steady her. But he was the reason she looked like that. "I should—I should go. I . . ."

He fell back another few steps, then turned away even though she was still staring at him, until she said, "Wait."

He stilled, except to look back at her. She didn't look any less terrified; she didn't reach for him.

But she said, "Be careful. Come back quickly."

"I will," he said. "I promise."

She swallowed visibly and nodded, and he fled as quickly as he could without breaking into a true run.

The tunnel was actually an aqueduct. Water from the reservoirs served the fields through channels aboveground—but the Well sent water *to* the reservoirs in giant underground ducts. Jae's magic made her a master of water and earth and tied her intimately to the Well, so stopping its flow for a day was easy enough, and opening a tunnel down to it from the surface was, too.

Elan carried a torch and his boots squelched as mud tried to suck them off with every step. It was slow going, dark and damp and *cold* in a way he'd never felt before. The desert nights had been cold but dry. This was something different. He shivered as he walked, and walked, and walked.

It would take several hours to reach the far end. He had to travel all the way to the cities, under half of one, and up to the surface. But he couldn't take any wrong turns: Jae had closed off the other branches, resculpted the world under the surface to make this easier for him. He wouldn't get lost, he merely had to walk through this strange, lonely, dismal tunnel.

He wished she was with him, but after what had just happened, he wasn't sure she'd ever want to be alone with him again. He was certain no one had ever kissed her before—at least, not when she'd had a choice in the manner. Maybe Rannith had.

Rannith had raped her.

Elan felt sick to his stomach. That had happened to her, and then he'd gone and kissed her, and the fear in her expression told him as clearly as words that he'd been wrong. He'd hoped she wanted him to do it, but she'd had no idea what he was thinking. Elan had seen her angry and defiant plenty of times, and he'd seen her broken and mourning. But he'd never seen her still with terror like that.

Dread wrapped further around him with every step. She was the center of his world, the one thing that had been steady and sure since he'd learned the truth about the War and the rest of it. Jae was always honest, forthright, even brazen. She didn't trust easily—and that made the fact that she'd come to trust him feel like a gift, one he'd now ruined.

Jae was strong and sharp and fascinating. He had no idea how this war was going to end, what the world would be like in its aftermath, but he knew that, if she'd let him, he would *stay* by her side. Before, he'd been sure she'd want that. Now . . .

It seemed like forever later that he felt the tunnel slope upward and saw light leaking down into it. He let out a deep breath, put out the torch, and climbed farther upward. The exit wasn't as steep as the entrance had been, thankfully, so he didn't have to scramble quite as much to keep his footing.

He listened but only heard distant murmurs, so he swapped out his boots and muddied robe for what he'd carried with him and carefully made his way up into the evening.

It took him a minute to figure out where he was. Yes, in a park, and in Danardae, no less. He could see a bridge in the distance and recognized it as one that led over to Caenn. That meant this park had to be near the fanciest shops and markets, where Andra had her workshop. He knew this area well, which was good—but he might be recognized, which was nerve-racking. Especially since he'd made himself so visible at the Break.

He pulled his hood up and headed toward the edge of the park, keeping to shadows as much as possible. Even out here it was muddy. The park was in bad shape. It wasn't the one that had been aflame during the Break, but weeks of wind and rain had felled some of the trees, and all the flowers and grass were drowning in mud. It squished unpleasantly underfoot as he walked, mud quickly coating his feet. He should have left the boots on.

Nearly no one seemed to be out. He shivered again as he slipped from the park down a street, heading toward the block with Andra's workshop. The streets were quiet, especially for a night with no rain. Normally, even in a market after hours, there would be people standing around chatting, cleaning their storefronts, trading gossip with each other from the day. Eating and drinking as they walked home. Calling out their windows to one another. Cities were never silent, but tonight, Danardae was as quiet as the Closest.

He saw why quickly enough: he turned down the street

that held Andra's shop and saw a notice posted. It said that the streets would be patrolled by guards from dusk to dawn, and everyone was encouraged to be home and stay inside. The shops in the market must have all closed early—if they had been open at all. Many of the storefronts looked like they'd been flooded or smashed. Frantic footprints were everywhere, and mud coated everything.

Even Andra's shop was in bad shape. The door and windows were hanging open but he couldn't see any of her wares inside—either she'd taken them somewhere else, or they'd been stolen. There were no lanterns lit, either. Maybe she was in her apartment instead.

Footfalls came from not too far away. He looked up quickly and saw two robed figures, visibly armed. From a distance and in this darkness he couldn't be sure, but he suspected they wore guards' gray, which meant he definitely didn't want them to bother him. He hurried along and turned onto another block. He'd have to come back and try to find Andra later.

At least on this block there was a little noise. There was a drinkhouse, still lit and buzzing with people. He slid inside, remembering everything he'd overheard with Lenni. Drunks were always willing to talk. The place was packed, people pushing elbow to elbow, most of them well on their way to drunk. He had to shove his way toward the back, where he could get a drink himself.

There was no chance of finding an empty cushion along the tables, but that was just as well. He wandered toward the walls, listening to snatches of conversation as he moved. He needed information, after all. He was rewarded quickly. No one in the drinkhouse seemed to want to talk about anything except—

"Well, we can't be *sure* it's broken, can we? I'd expect it to split the world, if the Curse really broke."

"Half the city was on fire. That's not broken enough?" someone returned. "And it's just as bad in Kavann. They're still flooded. Nothing's getting out that channel, either. I went, I looked. There was a mage, no doubt. Nothing could have done that naturally. It's all twisted up. Like a rock wall, where there used to be a park. You should look tomorrow. You wouldn't believe it otherwise."

"But they *can't* be free," the first voice returned.

Elan tried to listen in and get a feel for the speakers without being too obvious. The one who'd actually looked at the channel Jae had torn up was larger, boisterous, holding a mug of what was definitely *not* his first drink. There was a small crowd listening in. Elan wondered if any of the others had been to the decimated park themselves—or if maybe they were all too scared.

"If the Curse is really broken," a woman said, sounding bored—but it was an obvious put-on—"then we'd be at war right now."

"You think we aren't?" the loud drunk returned. "No one's allowed in or out of the cities. I heard there's rioting outside. Everyone from all around wants to come in—it's safe here, but out there, there are bands of Closest roving around, killing anyone they find."

That got a round of gasps. Elan took a swallow of the bitter drink he'd been given.

"How could you even know that?" the woman asked. "If no one can come in, then where are you getting your information?"

"One of my customers is a guard," the man said. "And he heard from *his* boss, who's a guard *captain*, that Her Highest says that's what's going on. They can't open the gates for anyone at all, it might be a ploy, an attack. The Closest are out there, all right. They're killing everyone. But we're safe."

"For how long?" someone else demanded. "What are the Highest *doing*? My wife is out there—my children! They need help!"

"And anyway, we're *not* safe," the woman put in, her disbelief forgotten. "If the Closest have a mage, then no wall will keep them out. If they're out for blood, they won't stop until they've overthrown all four cities!"

Elan almost couldn't believe how different this was from the conversation he'd overheard only days ago. It was a different crowd, but still all Twill. Now, none of them were outraged at the Highest for leaving them to their fates in the stone city. None of them were amused by the idea of a mage, or looking for a spectacle.

Everything had changed. They were all deadly serious, the dissatisfaction Lenni had taken advantage of turned to terror—and its target had turned to the Closest. Elan could feel the rising hysteria crackling in the air around him and took a risk. The biggest drinker's source was a bit distant, but he seemed to at least have some idea what was happening. That was more than anyone else. Elan cleared his throat to insert himself into the conversation: "Maybe the Highest have a plan? Lady Erra . . ."

"All Lady Erra's got is patrols in the streets, and it's too late," he said, voice full of disdain. "Half my cloth was stolen, and she's not even hearing complaints! Lord Elthis never would have stood for this."

No, he wouldn't have—and the way this man was talking, it was clear that Elthis was gone. When Elan had seen his body hit the ground, that really had been it.

His father was really dead.

"I think the Highest have a bit more to worry about than robberies," someone else said. "If there really is a war beyond the city walls, they've got to fight it."

The loudest man slammed his now-empty mug down. "*I'll* fight it. That's what I've heard they're saying. They want to raise us all together against the Closest—rid the world of the traitors once and for all, like their ancestors should have done in the first place. I'll help. And you." He threw an arm around one of the others. "Your wife's out there. You'll join, too. We all will." He raised his empty cup. "Someone refresh me, so we can drink to it!"

Elan made himself smile and raise his mug, too, as everyone started talking about that. But his mind was racing, already thinking it through, and he felt a little ill.

There were hundreds of Closest with Jae, and thousands more across the realm. If they could band together, they'd outnumber the Avowed easily. Their numbers combined with Jae's magic would win the day easily against the Avowed. But the Twill . . .

The Twill's fear meant they'd want their old world back— that they'd forget that life under the Highest hadn't been great, either. All it had taken was one change, big enough for everyone to see, and any thoughts of cheering Jae on against the Highest were gone. These people were all ready to join the Avowed.

The Closest army wouldn't just be facing the Avowed. They'd have to fight these people, too, and the Twill were nearly as numerous as they were. More Twill than Closest would have experience with weapons, and they'd be following well-trained leaders.

Which meant the Closest victory was no longer assured. Even if they did win, the cost would be that much higher. The lives lost . . .

He'd known everyone had looked down on the Closest. They carried traitors' blood, they were cursed, they were untrustworthy and chaos barely contained. Elan had felt that way once, too. But he'd never *hated* the Closest like this.

Maybe these people hadn't, either, until the Break. Everything was different now. But maybe it could be fixed, a little, maybe somehow these people could see who was really at fault. If they knew the truth of the War, and knew the Highest had been lying for generations . . .

But maybe not. The Highest's lies were easy to swallow, and the Closest outside the city walls *were* violent. For good cause—they fought to survive, they fought for freedom—but where the world wasn't flooded, it was burning. People were afraid.

"Elan?"

His name was hissed in his ear and he jumped, reaching for the knife he carried under his robe, just in case. But he recognized the smudge of mustache quickly and relaxed. "Osann. You startled me."

"That's obvious," Osann said, amused, and nodded to the door. "Not safe to say much more in here."

Elan followed Osann out. The guards seemed to have passed by, so Elan started back toward Andra's shop. "You didn't get out during the Break?"

"I tried. I couldn't get to the channel," Osann said. "I was stuck in the park until . . . People were terrified but the channel was the only way out. Those of us who managed to get to it before the fire . . . we had to crawl over the wrecked bridge to get back into Danardae. It was a disaster. There was a riot."

Elan shuddered. The survivors would have been angry and terrified, no one would have been quite sure what had happened, and with Elthis dead, the panic would have been even harder to contain.

The Highest kept the world in order. News of their defeat would have caused as much terror as the idea of freed Closest.

"Since I couldn't follow you all out, I fled to Caenn until the rain finally put the fires out and I could get back. How'd you get into the city?"

"There's a tunnel, in the park by the Caenn bridge," Elan said. "You can come back with me, and if we can get word to them, any other members of the Order who were stranded in the city can get out, too."

"I'll stay here, then, for now—spread the word," Osann said.

They'd reached the building with Andra's shop. "I need to stop in here," Elan said.

Osann gave him a confused look but didn't question it. It was easy enough for them to get in through the smashed doors. It was almost funny that the Twill and Avowed disdained the Closest, but they were the ones who'd done *this*.

Elan looked around. Andra's displays were empty, knocked to the ground. The cushions where she'd plied customers with tea and talk were in total disarray. Mud had been tracked in, footprints covered everything. He crouched to look at the overturned table and found a few papers that had fallen from it. Customer orders, at a glance—except the last one. That was in mage script.

He picked it up and walked to one of the windows, trying to stay out of sight while making use of the light coming in. He wasn't sure he was successful, but the only noises he heard were distant, so he read slowly and translated as he went.

No time to write—been summoned to estate house.
Will be with Lady E, learn what I can. I don't know if
I will be able to make contact.

It wasn't ancient writings. It was a message from Andra, left so they could find it.

"What's that?" Osann asked.

"A letter," Elan said. "She was trying to get in touch with me."

"Ah." Osann nodded, and Elan went back to reading.

Lord E dead. Highest just retook Danardae and
everyone is talking of war. No word yet but they ARE
going to strike. Taking time to plan first, I think. They
are afraid of J.

BE CAREFUL and do not trust anyone left in the city. Twill are rallying behind Highest, everyone is panicked.

Papers hidden in my bedroll. Keep them safe. Will contact if possible.

—A.

Elan slid the paper into his bag and made his way from the shop back and up to Andra's rooms, leaving Osann behind to keep watch. People had been up here, too—the looting hadn't been confined to shops. He wondered how many people had been attacked and injured in the midst of it, fighting off their own opportunistic neighbors.

Though Andra's sleeping mat had been knocked askew, blankets torn clean off, the thick roll itself was still intact. Elan groped his way over it and finally found a tear, hastily sewn shut. He pulled the stitches loose again and reached inside. It took him a few seconds to find the sheaf of papers.

More mage script including some of the more ancient texts. They were invaluable, and had nearly been lost. He slid them into his bag, too, grateful Andra had thought to hide them. Though if the Highest knew anything about them, they would have been proof Andra herself was a traitor. She couldn't afford that any more than the Order—the world—could afford to lose the ancient, hidden truths the pages might contain.

Elan looked around but didn't find any other papers, or anything else of value.

"I need to get back to Jae," Elan said to Osann, once

they'd met back up. "And we need to get the rest of the Order out of the city."

"I didn't know Andra was one of Lenni's—well, Lenni didn't like to tell anyone much of anything," Osann said, a little surprise in his voice. "But I know a few of the others, and since we've got a way out of the city now . . ."

"Get word to them if you can."

"The tunnel's big enough for everyone to pass through?" Osann asked, as Elan started down a street that would take him back to the park.

"Jae could *make* it bigger," Elan said.

"I'll let them know," Osann said. "We'll come through when we can—or when I hear from you. Good luck."

"And to you," Elan said, and they parted ways.

It was a relief to know that their few allies had survived the rioting. Osann and other members of the Order, and Andra, and . . . Erra, maybe.

Andra must not have gotten her the letter in time, but maybe it *still* wasn't too late. All she'd done so far was try to keep order in Danardae after the riots and fire—he could hardly blame her for that. Andra was with her now; surely Andra had given her the message. All he had to do was find a way to contact them.

Maybe it was good that Erra had so much power now. Not that he was happy his father had been killed—he didn't know *how* he felt about that. Their relationship had been so contentious, and after everything his father had done at Aredann, Elan knew he was a liar—and a killer, responsible for the deaths of hundreds of Closest. So maybe he should have been glad his father was gone.

But he wasn't. He knew that eventually he'd mourn—not just for his father's death, but for the death of who he'd believed his father to be. Steadfast and determined and always right. Honest. The father he'd *thought* he'd had, who he'd loved, even though his father hadn't thought too highly of him in return.

They were both gone—Elan's idealized version and the real man. Which just made reaching Erra and showing her the truth more vital than ever. Elan had lost his naïveté, his title, and his father. He didn't want to lose his sister, too.

Chapter 18

Jae wandered the captured town after Elan left, so dazed she barely noticed what was going on around her: the rows and rows of people training in every public space who went still as she approached, the Closest hanging out of windows to see her as she passed by, the way the already quiet groups went silent and hushed. There were hundreds upon hundreds of Closest in the town now, but Jae found herself stranded alone in her mind.

Elan had kissed her.

Her chest went cold and tight with anxiety just thinking about it. He'd *kissed* her. She hadn't expected it, hadn't known it was coming—hadn't known anything at all except that she was nervous at the idea of him doing something dangerous without her at his side. She wanted to help him and she worried for him, and before she'd had a chance to figure out what that meant, he'd kissed her.

The panic had hit like a sandstorm, sudden and overwhelming everything, burying her ability to move or even think. She hadn't known what to say, what to do, what she wanted, and then he'd looked so terrified, his voice had shaken, and . . .

She didn't want him to sound like that. She wasn't angry but she didn't know what she *was*.

She liked Elan. She trusted him more than anyone else alive—maybe even as much as she'd trusted Tal, as impossible as that seemed. Elan had sacrificed so much because he believed in her; he'd given up everything he'd known, he'd risked his life, he'd fought by her side, he'd followed her into the desert and back.

Maybe if she'd known what he was going to do, maybe if she'd *expected* it, she might not have panicked. But now she was sure he would never do it again—whether she wanted him to or not, which she wasn't sure about at all.

He would never do anything to hurt her. It shouldn't have been so terrifying to imagine him kissing her again—but it was, the thought of his lips on hers, of his hands on her body . . .

She tried to lose herself in work but just drifted from task to task for hours: using magic to help grow plants for food, washing and mending because so many of the Closest came with their clothes in rags, assisting in the kitchen. There were no decisions to make while Elan was gone, and she was too anxious to rest. She wanted not just to keep busy, but to be *useful*.

"Lady Mage." Karr's voice broke through the mist in her mind and she turned her attention to him. He was a large man, with dark skin marred by a still-healing wound on his throat that would eventually scar. He'd been at the Break, freed at the last moment as he'd cut himself, not deep enough or wide enough yet to kill him. He'd been at Jae's side almost since then, helping her handle all the Closest who needed her, though he had yet to find any of his own family among the masses. "Another group has arrived. If you have a moment, they'd love to see you."

She nodded. More and more Closest arrived daily, as the Order's messengers found them and as rumors about them spread. Jae tried to greet every group that arrived—to assure them she was real, that she was one of them, that she had magic and would wield it on their behalf.

Karr led her into the estate house's torch-lit room dining hall. It was the largest room in the house and could probably fit a hundred diners as long as they didn't mind bumping elbows with one another as they ate. Now it was packed, everyone shoved in so tight Jae could barely make her way up to the head table. She didn't bother trying to sit, just clambered up on top of it and stared out at them.

The group was quiet, even the children. They were wide-eyed, staring up at her, and she wondered what they'd expected. Someone older, probably, like Lenni. A leader, someone they could trust. Not her—young, nervous, awkward under their expectations. But she was the mage. She was the one who'd broken the Curse. They'd come here for *her*.

She made herself breathe, wishing Elan was with her. When she couldn't find the words for what was needed, he always seemed to. She glanced at Karr, but he was waiting just as expectantly.

Finally she spoke, forcing her voice to carry even though she was unused to letting it fill the quiet corners of a room. "My name is Jae, of Aredann. I'm a Closest. And I'm a mage."

As she always did, she held out her hands. This time, though, she didn't close her eyes. It was so much easier now that the Curse was gone and the Closest's energy was unfettered. She imagined a flower, grew it in her mind, but with so many people looking on, she didn't know if that would be enough. So she grew vines, too, long and chilly but smooth, let them climb her arms, pinching the sleeves of her robe inward.

The vines encircled her, wrapping down her bodice as she breathed and let them, feeling as if she herself was one of them. A vine, a weed, unwanted in the Avowed's gardens. She'd survived anyway, grown strong even when they'd tried to pluck her away, starve her, kill her. Weeds took hold, and if they were left unchecked, they thrived and took over entire gardens.

Yes, Jae was a weed. And as the vine wrapped around her waist, coming to rest at last, she found herself at peace.

Everyone watched her in awe now. She nodded, confirming whatever it is they were thinking but would never ask. Yes, she'd broken the Curse. She'd struck back at the Highest, felling one of them. Yes, she would lead them to victory.

"All the Closest here are training so we can fight. We've all gathered together, and if we *fight* together, we will win. We will never be enslaved again."

That earned not cheering, but nods and gestures, a few murmured words. Clenched fists from those who wanted to fight, anxious looks between others.

"We'll begin a meal for you now, and any who wish to may help with its preparation. You must be hungry," she continued. "You are safer here than you have ever been before. Please rest."

There wasn't really room for them to lie down, stretch out, but they must have been weary after traveling. Especially after the losses they must have suffered, fighting their way free, fighting just to get here—and now they could relax, because they'd seen her. She hadn't understood that at first, but Karr had helped her see it their way. The Closest would die to defend their freedom, but they'd never had it before. They needed a goal and a leader, someone to point the way as they figured out for themselves what they wanted—as individuals, as families, as a community.

"Perhaps you should sleep, too, Lady Mage," Karr said, as he helped Jae down.

"Lady Mage!" One of the members of the Order ran toward them in the hall. "Elan is back. He's waiting in the small study; he asked me to gather you and the others."

Jae wasn't sure if she was more relieved or nervous, and nodded. "Thank you. I should . . ." She glanced at Karr.

"Go," Karr said. "I'll set things in order here and then join you, if you don't mind, Lady Mage."

"Thank you," she said again, and let . . . Casinn, that was

the Order member's name, lead her out. They parted ways down the hall, him to find the other members of the Order, and her to the study, where Elan was indeed waiting. He was sitting on one of the cushions, looking tired, his hair pulled back and his face in shadows. His muddy cloak had been tossed down next to him, and he was examining a sheaf of papers, squinting.

"Perhaps it'll be easier to read in the daylight," she suggested.

He looked up, startled, and the levity in his voice was forced as he said, "You snuck up on me again. Of course you did."

She shrugged a tiny bit. He didn't say anything for a moment, and she didn't know what to say, either. It had never been like this between the two of them before. Finally she pointed to another cushion and said, "I could . . . sit."

He let out a breath and nodded, so she did. Near him, but not close enough to touch.

"Elthis is dead," he said, when she didn't say anything else. "Erra is alive. She's the Highest now."

"Oh," Jae said, not sure how to respond, no idea how Elan felt about any of it. He was furious at his father, but he'd believed in his sister. But if she'd now taken up their father's title, then the chances of being able to get word to her, or bring her over to their side, were vanishingly small. Jae wasn't sure they'd ever been higher, but Elan had insisted so many times.

"She might still . . ." He trailed off, shrugging awkwardly. "I left a message at Andra's workshop, but Andra's at the estate house with Erra. I don't know if she'll get it. I don't know . . ."

"Then you must think she didn't get the last message," Jae said.

"She couldn't have," Elan said. "Andra left me a note and didn't mention it, so she must not have been able to deliver it in time."

Jae didn't say anything to that. She hoped he was right, that Erra just hadn't gotten their plea for a meeting, but inwardly she didn't think the message would have made a difference. Everyone said Erra was much more like their father than she was like Elan—even Elan admitted that. Jae couldn't imagine anyone like Elthis caring more about the truth than about holding power.

"There were more ancient writings hidden in Andra's room," Elan continued, after a long pause. "Some of the Order's saved papers. I think they may have been about Aredann . . . actually, now that makes sense. I had no idea where Erra had found all those old papers about Aredann and magic she sent me off with, but she probably got them from Andra, who got them from Lenni."

"Ah," Jae said. She had never even thought to wonder, but it was one of those papers where she'd seen an inked drawing of the fountain that sat in Aredann's courtyard. That had led her to examine the fountain, since she had no idea what the papers meant, and that was how she'd stumbled over the Closest's hidden magic. Without those ancient, carefully preserved pages, she'd never have gained her magic and broken the Curse. Without the Order's help, even though she hadn't known about them at the time . . .

"Elan, welcome back," Lenni said. "Next time, I would

appreciate it if you'd tell me you were leaving. We could have slipped a dozen spies into the city. You didn't need to go."

"Yes, I did," he said, voice final.

"Well. Next time, then." Lenni's voice was just as short, the attempt at pleasantness in it poorly faked.

Palma joined them a moment later, yawning noisily, Casinn at her side. They both took cushions, Palma sitting near enough to Elan to place a hand lightly over his. He pulled his away.

Karr joined them a minute later. Jae caught his gaze, glad to have him there. She trusted Elan, but it was a relief to have another Closest in the room, someone who understood her in a way Elan couldn't.

"What did you find out?" Lenni said.

"Danardae is in bad shape," Elan said. "I didn't see the other cities, so I don't know if they had problems, too, but the rioting must have spread out of the park, because every street I saw was wrecked. There was so much damage."

He described it quickly—the broken walls and windows, the curfew and guards out walking the streets, the way everyone had been so scared and so ready for war. Finally he just shook his head a little. "I don't know what I'd hoped, but from everything I saw . . . Danardae is on the brink. I think one more gust will turn it into a storm, and the Highest want to unleash that storm on *us*. It'll be easy for them to enlist the Twill to help fight."

"But this isn't our fault," Casinn said. "The Twill should blame the Highest, not *us*."

"But they don't," Lenni said. "And even if we told them

how the Highest have been lying, they wouldn't believe it, or they wouldn't care. It's easier to blame the Closest. It just *is*."

Jae glanced at Karr, who was listening intently but silently.

"Not once they get to know . . . ," Casinn said, and he glanced at Karr, too.

"No one is going to *get to know* a Closest," Palma said.

Karr's expression finally twitched minutely. One of his hands tapped against his thigh for a moment. That was the only sign of his reaction—silent, understated. Jae wondered if anyone else even noticed it, but she could see his annoyance.

"We need to strike now, before the Avowed and Highest get organized," Lenni said. "If the Twill are so terrified, we can use that against them—give them something real to be afraid of. The panic will make it harder for the Highest to maintain control—that will hit the other three cities. And as things fall apart behind the walls, we'll be preparing. We can end this quickly."

"I'd like to know what you're thinking," Jae said. "About giving them something to fear."

"Actually, sending Elan into the city through the aqueduct just gave me the idea," she said. "Because the one thing the Twill and Avowed believe, above everything else, is that the Highest control the Well. All you have to do is show them the truth by draining the reservoirs. Then the whole world will know that you control the Well, and the Highest don't."

Jae stared at her, marveling, but she could remember too many dry days, dancing on the edge of sunsickness. She'd survived an estate with a drying reservoir. What Lenni proposed was horrific.

"It's still raining," Lenni said, after a long silence. "You won't do real harm—though I bet you can cause rain. If you could stop it . . . we could really weaken them, then. They'd be out of food and water both in short order. There's been one riot already. There'll be another in no time at all, and the Highest would destroy their own base of support putting it down."

"I can't stop the rain," Jae said, sharp. "And I wouldn't, even if I could." She could almost feel Tal's nod of approval at that.

"I would," Karr said.

Everyone turned to him, surprised. Jae cocked her head, waiting for him to say more.

"I've never lived a day unafraid," Karr said, his gaze meeting Jae's. "I'd let them know what that's like."

"Precisely," Lenni said. "Jae . . ."

"And you explained the binding to me," Karr continued. "That it depends on the Closest bloodlines. If we die, the Well comes unbound—they need to know that, and believe it. We make them afraid, and we make our point. If they fight us, they will lose, no matter what."

"They *will* fight us," Lenni said. "We know that. We have to *win*, no matter what, and we can use the chaos to our advantage. If you can't stop the rain, I still think draining the reservoir will be enough."

Elan shook his head a little. "I don't like this. We might still be able to convince Erra—"

"You still think that, even now that she's the Highest?" Lenni interrupted, incredulous. "When they bring their army against us, she'll be leading it."

"She might not," Elan said. "We don't know that for sure. She doesn't know the truth—"

"Are you so sure of that?" Lenni asked. "She's taken up Elthis's title, his responsibilities. The other Highest may well have told her anything she didn't know. She never answered your letter. She let the attempted slaughter of the Closest happen before the Break. She has done nothing, *nothing* to show that she could be brought to our side."

No one in the room said anything to that for a long moment, not even Elan. The anger in his expression turned to pain, one Jae knew only too well. She'd lost her sibling, too. At last he nodded, and said, voice hoarse, "I understand we can't act as if she'll be an ally. But if she *does* reach out to me . . ."

"Yes, we'll see what we can do then," Lenni said, but the dismissiveness in her voice made it clear how likely she thought *that* was. "Then we're decided. Lady Mage, Elan can help you write a message about the binding, and the Order will see to it that it's delivered—maybe we can use that aqueduct. We'll send it as soon as it's done, and you can drain the reservoir tomorrow, first thing."

"*Are* we decided?" Karr asked, though only a few people in the room seemed to realize how strong a point he was making by asking it as a question. "Lady Mage, *you* didn't say."

Palma rolled her eyes, and Lenni's expression went unreadable. "Of course. Jae, I *assume* you agree."

"Yes," she said. "I do. But . . . thank you, Karr."

He nodded.

"Until tomorrow, then," Lenni said, standing. She swept out, Palma and Casinn following, then Karr.

Jae glanced at Elan. She'd need his help to write the message to the Highest—not just with the actual writing, as she couldn't do that at all, but with the words. He was much better than she was at that kind of thing.

But now they were alone together again, and her pulse sped up as she realized it. He must have, too, because he looked away from her suddenly. She wanted to say something but couldn't—she didn't know what to say at all, didn't even know what she felt. She didn't want this, though, the strangeness between them. Elan was her friend and she needed him.

"Jae," he finally said. "About . . . about before I left, when I kissed—"

"Don't," she interrupted. She could feel panic at the edge of her mind again, a storm on the horizon.

He hesitated, then said, "I only . . . I won't. But please let me say this one thing."

Her stomach churned, but she nodded.

"I . . . I care for you, quite a bit," he said. "But I don't expect anything from you. We both have too many other things to think about anyway, and I won't bring it up again. I'll never, never kiss you or . . . or anything else, ever again, and I'll still be here for anything you need, anything I can do. It's all right if you want to pretend it didn't happen, but I just had to say that so you know—you know how I feel. In case you feel the same. But it's all right if you don't."

She stared a little, trying to hold off the anxiety, trying to make herself focus and understand. The words had washed over her, too much for her to take in, but she grasped for the few that made sense. That Elan wouldn't do it again. She could pretend it hadn't happened.

She really, really wanted to pretend that. So she nodded.

"I . . . It's all right," she finally said. "You're my friend. That's all."

"If you'd like, I'm sure Lenni or Palma could help you with the letter instead—if you don't want me near you."

"No," she said quickly, and focused on breathing for a moment. She could feel the ground under her feet, the air around her. She was fine. She *was*. "It's fine. Let's just put it out of our minds."

He nodded, his kind features gone serious, and he reached for the writing supplies. "If that's what you want, then let's get to work."

Chapter 19

"Highest!"

An Avowed scrambled into Erra's study, where she'd been meeting with Desinn Loerdan, who'd been at Aredann with her father, and several of her father's other trusted advisors. She looked up in irritation, but the man didn't even stop to catch his breath, let alone apologize for the intrusion.

"The reservoir—it's—come quick, Lady, *hurry*! It's all gone!"

Erra shot to her feet, instincts taking over. It was all she could do to keep herself to a quick walk, not a run, at the awful idea that something had happened to the reservoirs—but her father wouldn't have run. It wasn't dignified, and no crisis was more important than keeping the world's confidence.

A crowd had gathered before she reached the remnants of the park that overlooked the reservoirs, and her heart thudded as she saw. It was dim out, clouds covering the sun, though not thick enough that it threatened to rain just yet. But where there should have been the water of the reservoir, there was only silty, sandy mud and strange weeds curled in on themselves, drying for the first time. There was still a small ring of water around the central island, but that was all. Hardly enough to sustain the city for a day, let alone longer.

Horror hit her as she realized that the Highest might not be able to change this. The world thought they could—they needed the world to believe that. But after what Gesra and the others had told her . . .

She looked up at the clouds. It might rain. That would help. But . . .

The Closest mage had done this. She'd interfered with the Well, the delicate system of ducts and channels and reservoirs that kept the world safe from the desert. They had relied on it for generations. Now the water was gone.

She felt sick, suddenly, overwhelmed, and she desperately wished her father was there. He'd know exactly what to do, what to say. How to handle this.

She needed the other Highest, immediately, and turned to the nearest Avowed, not caring who it was. "Get Tarrir here, *now*, and Gesra and Callad—get messages going, *move!*"

The Avowed fled, grabbing others to help carry out the order. Erra gaped at the empty reservoir for a moment longer, then turned to see the people staring. Not just at the muddy hole in the world where their water should have been, but at her, too. Waiting for her to address them, to reassure them. Like her father would have.

She peered into the crowd. Halann was there with Efenn in his arms, and Andra, holding Jarren. Andra looked stricken. That was what finally got Erra talking—maybe she couldn't reassure the whole world, but she could reassure Andra.

"We will handle this," she said, trying to make her voice as thunderous as her father's always had been. Trying to make the lie as believable as possible. "The mage thinks she can interfere, but the Well is *ours*. Our loyal people will never go without, and the traitors responsible will be punished." She didn't spare a look back at the empty reservoir. "Their ancestors tried to take the Well from us once—and fell. We were merciful then. We will not be this time."

Someone in the crowd actually cheered, and Erra nodded curtly, not saying anything more. Halann fell into step with her as she strode back toward the house. Her mind was already racing, trying to anticipate what the other Highest would plan in retaliation for this—the Closest were gathering to the west of Danardae; there would have to be a way to attack them without the Closest knowing they were coming. . . .

"How could you let this happen?" Halann demanded as they walked. His voice was a hiss, not meant to be heard by the others, who were still too near, but his anger and anxiety were palpable.

"I said, the Highest will handle this."

"Without the reservoirs—"

"We'll get the water back," she said, trying not to let her

jaw clench, forcing out words she knew might not be true. Halann was annoying at the best of times, and she didn't want to deal with him right now when there was an actual crisis at hand.

"Your father would never have let this happen," he said.

She stopped short and turned to glare at him. He retreated a few steps, handed Efenn off to one of their Avowed servants, then squared his shoulders and glared back at her.

"The traitors who did this," Erra said, overly enunciating, "also killed him. Do you think I will let this go unpunished? Do you think I will do nothing to protect my people—our *children*?"

"As if you care about us at all," he said.

She wanted to lash out, unleash her fury on him. But her father would never have done that—he never fought with people in public. He always stayed calm as he destroyed them, ensuring that everyone would respect, even fear, the Highest. So she tried to make her expression as unreadable as his had always been.

"Keeping the order, protecting the Well and its reservoirs, is *my* duty," she said. "Do not question me."

She waited to see if he would, pressing his luck because they were married. If he did, she'd have to find a fitting way to silence him. He should have been her staunchest supporter, and she couldn't afford to have him speak against her now.

Maybe he realized that, remembered that her father was gone. Elthis's approval didn't matter anymore, only Erra's, and if he wanted to maintain any of his influence after the Closest had been put down, he would have to get in line.

He bowed his head, acquiescing. "Yes, Highest."

Good. She nodded at him and then started back toward the house, grabbing Avowed and dispatching them with orders as she went. The curfew would need to be enforced again, and more strictly; she wanted every guard they had out in the streets, keeping the peace. Her people would be scared and she couldn't afford another riot. She couldn't fight her own people and the Closest at once.

"Erra?"

Andra was hovering nearby as they finally reached her private study. Erra gestured at the door, saw Halann still following them, scowling, and pointedly ignored him. "Give us privacy," she informed the nearest guard, and then gestured Andra in, shutting the door after. Yes, Halann had finally quieted when she'd confronted him—but she didn't mind reminding him of his place, either.

"Don't worry," Erra assured Andra, before Andra could even speak. "I will handle this, and I'll keep you safe."

"I know," Andra said, her voice heavy with emotion. "I just . . . Erra, what will you do?"

"Strike back," Erra said.

"Against the mage?"

"Yes," Erra said. She had the brand at her hip again, still tangling with her robe if she walked too fast. When she confronted the mage for this, the mage would fall.

"How?" Andra stared at her.

Erra shook her head. She didn't like lying to Andra, but this was too important. "I can't tell you—as much as I trust you, it's a secret that only the Highest can know. But once that girl falls, the rest of the Closest will, too."

Andra swallowed, nodded. "I see. But what if . . . what if there are other mages?"

"Then we'll deal with them, too," Erra said. "Mages, Closest, and anyone else who dares defy us."

"Of course, Highest," Andra said, but she still looked uncomfortable, not reassured.

Erra sighed and tried to soften herself—this was Andra, after all, not anyone else. She could allow herself this one moment. She took Andra's hand and squeezed it gently. "You just need to trust me, and the rest of the Highest. I won't let anything happen to you."

"I know," Andra said, and squeezed back. "It's just, if there *are* more mages . . . what if . . ."

Erra started to give her another reassurance, wanted to hold her and make promise after promise, but before she could say anything at all, the door rattled and was thrown open. She looked up in irritation and found Desinn wild-eyed and clutching a scrap of paper. His robe was in total disarray, and there were guards flanking him.

"Highest, this is . . . it's a message. From the mage." Desinn held the paper out, his hand shaking.

Erra braced herself and pulled away from Andra. "You'd best go."

"Yes, Highest," Andra said, but she hesitated for a long moment before finally walking out. Erra dismissed the guards who'd come with Desinn, but she kept Desinn himself in the room. She shut the door and looked at the letter.

It was written in Elan's handwriting.

Highest,

The Curse is broken. My people are free. You have seen my power for yourself. Let the draining of your reservoirs be a lesson: if you fight us, you will lose. Even if you slaughter every last one of us, you will doom yourself.

The Well was crafted by Closest and is our birthright. Despite the lies you have told for generations, only I control the Well's power. Further, its magical binding is tied to the Closest's very bloodlines. The Curse nearly eradicated that binding and caused the drought. Our freedom ensures the Well's continued glory—but if there are no Closest, there is no Well.

If forced to, we will fight for our freedom with every breath. There is not one Closest who would not die before bowing to you again. So as I said: if you fight us and we defeat you, you lose your power and your lives. If you fight us and you conquer us, we will die rather than allowing you to rule us, and the Well will die with us.

But if you relinquish your power and raise no force against us, we will allow for peace. That choice is yours.

The signature was a scrawl, barely legible—it looked poorly copied, handwriting worse than a child's. Even so, Erra could read it: *Jae Aredann.*

A letter from Jae—but in her own traitorous brother's

handwriting. So much for the message he'd sent her before the Break. He'd stood by then, while their father was killed, and he wrote this now, a threat on her enemy's behalf. He'd chosen his side.

She willed her back to stay straight, unbowed, and unbent. Andra was one thing, but she couldn't show even a moment's worth of weakness to Desinn. She set the letter down and demanded, "Where did you get this?"

"I was accosted," he said, straightening his robes. "Two thugs in black robes, like at the vow ceremony and the Break—"

"Did you read this?" she interrupted.

"Yes, Highest. I didn't know what it was at first—"

"Do you believe it?" she demanded.

"Yes . . . yes, Highest," Desinn said, hesitant. "I heard your father say some . . . some things at Aredann that made me wonder if . . . but . . . I don't know. It isn't a matter for *me* to discuss."

"That's right, it's not," Erra said. "So don't, not one word to anyone."

"Yes, Highest," he agreed quickly, and fled when Erra gestured him to the door.

Erra took a moment to herself to contemplate it. Now that she knew the full truth of the War and the Well, she couldn't deny that fighting the Closest could spell disaster. It was possible that it *would* destroy the Well.

But at the same time, she could hear her father's voice reminding her that it wasn't the Well that protected the world. It was the Highest.

The mage's threats didn't matter. Even the Well itself

barely mattered now, especially since the rain had returned—the reservoir would fill itself with that; the channels would flow, the crops would continue to grow. The Well was important, yes, but not the most important thing.

No one could ever doubt the Highest. *That* was the key to keeping the world safe. Which meant this rebellion had to be put down—no matter what it cost.

Chapter 20

JAE WAS TAKING WEARY STEPS TOWARD HER ROOM BUT HEARD A footfall behind her. She went still and forced herself to breathe slowly as she turned around to see who needed her now, what would keep her from sleep. She was tired, and not just physically. Draining the central cities' reservoirs had taken a lot from her, even with her increased power, and someone had needed her attention every moment since. The Order, to talk about strategy and how they'd strike next, if they should attack or retreat. New groups of Closest arriving. The squads that were now training, the volunteer kitchen workers in the estate house who were preparing food for the entire thriving town of Closest, the handful of volunteers who watched all the children. Everyone had questions about where they could go, if it was safe, how much they could consume or should cook, what they should do next. Somehow, they all expected her to know the answer.

She tried. She really did. But now all she wanted was to lie down on her mat, shut her eyes, and be alone in the dark and the quiet.

Elan was the one who'd followed her. He held up a single hand, palm open. She sagged in relief and jerked her head toward her room and he fell into step with her.

"I won't keep you long," he promised. "And I'll make sure Karr knows to keep everyone else out. You need sleep or you won't be any good to anyone."

Jae wasn't sure she was much good to anyone now, but she didn't say so. Just waited. As always, when she didn't react, Elan continued.

"I thought you'd be interested in hearing what I've translated. But it can certainly wait—I can see that you're tired."

She was, but Elan was still acting a little awkward around her, as if he was afraid she'd throw him out at any moment. So she nodded and led the way into her room. "Yes, of course."

He sat cross-legged and shuffled the papers he'd been carrying. "It's about the founding of the Well. Letters between Janna Eshara and the other Closest of the time—and mages of the Highest as well. It keeps mentioning the cursed Rise, but I still have no idea what it is. Magic gone wrong, somehow."

Jae waited, listening, longing to shut her eyes.

"It does explain a little about why there have been no mages in so long, though. The whole reason the Highest refused to join Janna's mages was because of the Rise. They believed any great work of magic had the potential to destroy the world. So they refused. Then, after the War, the movement against magic—magic that *had* killed thousands—was so strong, they decided to seal their magic off entirely."

"That must be part of what the vow ceremony does," Jae said. "I know it was part of the binding of the Curse, but the way Nallis's energy dimmed after his vow . . . I think the ceremony also siphons off the Avowed's magic. And since the Closest's magic was hidden away, that only leaves the Twill . . . and any Twill mages, they kill."

"I wonder how," Elan said. "You'd think mages would be able to defend themselves."

"You'd think. But at the Break . . ." Jae had lost her magic. She still didn't know what had caused it there, or at the vow ceremony. It hadn't lasted long, but if it had been the Highest's doing, that would explain how they'd been able to murder Twill mages through the years, including Lenni's mother.

Jae started to answer, but before she could, heavy footfalls hit the corridor outside her room and someone called, "Lady Mage! Lady!" She stood, startled, and Elan climbed to his feet and jerked the door open. Minn was outside, frantic. "Come fast, there's fighting—we're under attack!"

Just like that, Jae's exhaustion vanished and she ran back the way she'd come, Elan and Minn at her elbows. They dashed down the corridors, downstairs and out, and then the noises were unmistakable. Screams and weapons clanging and people shouting. It was happening in the town square, and a thread of smoke rose from that direction, too.

She skidded to a stop at the edge of it, trying to figure out how to help. Elan and Minn pushed their way in, Elan stooping to pick up a knife off the ground, Minn producing one from her belt. Jae was unarmed and felt helpless. She reached for the energy around her, watching the fight in both true vision and other-vision, but she couldn't figure out a way to intervene. She could shake the ground, open up a chasm—but the groups of fighters were so intertwined she couldn't be sure she'd only knock over the attackers.

The far edge of the square was on fire. At least one torch had been dropped and caught. It wasn't an enormous flame yet, but she couldn't let it spread. She couldn't control fire, though, so instead she reached for the air around it. It was thick with water, and fire needed air to survive. As a body collapsed at her feet and a wide-eyed Closest slammed into her, driving someone else back, she raised her hands and pulled the elements apart.

Air rushed out. Water rushed in, a lightly misting rain covering the whole square. The fire died almost instantly, turning to sizzles. Someone began cheering, realizing she was there, but the attackers didn't slow even as the cheer spread. Jae tried to figure out where her people were in the crowd—maybe she could at least separate everyone into groups, try to contain the fighting that way—but then it was clear, the attackers were grouped together, yes, but trying to get to her, now that she'd shown herself. Before she could stop it, Lenni yelled, "Here! Everyone, here!" and shoved between Jae and the crowd.

"No!" Jae yelled, but it was too late. The fighting was too intertwined again, members of the Order following Lenni deeper into the fray, trying to protect Jae from the onslaught.

She ducked back, frantic, looking for a way to strike, but one of the attackers saw her, broke away, and went right for her.

She didn't have time to think, and let instinct take over instead. The ground trembled and her attacker slid, hitting the mud that had formed when she'd put out the fire, landing square on his back. Three Closest closed in on him, outnumbered, and she heard him scream—

The mud gave her the idea. She raised her arms and shouted, "Enough!"

She called on the water again, and the earth along with it, releasing a torrent of mud. It burbled up from the ground, first ankle height, then knee. She didn't dare raise it farther, in case injured people were trapped, but it was thick and heavy. It seemed to mute the noises of the night, and everyone who'd been so frantic was now slowed down, trapped, unable to pull their way through the sludge.

It wasn't a perfect solution. People who were close enough still fought, at least for a moment, before everything fell still and everyone stared at her. She let out a breath, looking around desperately, and saw Elan—just as trapped as everyone else, a knife still in his hand.

"Tell me what happened," she demanded, using the energy of the air around her to carry her voice, unnaturally loud, to everyone. "How they got in."

"The Closest let them walk right in!" one of the members of the Order said—Casinn, the young, nervous one. One of his arms was limp at his side, blood gushing from a wound on his shoulder.

"They were disguised." That was barely a murmur, from

one of the Closest nearest her. Jae turned her attention to the young woman who'd spoken, who immediately shrank under her gaze. "I'm sorry, Lady Mage, they were . . . they were dressed like Closest. We thought they were just another group, ready to come in and help, wanting to see you for themselves, but . . ."

Someone else chimed in. "We realized they were too loud, something wasn't right. I tried to check so we could be sure and they attacked."

Jae now stared around at the attackers. Avowed guards, she assumed, but of course she didn't know any of them. Given how they'd turned toward her as soon as she'd shown herself, that must have been their plan: get to the house, and get *her*. At least her magic had held. Whatever had happened at Danardae, during the Break and the vow ceremony before it, hadn't happened again.

"Throw down your weapons," she said, voice carrying again.

There was a long, horrible pause. No one moved.

"Drop your weapons," Elan said, calling out to the whole crowd, "and we'll spare your lives, for now."

The threat must have done it, because finally one of the attackers did so, discarding a sword and a knife into the muck. The rest followed suit. Their weapons would go to the Closest, help arm them.

Freeing everyone from the mud was a trickier matter. Jae could dry it, so it turned to powder they could easily kick through, but they had to do it one person at a time, freeing the Closest quickly, and the attackers more slowly—and only after their arms had been tied behind them, securing them so they couldn't fight again. Closest who had experience patching wounds up helped those who'd been injured, while Lenni and Casinn led the captured Avowed to the house. They joined the handful of captured Avowed in the basement, one of the only rooms that locked. Jugs of water were usually kept there, underground to keep them cool, and locked in because they had been so precious during the drought. It was the nearest thing the house had to a dungeon or cell.

It was well past the middle of the night when Jae finally limped back into the house herself, everyone freed and cared for. She was so tired her head was swimming, but sleep was now a distant fantasy. There were more important immediate matters. Instead of her sleeping room, she walked to the study.

Within a few minutes, a small group had gathered to join her. Elan, of course, sporting a bandage around one of his calves. Lenni and Palma—Lenni had run out to join the fray, but Palma hadn't. And Karr, joined by Minn, the Closest woman who'd come in with the same group as Palma. Minn alone in the group still looked scared, her anxiety obvious in her expression, her gaze darting around as if she thought someone might attack again at any moment.

"It's all right now," Elan assured her, helping her sit, even though he'd been injured worse. "I take it you've never been in a fight before."

"Of course not," she said, barely a murmur. Even Jae had to strain to hear her.

"Of course," Elan echoed. Even if Minn had been attacked before, she'd never have been able to fight back. She must have seen bloodshed and violence during the Break if not well before it, but it was possible she'd never taken part in it. Had never hurt anyone herself.

Jae glanced at Karr. If he was similarly affected, it didn't show.

"Well," Lenni said, drawing their attention. "That was certainly . . . eventful. We probably should have expected it. It means we really did scare the Highest—and it means that was the best idea they could come up with. An assassination attempt that didn't even get near you."

"The next one might," Elan said.

"We won't let it." Karr's voice was soft but certain.

"What do we do with the prisoners?" Palma asked, and then, as everyone else gave her pointed looks, she rolled her eyes. "It's just easier to ask it like that. I don't mean anything by it."

"It *is* a good question," Lenni said. "More than a dozen of them survived. It would make quite a statement to the Highest if none of them came back. Or at least, not alive."

"No," Elan said quickly, vehemently. "They're our prisoners, we're not executing them."

"Why not? We're at war," Lenni said.

"They're Avowed," Palma said. "They were just doing what the Highest told them."

"I don't have much sympathy for Avowed," Karr said, pointedly. "Anyone who does shouldn't be here."

Palma crossed her arms, huffing, and a small part of Jae enjoyed her discomfort. But still, Jae said, "We aren't going to execute them. We aren't like Elthis. But we need to figure out what to do next."

"We don't have enough food," Minn said, her voice trembling. She looked around the room, then seemed to gather herself up. Her voice was a little louder as she continued. "We *don't*, and more and more Closest join us every day. We need more food and space and . . . and everything else. We need to move, and we need to find the rest of the Closest survivors from across the world."

"Gather a *real* army, and find a place to settle down," Karr said, nodding. "Somewhere secure."

"Nowhere is secure," Lenni said. "We gave the Highest a chance at peace, and they attacked instead. They don't care what happens—they don't care about anything except killing Jae, and all the rest of us. You all must know that's true."

Jae waited for someone to speak—for Elan, especially, to object. But instead, he seemed to fold in on himself a little. "I hate to say it, but Lenni is right. I wish . . . I'd hoped Erra would . . . but we know she got our message and this happened anyway."

"She's with them," Lenni said, but her usual hostility at Elan was gone. For a change, she sounded a little sympathetic.

"And now we can't just sit here and do nothing, either. Minn is right, our supplies are running short," Elan concluded. He sounded miserable.

"Then we should end this as quickly as possible," Lenni said. "No more warnings, no waiting for another attack. *We* can strike, really strike this time. Instead of their water, we go after their lives."

"Or we could go to Aredann," Elan said. He caught Jae's gaze, and for a moment her whole body sang with agreement.

Aredann—*home*. "There are no Avowed to fight with there, and it's isolated enough that no one could sneak up on us."

"That's too far away," Lenni said. "Besides, if we flee, we give the Highest time to rally their resources, to plan, and instead of a useless force like tonight's, *they'll* have an army, too, with the Twill fighting under the Avowed. Exactly like *you* saw in Danardae. None of us will be safe until the Highest are toppled. We aren't safe until we rule."

"We," Karr repeated. "Do you mean the Closest, or the Order?"

For a moment, the whole room held its breath. Even Jae gaped, staring back and forth between Karr and Lenni, the tension in the air as thick as any of the elements.

Finally Lenni said, "We're on the same side. And all I've done—all the Order has done—is help. The Break wouldn't have happened without us."

Karr eyed Elan and Jae, and said, "I'm not so sure of that. It seems like Jae could have managed it on her own."

"It's all right," Jae said, surprised to hear so much doubt from Karr. "They're our allies. They *did* help."

Karr gave her a long look, and finally said, "Of course, Lady Mage."

"What we do next is up to you, Jae," Lenni said, and now her pointed looks were all at Karr. "But I vote we attack."

"I agree," Palma said. "I just want this all over."

Jae looked at Karr and Minn. Neither one ventured an opinion, just waited expectantly. They'd already given her their input anyway, and Closest who weren't used to speaking at all certainly weren't used to repeating themselves. They'd both voted to find somewhere more secure.

She looked at Elan, wondering what he felt about Erra. He'd finally admitted that she must have been turned against them, but Jae still had a hard time imagining him striking against her. He gave a tiny shrug. "I'll follow whatever choice you make, Jae."

"With your magic, we can win the day," Lenni said again. "Quickly, decisively."

Jae looked around the room again, trying to think it through. She needed to be rational about this—because her first instinct was to attack. *Not* because of Lenni's tactical concerns, but because after so many generations of sorrow and anger, the idea of leading the Closest against the families that had enslaved them sang in her blood. She couldn't help but remember the moment she'd realized Rannith was dead, that he would never hurt her again. That no one would, at least not like that. There had been a ferocious joy in unleashing her anger.

But she could almost see Tal shaking his head in disappointment. He hadn't understood then, and he wouldn't now. His concern wouldn't be revenge—it would be saving the most Closest lives possible.

That led her back to Lenni's plan. The sooner this ended, the more lives they'd save, in the long run. There wouldn't need to be a huge clash of armies, Twill and Closest fighting one another on a battlefield, so intertwined that Jae could barely help them. *That* would bring Tal to her side.

The sooner this ended, the better. So she said, voice steady, "We attack."

Chapter 21

It was probably after dark, but impossible to tell from within the tunnel. Jae could sense the cities as they approached, though—the tangle of elements and people, all that flaring, roiling energy. She reached out with her mind, trying to ascertain if it was safe at the mouth of the tunnel, but the thicket of elements and humans was so tightly interwoven in the city that she couldn't sort it all out.

Her army, small though it was, trekked toward it all. There were several hundred of them, but only the dozen members of the Order were fully trained in how to fight. They'd be leading the way, with the Closest broken up into smaller groups, following them.

Jae had widened and reinforced the aqueduct that led to

the park in Danardae. It had worked to sneak Elan in, and the members of the Order who'd delivered her ultimatum— and though there was no way the army would stay unnoticed for long, the duct would still serve to get them in, past the walls, and even relatively close to the estate house. Danardae was the weakest of the four cities right now, so they'd take it first, solidify their hold, and continue the fight from there until they'd conquered all four cities, and all four Highest.

Something like excitement gripped Jae. Everything would be over soon. Her people were free now, and soon they'd be rid of the Highest once and for all.

"We're almost there," Jae said, as the tunnel began to slope up. She hadn't enlarged the opening yet—there was too much chance that opening up such an enormous pit would be noticed. So she waited, while her force crowded as close together as they could.

She looked over at Lenni and the other members of the Order, saw them nod in signal. They were all ready, some of them even eager. The Avowed inside the city would be un-prepared, and Jae's magic would further ensure a victory—*if* it held the way it had when the Avowed had attacked their town. She nodded back, shifted the earth above them, and opened the aqueduct tunnel to the park above.

One of the members of the Order led the charge, dozens of Closest following, hurling themselves past Jae and up into the night. She took a moment to brace herself, found Elan on one side and Karr at her other, and joined the next group that made for the open air.

Screaming filled the night almost as she reached the ground. She looked up, grateful that the night was dark enough that she wasn't blinded from coming out of the tunnel, and then recoiled in horror.

The Avowed were waiting for them. The fight was already raging, as Avowed pressed forward—but not just Avowed. There were others, not as well armed or uniformed. Twill who'd joined their cause followed the Avowed guards' leads and attacked the Closest.

The shouted warning echoed back into the tunnel, but it was too late. More and more Closest broke through, running past Jae as she tried to figure it out. The Avowed had known—somehow they'd *known* this was happening.

"Jae!" Elan pushed her sideways as someone rammed into them. She danced back, whirling around, trying to find somewhere she wouldn't get stabbed or trampled while she called up the magic. Once she had a plan, it would only take a heartbeat, but the further embroiled the two sides became, the harder it was to act.

"This way," Elan continued, pulling her. She didn't know if he'd spotted somewhere safe or if he was just determined to get her out of the thick of it, but she followed, dodging between fighters, over bodies.

The violence was cacophonous and overwhelming. The park stank of blood and mud and echoed with screams and shouts as the plan they'd laid out had fell to bits. Two of the Order leaders were still attempting to push forward, Closest following them, but Avowed and Twill had driven the groups apart and closed in to devour them. One of the Order members fell, and the Closest following him panicked, losing what little formation and togetherness they had.

They weren't well enough trained—barely trained at all.

No one was supposed to know they were coming; that had been their biggest advantage, and without that it would be a slaughter.

Jae's mind went blank. She couldn't drown or bury the armies, not without sacrificing her people, too. She couldn't even raise the mud the way she had when they'd been attacked—there were too many people around who could strike from a distance, throwing rocks, or setting the park on fire and letting everyone burn—

"We need to retreat!" Elan shouted, trying to catch everyone's attention.

Jae dodged as someone else rushed toward her, unthinkingly raising a wall of muddy rock. Her would-be attacker hit it, and someone shouted. She heard the word "mage" repeated, and then one of the groups of Avowed started straight for her.

They knew who she was now, where she was in the crowd. Though Closest threw themselves in the way, trying to keep her safe, they were going to lose. Outnumbered, untrained, dying for *her*, to protect *her*—

She threw her arms up, raising another wall, longer and larger. It was imperfect, it wouldn't do more than slow the Avowed attackers down, and it cut off as many of her own people as it helped. But she couldn't stand not acting, and she couldn't sacrifice her own people, and she couldn't let them all die for her.

"Jae, get back to the tunnel," Elan said, shoving her, then shouted, "Karr, get her back!"

Karr grabbed Jae's arm and pulled her back the way they'd come, but they were surrounded. She raised another muddy wall between her and an attacker, knocking the Avowed over and sending a blade askew moments before it would have reached Karr. He yanked her again, but something at the side of her vision flared bright with magical energy.

She blinked into other-vision. The world was just as chaotic like that as people twisted around, covered in mud and blood and pain, throwing themselves toward her frantically. A handful to protect her, most trying to get closer—leading a strange null spot, like she'd seen at the Break before her magic had faltered.

When she looked in true vision, she could see it clearly. Erra. The Avowed were rallying around Erra, who somehow carried the void with her, wielding it along with the weapon in her hand.

Jae turned toward Erra, grabbed energy from the earth beneath her feet, and *threw* it, sending the world trembling and shuddering, splitting apart. If that null spot reached her—

Her magic reached Erra and flared for a split second, then—then went dark, completely gone, as if it had vanished. The chasm she'd opened tapered off, a crack in the battlefield that didn't even come near the approaching force. It just suddenly *stopped*, not big enough to do more than trip and confuse people.

The Avowed pressed closer. Karr punched someone, trying to keep her free, and she ran toward the tunnel again. The way was thick with bodies, some upright and fighting, but more and more on the ground, dead or dying.

She tripped on one and went down hard, jarring one of her knees and elbows. She rolled as someone closed in on top of her, but Elan was there. He was fast, but not fast enough: he could block her, but not the blade itself. He tried to dodge but it was too late, and the blade bit into his side. He screamed in pain and the world seemed to slow down around Jae as he fell.

He landed a few hand spans away. She struggled to her feet, trying to get to him, but people pressed between them. He'd be trampled. She screamed as she grabbed at the earth again, pulling it upward this time, a peak rising, sending everyone skidding down and off. His body slid, he grabbed desperately for a handhold. She pressed the ground up under his feet, but Erra was too close now, and —

Jae's magic stopped. Again. Erra was close and getting closer, only a few people between Jae and the awful approaching edge of that blank area.

Karr fought someone off, Jae lost track of Elan in the mess, and Lenni ran right for the null area but was pushed aside. The null area hit Jae and she was dizzy, overwhelmed, and confused, as the magic she always sensed around her vanished. She groped for it but couldn't find anything, earth or water or air, and she wilted as if her own energy was being sucked out, too.

"I can't," she tried to say, not sure who she was speaking to, as she swayed on her feet, so weak she could barely stand. She stumbled and one of the Closest hit her in the midst of a fight with a Twill. She barely caught a glimpse of Elan as she fell, still on the ground on the side on the hill she'd raised. He wasn't moving.

Someone closed in on her. She struggled up to her hands and knees, and as the Avowed raised a blade, Lenni slammed into him. Jae could barely stay upright, barely keep her eyes open even in the midst of all this, now completely useless. She didn't even have a weapon, didn't know how to use one anyway, and even though at the vow ceremony her magic had come back after a moment, now it didn't.

Violence closed in around her. More Closest killed, more Avowed pressing them all back. She saw a knife stuck in a body—*Minn's* body—and managed to crawl forward to reach for it, but before she could get there, someone kicked her and she hit the ground again, sprawling in the mud.

Desperate, she tried to reach for magical energy, but she couldn't find any. She clawed her way through the mud, trying to get away before whoever was attacking realized exactly who she was—

Then the body that had kicked her fell back, and Karr was there. He leaned down, grabbed her arms, and hauled her up.

"Find Elan!" she tried to say, but she couldn't get her mouth to work. She'd hit her head when she'd fallen, her magic was gone, and she was lost and couldn't make sense of the world around her. She couldn't see Elan anymore, even as Karr shouted something and the Closest seemed to rally around him. Even as he picked her up, when her legs wouldn't work right, and ran for the tunnel mouth. Even as they retreated.

She wanted to use magic, close the tunnel behind them. But her magic was gone.

So they ran, still fighting, until finally there was enough distance that the Avowed fell behind. But they still didn't slow.

Jae tried to tell Karr she could walk—she could run—but

she couldn't. Couldn't talk, certainly couldn't hold herself up. All she could do was picture Elan falling, clutching his bloody side.

So many people had died tonight, trying to protect her, following her orders to attack. She should have saved them but she hadn't been able to, and not even a quarter of the force that had attacked were with them as they retreated. Minn was gone. She didn't know where Lenni was, if she'd survived. And Elan . . .

"I need Elan," she finally managed, making Karr hear her at last.

"He's lost," Karr said. "We're retreating. We're going to take you to safety."

Jae went cold and gave up struggling, totally numb and too weak to protest. She lost track of Karr, of the other Closest who'd survived, of the tunnel and the world and everything else. She couldn't focus on any of it, because Elan was gone. Just like her magic, Elan was *gone*. She'd freed the Closest, but now they'd be killed, because she was useless, and the Highest would follow them, would attack anywhere Karr took her. They'd lost, and there was nowhere safe.

Except . . .

Her head was swimming. She grabbed Karr's arm, not sure he'd hear, or that he'd understand even if he could. It was all she could do to make her mouth work, get out one single word: "Aredann."

Chapter 22

THE LAST THING ELAN REMEMBERED WAS SKIDDING DOWN A HILL in a slide of mud and bodies, clutching his side, pressing his drenched, sticky robe against it in an attempt to stop the bleeding. But he already knew the wound was too deep, that he was too weak, that he wouldn't be able to save himself. Footsteps crashed around him, everyone frantic and shouting and running toward somewhere nearby. . . .

The world faded to black.

The next thing he knew, he was being yanked up. He couldn't really see, didn't know where he was, who was grabbing him. He shouted but couldn't form words, and it didn't matter, anyway. He was pushed back down somewhere else, his body lit with pain, his mind unable to focus.

Moments of awareness came to him like sparks flung from a fire. As they blazed, he'd see faces, hear voices, know someone was speaking his name. He'd remember that he'd been in a battle, try to ask about Jae, but the spark would fade quickly and his mind would go dark again.

Then the real pain started.

He was hot everywhere, aware only that he felt like he was on fire. Someone poured liquid down his throat but it didn't help. He screamed in agony as something was done to his side, realized that was where he'd been wounded, but soon that pain faded back into the burning that consumed him.

Every movement he made, every single twitch, was a torment. He was naked on a cold stone floor, and the coolness of the stones was mercy against his heated skin. Slowly he recognized a little more—that someone had come and bathed his wound in wine, that it was infected, that they slathered it with salve and made him drink, and that if he didn't stop burning soon, he would die.

Try as he might, he couldn't force himself to cool down. He couldn't even force out words, thank his caretakers for the water, for cleaning the awful, cursed wound that had done this to him. He didn't know where he was, how he'd gotten there. His world was searing agony, worse even than when he'd been lost in the desert and almost died. At least there, he'd had Jae.

Jae . . .

He had no idea what had happened to her, what had happened on the battlefield. He tried to ask, but his throat was too parched, his caretaker didn't listen, he wasn't even sure he was making real words. As he thought of her he struggled, tried to find himself, tried to wake himself up, but still he burned.

❖❖❖

For the first two days, they didn't let Jae walk. She wasn't sure she was strong enough to walk, anyway. She sat on a cart pulled by a stolen horse, along with sealed water jugs and carefully preserved grains and dried meat. All the food they'd been able to take from their captured town had been placed on carts, most of them pulled by humans because there weren't enough animals, and the entire, massive enclave had retreated.

Jae didn't want to speak to anyone, and she didn't want anyone to speak to her. So they left her alone, which was just as well, because she was useless now.

She couldn't fight. Her magic was gone, and she was terrified every time she even tried to look into other-vision. There was no reassuring pulse of energy, no glow or swirl of light, no sense of the world around her beyond what she could see and hear. She couldn't rise above her retreating army and seek out friends, assure herself they were safe, or look into the distance and sense coming threats. All she could do was stay huddled under a blanket, her skin clammy from all the moisture that hovered in the air. Storm after storm opened up, but the air never lost its moist edge, and sometimes she could barely breathe through it.

The retreat was plagued by rain, which also meant mud—and that made retreating even slower. As if moving an enclave of well over a thousand hadn't been slow enough.

After two days, though, Karr told her they'd picked up new groups, Closest who hadn't made their way to the original encampment but now had found and joined them. Their army was still growing, and the newcomers wanted to see her. Even if she was useless.

So she managed to stand on her own, discovered that though she was weak, she *could* walk, and she greeted them, not offering up her usual display of power. She walked throughout the army as it paused for the night and saw some familiar faces: Lenni, Casinn, Palma. Karr, and some of the other Closest who'd attached themselves to her since the Break. Many of them were wounded, slowing the retreat further still, but at least they were among the quarter of the force who had made it back.

Elan wasn't.

Jae still expected to see him in the crowd, for him to break away and wave. For him to come up behind her, put a gentle hand on her elbow and smile as he tried to remember not to talk—and then to talk anyway, because he hated the quiet. She saw him in every shadow, heard his voice in every distant, hushed conversation. But, like Tal, he was gone.

No one had any idea if he'd survived or been killed in the battle. Jae had seen him fall, and so had Karr, but there was no way to guess if that blade had killed him. If he'd survived, only to be left behind, he might have bled to death in the park. If he hadn't, somehow surviving all that, then he'd certainly have been taken prisoner.

Jae bowed her head every time she thought about it. He was the only person the Highest hated nearly as much as they hated her. After all, she was an outsider, but he was a traitor.

He'd broken from their ranks, defied them, helped their enemies. Sworn himself to Jae and the Closest, devoted his life to finding and telling the truth. She doubted that any of the Highest or Avowed would believe how desperately he'd tried to remain loyal to his sister—all they'd see would be the way he'd defied his father at the Break. Erra herself was against him now, too.

The first attack came on the third day, as they passed near an estate where the Closest who'd risen up had been slain. Their frantic efforts hadn't been enough, and neither had their number—and when the Avowed learned that even those who hadn't been involved with the attack were free of the Curse, the rest had been put to death, too.

It was those Avowed who attacked. But their number was small, compared to the growing army, and though they did damage, they were defeated. But Jae had nothing to do with that defeat—without magic, she couldn't help at all. Even had she wanted to fight, she wasn't allowed. Karr made that very clear. Magic or no, the Closest considered her too valuable to risk her life in a skirmish.

They were retreating to Aredann, where they'd all be safer—and where they could keep *her* safe. She didn't understand why, when she'd messed so many things up so badly. She was the one who'd ordered the attack that had cost so many lives, including Elan's. Even when she'd had magic, it hadn't been enough to win the day for them, and now she didn't even have that. There was no reason for them to protect her anymore.

She felt like a flame that had been doused by the endless, cursed rain. She couldn't even call up her rage, which had always been so endless. Tal was gone, Elan was gone, her magic was gone. She felt like she was gone, too, empty and exhausted and useless.

But it rained, and they retreated, and at least she could walk under her own power again.

※ ※ ※

Elan wasn't sure if he was delirious or dreaming or if it was real when he saw Andra. He blinked a few times, not quite able to get his throat or mouth to work. She knelt next to him — he'd been dressed and moved to a sleeping mat, though all he could remember was cold stones. She had a lantern, and there were no windows around.

She peeled off the bandage that had been wrapped around him and washed his wound gently. He hissed with pain and she looked sharply down at him and said, "You're awake."

"Yes," he said, barely able to force the word out.

"Hold on," she warned him. She finished cleaning and then smeared something else sticky and sweet-smelling over the wound. He tried to push up onto his elbows to see how bad it was, if it had closed up or been sewn shut or if it still gaped and bled, but the movement hurt too much.

She finished and wrapped the bandage back in place, then moved to where he could see her, sitting back on her heels. She pressed a hand to his forehead and let out a breath.

"Keeping you alive was a cursed close thing," she said. "You were sliced across the side, and then it was infected. You're still warm, but I think the worst has passed."

She moved to help him sit a little, folding the sleeping mat under him so his shoulders were raised. Then she poured a mug of water and helped him drink it down. That soothed his parched throat, but even just that motion exhausted him.

He forced out, "What happened?"

Andra was silent for a long moment, smoothing his hair back from his face. His skin crawled with the want of a bath, and he itched from dried sweat. Finally she said, "It was a rout. Jae and a few others escaped—not many, as far as we can tell, but it's hard to say. And now the whole Closest army is fleeing. The Highest will be after them soon, but they're taking some time to gather their forces. They want to show strength. I think . . . I'm afraid that's why they let you live."

Elan grimaced, knowing exactly what that meant. It would have been easy for the Highest to leave him for dead on the battlefield, or to step aside and let the infection take him. But they'd dressed his wound, helped him fight the infection off, because they wanted him to live, for now. So that when he died, it would be in public, an execution in front of a crowd. Another spectacle.

Andra sighed and folded her hands in her lap. "I wish I could. . . . There's nothing I can do. Erra keeps me close. She doesn't suspect me; she's trying to protect me. I'm housed with Halann and the children now, can you believe that?"

He couldn't even shake his head in surprise.

"I'd send word to Lenni if I could, but I can't reach her, not without raising suspicion. Maybe not at all, now that the army is gone. And Erra won't listen to me. I've tried to make her see reason, but she—she won't even tell me how they found out about the attack. Someone in the Order is disloyal and I don't know who, but someone betrayed Lenni and Jae."

Of course. He hadn't been coherent enough to even wonder, but since the Highest's forces had been waiting for them, that meant they'd known about the tunnel exit and either known or suspected an attack was coming. Someone from the Order who'd been stranded in the city must have found out and switched sides after he'd told Osann about the tunnel. Or maybe it was Andra herself, loyal to Erra after all . . .

But no, because she hadn't known about the aqueduct. He hadn't been able to get word back to her after using it and he doubted Osann would have been able to reach her at the estate house, either. So she couldn't have known about the coming attack.

"Did . . ." It was hard to talk, but he made himself. "Did Erra get the message from Jae?"

Andra nodded. "She wouldn't tell me what it contained, but whatever it was, she didn't believe it."

"The Well," he said. "If the Closest die, its magic will come unbound. The Well will dry up if all the Closest are killed. They have to stop this war. You have to convince her."

"She won't listen to me," Andra said. "Only to the other Highest. She's changed since her father died. I've never seen her so . . . so emotionless before. I'll keep trying, but . . ." She didn't sound hopeful. "Did you find the papers I hid?"

"Yes." Elan's throat hurt. He tried to keep his eyes open, stay awake, but he wasn't sure it would last for long.

"Good. I think there are more here, in Danardae—and probably the other Highest's houses, too. Their own histories, if they can even read them. I caught a glimpse in Elthis's study once—Erra's now, when I was in to see her, but . . . I couldn't get close enough to check, and I certainly couldn't have explained to her why I can read it."

He gave a tiny fragment of a nod.

"I'll steal it away if I can. Not that it'll do any good now." She sighed and stroked Elan's face again, her fingers gentle. "I can't stay. Erra's been letting me play nurse, but if I linger, she'll think you're well enough to question. I'll keep you safe as long as I can. I promise."

He didn't even have the energy to thank her. Just waited as she walked out, too weak to stay awake for more than a minute after her footsteps faded.

✿ ✿ ✿

"Lady Mage," Lenni said, and Jae braced herself. She was sitting on a muddy square of carpet, set on the even muddier ground, in front of a campfire. The rain had let up, but she was sure it would come pouring down again soon. Not that she could sense it in the air, feel the energy of the water grow thicker and thicker until rain spilled out. It was just that the clouds hadn't given way once in the week they'd been traveling. It was hard to tell that this was dusk, not dawn or midnight or noon, with thick gray clouds blanketing the whole sky.

Jae looked up at Lenni and then back at the flames, raised the mug of tea she held to her lips to drink, and waited.

"Why did you tell everyone about your magic being . . . lost?"

Jae frowned, both at the rudeness of the question and that

Lenni thought it was worth asking at all. Jae had told Karr and a few others, not to excuse how little help she'd been in the fight, but so they'd know she couldn't protect them anymore. But Lenni waited, so she answered, "Because it's the truth."

Lenni sat in silence for a minute, and finally said, "I don't think I understand you very well. All these people need you to be a leader, but you tell them you're weak. Their faith in you is the only thing holding this army together. If they lose that . . ."

"I don't want them to have faith if I can't help them," Jae said. "I won't be like the Highest. I won't let anyone follow me because of a lie. And . . . and after the slaughter at Danardae, maybe they shouldn't follow me anyway—"

"You couldn't have known that was coming," Lenni said. "It was my idea. It's my fault."

"No. It was my decision," Jae said, because she was certain of that much. Even though Lenni had pushed for it, if Jae had refused, the Closest would have followed her, not the Order. She'd given them their freedom, and she was also responsible for their deaths.

"Do you . . ." Lenni trailed off, then started again. "You know more about Aredann than I do, so I guess you really think we'll be safe there."

"As safe as we can be," Jae said.

"That doesn't really inspire confidence, either."

"I'm not going to lie," Jae said. "Not to you, or anyone else. I think we'll be safest at Aredann, but there's nowhere safe while the Highest reign. Pretending we are would only make things worse."

"I suppose that *is* true," Lenni agreed, and stood. "Rest up. Magic or no, you *are* their leader—our leader."

She walked off, but a moment later Karr was there, taking her place. "I didn't mean to overhear that, Lady Mage, but . . . well, I did."

Jae cocked her head.

"We'd follow you anywhere. But she's right, we do need you to lead us. We need your strength," Karr said.

"But I don't have magic anymore—"

"I know. But that isn't what I mean. You told us you're vulnerable, but that doesn't make you weak. Your magic being gone . . . that doesn't, either."

Jae waited, not quite sure what he was getting at.

"You freed us. You gave us this chance. There's not a man, woman, or child in this camp who wouldn't follow you into the desert and give you their last drop of water."

Jae shook her head. "I don't deserve that. I broke the Curse, but look at everything else that's happened. Whole enclaves were killed when they rebelled, and I led *you* directly into danger."

"The Closest who died, died free," Karr said. "If they were here to ask, they'd tell you the same as I will now. None of them would rather live cursed. Not after taking a single free breath. You must understand that. You were cursed, too."

Jae did. It hadn't been more than a few months ago, though it felt like a lifetime, but she could still remember the rush of realization. The Curse didn't shackle her anymore, and—like Karr had said—she'd die before she'd return to slavery. But still.

"With my magic gone, I'm useless."

"No. You're our leader. I think Lenni . . . she tries, she means well, but she's not one of us. You are. You're *ours*," Karr said, and then stood. "Eat up. You still need your strength."

It rained, and they retreated. Jae walked shoulder to shoulder with different Closest every day, but not one ever blamed her for the lives she'd cost. Maybe they were simply keeping silent, until she realized the reason there were different people with her every day was that it was a position of honor. Karr was right: the Closest still followed her, even knowing she had no magic. Even though she'd made the wrong choice and cost yet more Closest lives. Even though Elan was probably dead somewhere.

Lenni was more distant, but Jae could hear her sometimes, helping direct people, keeping the army moving. If she had reservations about the retreat to Aredann, she wasn't making them known. Jae marveled a little at that—that Lenni, who had built the Order up from ashes, was now willing to follow her, too.

Yes, they'd always been on the same side. But as Jae looked back, she couldn't help but see them very differently. Jae and the Closest had been fighting for their freedom; the Order had been fighting against the Highest. No wonder Elan had been so suspicious of Lenni and her people. The two causes had the same end goal, which made them natural allies, but the Order also had people like Palma—people who didn't seem to care about the Closest much at all.

Palma had expected the Closest to be grateful. A thankful, docile mass that would put the Order in charge—put *her* in charge—and thank her for it. It had probably never occurred to Palma that the Closest wouldn't be any more interested in the Order ruling them than in letting the Highest continue to do it.

But the Closest had made it clear that they would follow Jae, not the Order. Lenni seemed to have accepted that, which was a relief, since the Order would follow her. Jae was grateful Lenni was with her, even if she didn't want to be the kind of leader Lenni was. The kind who refused to be vulnerable and could only think of ways to attack.

The army's movements were slow. Jae tried to picture the future as she walked, to figure out what kind of leader she really wanted to be, and was so distracted that she barely noticed the low, slow pulse of the earth under her feet. When she did, she stumbled, and it was gone.

"Lady Mage . . . ," one of the Closest started, reaching to steady her.

Jae waved her off, staring at the world around her, concentrating, reaching—and yes, there it was again. Not as bright as she remembered, as if the energies were distant and weaker. But she could feel the earth.

"I'm all right," Jae said, her heart beating too fast. She didn't crow out the knowledge, since she wasn't sure if this would last. She had no idea if her other-vision would get stronger, if she'd be as powerful as she had been before, and she knew for sure she wouldn't be able to count on the magic to save her people. So she kept it to herself.

But with every step, she sensed the steady, glowing earth under her bare feet, and she'd never been so relieved.

✦✦✦

Elan didn't know how many days it had been when he was finally able to stay awake more than asleep. He could stand and pace the length of the tiny, locked room. He could eat and drink on his own. He could talk again.

So he should have expected it when, instead of Andra, two guards came in. He braced himself, but they moved efficiently, not bothering with words. They grabbed him, yanking him upward. He struggled, but he was too weak to shake them off or jerk free. One held him while the other yanked his flailing arms behind him, clapped shackles around his wrists, and shoved him forward. He stumbled, crashed to his knees, and the guards each took one of his shoulders, holding him there.

Only then did Erra walk in. She stared down at him, and he stared up at her.

"Hello, Elan," she said. "I think it's time we talk."

✦✦✦

Every day, Jae's thoughts grew clearer. She still marveled at the idea that the Closest wanted her to lead them, and she was honored that they hadn't abandoned her even knowing she had no way to protect them. They were still determined to stay with her and protect her and follow her—despite what Lenni had thought, telling the truth hadn't weakened them at all.

The Closest wanted her to lead them. So she would, and

she pledged to herself that, above all else, she would always listen to the Closest. She wouldn't always be right, but she would do the best she could to always make decisions with the Closest's needs in mind. Because their needs were hers, too. She was one of them, after all, and if she'd listened to Minn, Minn would still be alive.

It was too late to go back and undo the mistake she'd made by attacking Danardae, or to bring back Minn and the others who had died. It was too late for Elan, though her heart ached when she thought of him. It was raw, like when she'd lost Tal—but different. Tal had been her whole life, until that moment, where Elan was only part of it.

But now, when she thought of how he'd kissed her, she wished desperately that she hadn't panicked. Or that when he'd tried to talk to her about it, she had known enough to tell him the truth: that she cared for him, too. His absence left her empty the same way her vanished magic did, as if a part of herself was gone.

Now, even though her magic slowly but steadily seemed to be returning, Elan was gone forever. She'd never get to tell him how she felt.

So she mourned him, just as she mourned Tal, and Minn, and the other Closest who'd given their lives for her, and for their freedom. And she kept walking forward.

Every day, she grew more comfortable with the way the other Closest looked at her, spoke with her, hoped for her nods of approval. Every step carried them closer to Aredann, the only home she'd ever known. Every day brought more Closest to their fold, their ranks swelling now to double what they'd been by the central cities, and still growing. And every time she let herself try to use other-vision, she could make out more energy, see further, sense more.

As they crossed from cultivated lands into the open desert, she found she could once again pick out the energy of water in the air. By nightfall, she could feel the air itself, its angry buzzing a reassurance. By noon the next day, she could sense Aredann ahead of them, in all its isolated glory. The reservoir, brimming with water and magic both; the fields, the stones of the estate house. The *people*.

The Closest sent messengers traveling quicker out ahead, so everyone had gathered by the time their army arrived. Jae's heart pounded as she saw the gathered group, the familiar faces, Shirrad and Gali standing at the front. Tal's absence hit her, but it was tangled up with a strange kind of relief. When she and Elan had first come back to Aredann after Tal's death, she'd thought it would never feel like home again without Tal there. Now, as she looked up at the estate house where she'd lived her entire life, she knew it *was* home, and though Tal was gone, when she walked its halls, she would remember him and feel him with her.

Jae didn't have words for it when Shirrad held out her arms, but Jae let Shirrad hug her, and then Gali, and her eyes went damp and watery as they treated her like a friend and sister, until Shirrad finally said, voice thick with emotion, "Welcome home."

As groups of Closest split off to get to work, building out the town and pitching tents because there was no way Aredann's few buildings could hold the whole gathered Closest force, Jae and her friends and followers were led inside. Jae walked the familiar halls, hands tracing over the tile mosaics, picking out the imperfections that she'd caused with earth-quakes.

"You must need rest," Shirrad started, but Jae shook her head, walking not toward the kitchen or any of the sleeping quarters, but to a hall that would lead up and out—to the roof.

"There's something I need to do first," Jae said. She glanced back at her friends, saw Karr and Gali walking side by side while Lenni followed with Casinn and other Closest. "But it won't be easy. I may pass out. Please catch me if I do."

"I don't understand," Shirrad said, as they stepped out into the misty day.

Though Aredann was only two stories, this was the high-est point around. Jae looked out at the town and the mass of people, into the distance. She shut her eyes and *felt*, sensed the ground as it spread forward out of her range, reached for as much of its energy as she could.

She didn't open her eyes, instead using other-vision to see where the crowds ended, give them some room to spread, to measure the span of the fields, the distance to the reser-voir . . . she held it all in her head, this oasis in the desert that would have to become a home not just for her, but for everyone here.

Then, bracing herself and bringing all her willpower to bear, she took the energy of the earth and *pulled*. There were gasps and shouts of shock—and then applause and cheering. Jae opened her eyes, the world fuzzy around her, and smiled.

A wall ringed the whole estate and town, thick and high enough that the Highest's forces would need to spend time and lives to breach it. It was the first magic she'd done since Danardae.

Her vision swam and she was dizzy, exhausted. She took a precarious step backward. Gali reached out to grab her, hold her upright, but Jae didn't pass out, though she needed to rest immediately. But before allowing herself to do so, she took one last look out at Aredann.

She wasn't precisely safe, but it would do for now. She was home.

Chapter 23

ERRA STARED AT ELAN, BUT IT WAS LIKE LOOKING INTO THE FACE of a stranger. She knew his face so well—it was so similar to her own—but it wasn't his newly grown beard or too-long hair that had changed it, or even the way his cheeks were gaunt and his skin was dull from fighting off the infection. It was that he didn't smile; there was nothing naïve in his expression. She'd rarely seen him this serious.

"Well," she said, oddly at a loss when he didn't flinch or cower. She half-expected him to start laughing, as if the last few months had all been a joke or a dream. But he didn't, just stared up at her. Her younger brother, her enemy.

Finally he was the one who broke the silence, asking,

"Did you not get any of my messages? Or did you really ignore them?"

"I had no interest in listening to the ranting of a traitor and a madman," she said.

"I see." Something in his face hardened. "It's funny. Everyone in the Order thought I was mad for believing you *would* listen. Because I did, Erra. I told them again and again—you were lied to, just like I was, and if you heard the truth, you'd never stand for it. I told them, you're not like Father—"

"Father—*my* father—is dead," she interrupted. "Your friends killed him, while you stood there and let it happen. And yes, I am like him. He didn't stand for your rebellion, and I won't, either."

Elan took a breath, as if steadying himself. He didn't argue, didn't plead. Just waited.

"Your friends have lost," Erra said to his silence. It was frustrating that they hadn't killed the mage girl and ended the whole cursed rebellion at Danardae, but the mage *had* lost her power. That was obvious. Gesra said that with enough time and rest, the girl's power would restore itself, but this time, Erra had finally stayed composed despite the visions. The world had burned around her and she hadn't cared about anything except reaching the mage. Even if her power did come back, next time, Erra would win.

"I doubt that," Elan said.

"They may not know it yet," Erra said. "But their cause is lost. Jae Aredann's magic is gone, and without her protection, the Closest stand no chance. They've retreated—and tomorrow, we will pursue them."

"You really shouldn't do that. If you got my other message, then you *must* have gotten our warning."

"And dismissed it, just as easily."

"Then the Highest never told you the truth of the Well," Elan said. "But Father knew. The War was—"

"You two are dismissed," Erra said sharply to the guards, cutting him off.

One released Elan, but the other said, "Highest, are you sure it's safe to . . ."

"Are you questioning me?" she demanded, and the man actually fell back a step.

"No, Highest, forgive me." They both fled, and she turned back to Elan.

"So you *do* know," he said. "You just don't want anyone else to. How can you stand there and know our ancestors lied about—"

"The Closest were maniacs," Erra said, remembering Gesra's words. "They were selfish; they wouldn't allow anyone use of the reservoirs. The world needed the water—"

"So you stole it," Elan said, disgusted. "If the Highest lied about the War, what makes you think they told the truth about the Closest? I'm telling you—I'm *telling* you the *truth*. That because they crafted the Well, its binding will unravel without them. The more Closest who die, the weaker it becomes, and if you wage this war on them—"

"*They* started this," she interrupted him. "Before the War, when they were cruel. We're only finishing what our ancestors should have. You know what a threat the Closest are—if we can't control them, they can't live."

He shook his head. "They're not like that. I used to think . . . but they *aren't*."

"Everyone knows what they're like." Her words were clipped with anger. The Closest were a danger, rebels and traitors, now free to destroy the world her family had worked so hard to protect.

"No. Everyone knows the Highest's lies about them. Everything about them, the Curse—*all of it* was a lie. Even if I didn't believe Jae, it wouldn't matter, because I heard Father admit it!"

"Stop calling him that!" she half-shouted. "He disowned you. You are nothing but a traitor. Not his *son*."

"Not your brother," Elan said.

She didn't flinch from the truth in that statement. The man in front of her wasn't her brother, the smiling, naïve young man who'd been sent to Aredann. The brother she'd loved was gone, and the traitor in front of her was no one.

"The only reason you're alive now is so I can make that girl watch when I execute you," Erra said. "You'll die in front of her—all her people."

"Do you think that'll stop her? The only person Jae loved is already dead," he said. "She'll mourn me—but she won't stop, not until you've surrendered or you're dead next to me. And the Highest won't ever surrender, will they? Not even when it costs you the whole world. Because the Well *will* dry if you kill the Closest. If you fight them, you curse yourself."

"We will handle it," she said. "The Highest will protect our people."

"You sound like a fanatic, not a leader. The Highest have no idea what they're doing," Elan said.

Shock hit Erra, and she let her anger unfurl and slapped him. He rocked on his knees but didn't recant, though part of her had actually expected him to. It wasn't rational, but she'd never heard anyone talk about the Highest like that before.

"I'm not the only one who thinks so," he added. She balled her fist, but he kept talking. "The Twill who've joined you might fear the Closest now—but they hated you, just weeks ago. And they will again, when the reservoirs run dry. Even if you win this war, you'll be fighting another one within years."

"Enough!" She hadn't meant to scream, but she couldn't stop herself. "You are wrong, you're a liar and a traitor and a vow-breaker. And you're nothing to me, no one at all. I don't even know you—I never did."

She turned away, but not quickly enough.

"But I know you," he said, his voice steady again. "I do. I think *you* think you're just trying to be a fair ruler, and that you *do* want to protect people. But right now, all you're protecting is your own power."

"Power I will use to make peace!" She turned back toward him despite herself. She'd condemned him, this traitor who wore her brother's face, and now she couldn't stand to look at him. But she couldn't just walk away.

"Power you want to use to slaughter people you kept enslaved for generations," he said. "Because they challenge you. Power *our* ancestors wielded to force everyone to obey them. Power because you just want power, and you don't care what you do with it!"

"You're wrong," she said.

"If I was wrong about anything, it was about you." He stared up at her, his face not a mask now, not desperate, but twisted into something much angrier. "I thought you were better than that. But I'm telling you the truth, and if you're too determined to rebuild a world order that has you at the top, you as *Highest*, then you're not. Jae and Lenni were right when they said you wouldn't understand. That you'd condemn the world rather than let someone else rule it."

Erra turned away again, not letting him see how much his anger stung. It shouldn't matter. He was the vow-breaker, not her, and she shouldn't care what he thought. The only thing that would matter now was that she'd condemned *him*, that the whole world would see that she had no mercy for their enemies, not even for her brother. They would have faith in her to protect them, and she would keep the peace.

"I warned you," Elan called from behind her, as she walked through the door. He wasn't going to stop, so as much as it irked her, she'd let him have the last word for now—it didn't matter; he'd be executed soon enough. "When the next drought comes and the Well goes dry, remember that I warned you."

She locked the door behind her.

Chapter 24

JAE SAT ON A CUSHION IN WHAT HAD ONCE BEEN THE AVOWED'S
private study. Now it was the one room that wasn't stacked
with equipment or food or other supplies, as Closest stock-
piled everything they could. Aredann's resources weren't
exactly vast, but with Jae's magical coaxing, the fields were
yielding far more than they would have naturally, especially
in light of overwatering from the storms. Any blankets that
weren't desperately needed were being cleaned and con-
verted to clothes; any older clothing repaired and parceled
out to those who needed it. With thousands of people living
in an estate and town meant for a quarter of their number,
every room was crowded, and everyone was a little hungry
and desperate and irritable.

"I admit, I didn't expect us to have anywhere near enough food," Lenni said, coming to sit across the small table from Jae. This was their impromptu conference room, where she, Lenni, Palma, Shirrad, Gali, and Karr had taken to meeting. "Your magic can do incredible things, Lady Mage. But it isn't enough."

"I'm not sure what you mean," Shirrad said. Jae almost smiled at how Shirrad had started speaking like one of the Closest.

"When the Highest arrive, we can't just hide behind the wall and wait. I know—I know you won't like that. I know it sounds exactly like what I said about Danardae—"

"Yes, it does," Jae interrupted. She was *not* going to rush into anything this time.

"But this *is* different. When the Highest arrive, they'll surround us. We'll be safe within the wall for a time, but we have nowhere to go. No escape. Aredann may be safe, but it's still going to be a battleground, because sooner or later, either they'll attack or we'll run out of supplies. We'll *have* to fight eventually. We didn't at Danardae—I was wrong. But here . . . I can't see any other way, and I'd rather fight while we're well fed and ready."

"And get it over with," Karr said, nodding in agreement. "While we're in a stronger position. They can't get past the walls, so *we* can decide when it's time to fight."

"But my magic might vanish again," Jae said. "If we attack and I can't help . . ."

"Then I suppose you're certain they have a way to drain it," Lenni said.

"It's happened every time I've been near them. At the vow

ceremony and the Break it was only a few moments, but after Danardae . . ."

"Then we can't strike," Shirrad said.

"Then we *have* to," Karr said. He and Lenni exchanged looks, and Jae wondered when the two of them had become so aligned. Or maybe they always had been. Karr hadn't been in favor of attacking Danardae, but he hadn't shied away from the fight, either. "If we can't rely on your magic, we have to rely on ourselves. They'll get to the wall and wait, and we'll take them unaware, and end this war for good."

"But just ending the war isn't enough," Jae said. "We need to know what to do next."

"Next, we see the Highest executed for their lies and their crimes," Lenni said.

"Yes, but something needs to come after that, too," Jae said, pressing again. This was the piece she'd been missing, that she'd never understood. Everyone could agree that they needed to win the war, and that they'd never be ruled over again. But no one knew what that would really *mean*, how it would work. Jae certainly didn't. "The world will be in chaos. Everyone who survives will be desperate and terrified. Elan saw that in the cities—how much looting and violence there had been. We can't allow survivors—on either side—to just destroy themselves."

"If we topple the Highest, then *we* are the ones who rule. All of us, together—under you, of course," Lenni said.

"Of course," Palma said, rolling her eyes.

Shirrad shot a glance at Palma, but when she spoke, it was to Lenni. "You say under Jae—but your *friend* doesn't seem eager to listen, let alone obey. Somehow it seems like when you all say *we*, you don't mean all of us."

"Who should she mean, you?" Palma returned. "You're here for the same reason I am—the Highest took away your estate. And you *know* we're more fit to rule than . . . Be realistic. Who would say vows to a Closest?"

"I would," Shirrad snapped. "To Jae, in a heartbeat. And I'm *not* here because of what the Highest took away from me—it started out that way, but now I'm here because this is where I belong. The Closest at Aredann are my friends—my family. And I'd die to protect them. If you won't do the same, *you* don't belong here."

Shirrad's fists were clenched, and the funny thing was, Jae recognized the look of rage from the days when Shirrad had ruled over her. Back then, Shirrad had been as much a tyrant as any Avowed—but she'd also been desperate, scared, and young. Trying to protect the people of Aredann inside a system of vows and obedience, and it was that same system that condemned the Closest.

Shirrad hadn't done anything to help them, but Tal had always thought she might, given the chance. Jae wished he could hear Shirrad protect them so fiercely now. The thought actually made her smile just a little.

"Enough," Jae said. "Lenni, there are people in your Order who are here because they want to see justice—but there are some who only wanted power the Highest wouldn't give them. I know where you stand, but I think you may need to look at your friends and figure the rest of them out."

"I hate to admit it, but you're right, Lady Mage," Lenni said. "Palma, I think you'd best leave."

Palma's mouth fell open. "And go *where*? I'm stuck here now—stuck with all of you!"

"Then you'd better hope we win," Karr said, with a little dark humor in his voice.

Palma stood up sharply, glared at them all for just a moment, and then stomped out. Karr smiled, and it wasn't very kind, but so did Jae.

"Unfortunately, none of *that*"—Shirrad nodded toward the door—"solves the problem. What do we do when the Highest army arrives?"

"I don't know," Jae said. "I decided too quickly about Danardae. I want to think about it more—hear more people's thoughts."

"We'll gather anyone you want to speak to," Gali said, shifting so she'd be able to stand up quickly and follow Jae's instructions.

Jae considered it for a moment, then sighed and said, "Everyone. I want to spread the word to everyone, the full truth of the matter, that I might not be able to protect us. And anyone who wants to can come speak to *me*. Once I've got an idea of what people want, I'll make up my mind. We have time before the army arrives. The least I can do is listen."

"And that's why we'll keep following you, Lady Mage," Karr said. "Magic or no, until this is over. And after."

He stood to join Gali in spreading the word, and Jae couldn't bring herself to say that no one, least of all her, had any idea if they'd even survive until after.

❖ ❖ ❖

The forced march toward Aredann was slow. Elan had made this trip before, but being surrounded by an army meant it all took three times as long. The infection and the wound itself had sapped much of the stamina and strength he'd built up over the past months, so just the daily grind of walking, walking, walking was exhausting.

Walking with his arms shackled in front of him, four guards surrounding him, and what felt like half the army jeering and laughing when they saw him was harder. He understood it, in a sick way. Jae and her people were out of the Avowed's reach for now, but here he was, and they hated him even more. As shocking as the Break had been to everyone, they already thought of the Closest as untrustworthy, nothing but carriers of traitorous bloodlines, so the fact that their freedom had started a war didn't surprise anyone. Jae was an easy enemy.

But Elan had turned his back on the people who now surrounded him. He'd broken ranks, broken *vows*, and willingly joined their enemy. It was an insult.

So all he could do as they taunted him was keep walking forward, keep his head held high, and try not to stumble. When he inevitably did, he had to catch himself. When he couldn't, he picked himself back up, even as the guards shouted at him, occasionally kicked him when he was on the ground, trying to get his breath.

He remembered his life from before he'd been exiled to Aredann and summoned his ancient, disdainful mask, looked at everyone as if *they* were no more than mild irritations. But the mask felt wrong. He'd never realized how hard it was to maintain—not just now, but how hard it had always been. It had never suited him, which was part of the reason his father had never been interested in him. Elan simply wasn't meant to be a politician who could play it cool, never let emotion rule him. He *liked* having feelings, and he liked helping people. He would even help the army who surrounded him now, if they'd let him.

But they wouldn't. They were going to fight the Closest, and once the Closest were dead, the Well would dry, and all these people . . .

They wouldn't listen to him.

They'd been traveling for weeks, long enough that some of his stamina had returned, when Andra finally slipped into the tent where he was kept at night. It was a small, tattered affair, but it kept him separate from the rest of the army so he couldn't talk to anyone—and no one could try to kill him before Erra was good and prepared to have him executed.

Andra presented him with a bowl of bread and lentils, not much of a meal, but about what he'd had every night. He glanced at her.

"Erra trusts me enough to let me near you," she said. "She's meeting with the other Highest, so she isn't near enough to supervise."

"Ah." He nodded and then ate, the chains on his wrists rattling. Erra hadn't been in to see him, but he could often hear her through the flimsy tent fabric. She was usually somewhere nearby, keeping track of every single person who was allowed to see or speak to him. Except Andra, who was still her confidant. Except . . . "I don't understand you. Whose side are you on?"

Andra hesitated, tapping her fingers against the satchel she had over her shoulder. Her hair, usually pulled back into a cloud around her face by a headband, was contained in a large puff at the back of her head. "I don't . . . don't know. Yours. Jae's, I mean. But I wasn't at first. Lenni *did* blackmail me, but if she hadn't, I'd never have seen the Highest's hypocrisy. But I can't . . . I'd help you if I could."

"I know," he said. "I didn't mean that. I just don't understand how you could love Erra and still betray her."

"I didn't have a choice before. Now . . . I want to help the Closest, but there's nothing I can do. I tried to make Erra see reason. I really did try," she said. "But Erra won't. I swear, she didn't use to be like this. It's like she's gone mad."

It did feel that way, but Elan knew his sister too well to believe it. "She thinks this is what she has to do. What our father would have done."

"I miss her. How things used to be . . . ," Andra said softly, then cleared her throat. "Quickly, now, before she returns. I brought all this." She pulled a sheaf of papers from her bag. "I know you won't have time to read all of it before she returns, but I thought maybe if you could write out the translation key for me. . . ."

Elan nodded. It wasn't as easy as a key, it was the way to rearrange the sentences, but he could jot down those instructions, too. He wiped his hand on his dirty pants and reached for one of the papers, reading to make sure he could still puzzle out the ancient script. It had been weeks since he'd last seen any of it. But he could, because he recognized the note scrawled at the top easily enough: *Saize Pallara, journal—after the Curse?*

Someone from the Order, making notes, trying to make sense of the few remnants of papers that had survived the Highest's purging. The fact that even one of the most revered Highest of all time had had most of his papers destroyed showed just how determined they were to erase everything they could.

His gaze flitted down the page.

> *. . . have feared magic since the Rise in the*
> *west. Eshara was right on that count. Even my*
> *own allies have never understood and now I*
> *must protect them from their own shortsighted-*
> *ness . . .*

Eshara—Janna's surname. He glanced down another paragraph.

> *Taesann was a greater mage than the cursed*
> *idiot who joined us, who wasn't even smart*
> *enough to question his brother before killing*
> *him. This idiocy could have been avoided, but*
> *instead the demands I face are reactionary.*
> *I should refuse, but we've only just finally*
> *consolidated our power. I must serve the*
> *decisions we all reached, foolish though they*
> *are, but at least I can do this much.*
> *For whichever of my descendants reads*
> *this, I hope you are wise enough to use it. The*

very brand we seal our vows with also seals
away our magic. There will be no more mages
among the Highest or Avowed. This is to meet
the demands of my foolish allies and their
cowardly fear of another Rise—as if the mages
who might arise from the ranks of the Twill
wouldn't pose a more immediate threat!

Jae had guessed right. The vow ceremony didn't just provide energy to the Curse, it *did* siphon away all the Highest's
potential mage powers.

But I will protect my descendants, and curse
what the other Highest think. And so, to
whoever of our bloodlines reads this: the very
brand that stole our magic can do the same
to others. There will be one per generation
who can wield it against mages to drain their
power.
 Fire is my element; with fire, I seal it to our
blood. As long as we hold this, we will never be
truly powerless. But should our bloodlines be
broken, no one else can yield it . . .

Forged with fire, bound to the Highest bloodlines—and
only one of them in each generation. Elan swallowed a wave
of revulsion and he remembered the brand in Erra's hand,
perpetually hanging at her side. She'd been at the fight in Danardae. She was the one who would lead the charge against
Jae—and with the brand, she'd succeed.

But no one else could use it.

Even after everything, it was too horrible to contemplate, but he had to get the message to her. "This explains how to stop the Highest from stealing Jae's power. To ensure she'll win."

"How?" Andra asked, eager.

Elan couldn't meet her eyes as he said, "She has to kill Erra. Either that or unbind the magic, but it's sealed with fire—and Jae can't touch fire, not at all. So it has to be Erra."

Andra opened her mouth, as if to speak, but shut it after a moment and shook her head.

"It has to be," Elan repeated. "I have to get word to her—"

"No," Andra said, firm. "You can't . . . I won't help with that. I *can't*."

"Andra, we *have* to. If the Closest are defeated, they'll be killed—slaughtered, all of them, if they don't take their own lives. And without them, the Well itself will come unbound. The world will be doomed. I love Erra. Even now. But we can't let that happen."

"But . . ." Andra shook her head again. "I can't help you escape, anyway. Anyone in this army would recognize you and you'd never make it."

Elan hadn't really expected her to do it. She wasn't one for risks, that much was clear, and as twisted up as she was about everything, she still loved Erra. He understood that— he'd been honest when he said he did, too. Even though he thought she was wrong, dead wrong, and even though sending Jae this message would seal her death.

It was awful to ask Andra to take part in that. But he had no other choice.

"Then leave me here, and go yourself," Elan said. "No one in the camp would stop you."

"I can't," she said, shrinking further. "Erra would notice my absence, and if she ever found out . . ."

"Erra is the one who won't listen or believe when we tell her the truth," Elan said. "I've begged her a hundred times to listen to me—to stop this. But she won't. And if the Highest continue this war . . . Getting this information to Jae could save thousands of lives. You have to do something, Andra, whether it's freeing me or going yourself. Unless you want the Well to dry, you have to!"

When Andra looked up, her eyes were shining with unshed tears. "All right. I'll go. I'll . . . I'll . . ."

"Thank you," he breathed.

Andra gathered the papers and stood, though she had to hunch to avoid hitting the tent's low roof. But as she opened the flap to step out, Elan saw that there were people outside.

One of them said, "I told you, Highest. She's a traitor, just like he is."

And Andra gasped, "Erra, *no*, please!"

Chapter 25

ERRA STARED AT ANDRA, SHOCK OVERCOMING HER NEED TO appear untouchable. Andra couldn't have—Andra would *never*—

But it was just as Osann had said. They'd taken the cursed mason prisoner after the Break, and he hadn't needed any convincing to tell them everything he knew. Then, in exchange for his life, he'd agreed to become a spy for them. To contact the few other members of the Order of the Elements he knew of and find out what *they* knew, spread misinformation. Do anything the Highest demanded of him.

It had paid off more quickly than they'd hoped, when Osann had found Elan and learned about the Closest's tunnel into Danardae. After that it had only been a matter of keeping it guarded. When the Closest had attacked, they'd been ready.

Now, though, Osann had broken into a meeting of the Highest and begged them to come quickly. He said he'd finally gotten confirmation of an Order spy among their army—that they wouldn't believe who it was. But if they'd only come listen to what was happening in the traitor's tent . . .

Erra stared at Andra. Andra, her lover, her most trusted friend. The one person who had always seen her for exactly who she was, not just as a member of the Highest, and who had cared and loved her anyway. Not like Halann, only worried about his own power, and not like Elan, who'd turned his back on her.

It wasn't possible.

Before Erra could do more than clench a fist, Andra said, "It isn't like you're thinking. I'm not—I'd never betray you. I love you!"

"We heard you," Tarrir said, stepping forward when Erra couldn't find any words through her anger. He raised his voice further, calling, "Guards! Bring shackles—"

Osann burst toward Andra, grabbed her, and knocked her over. Andra shrieked and flailed, and a moment later, fire erupted next to her. It caught Osann's robe and he shouted in surprise and pain as Andra rolled away and sprang to her feet. There were people pressing in around her now, but Erra was pushed toward her, Tarrir at one of her shoulders and Callad at her other.

"It wasn't like that, I had no choice," Andra said, and she was looking directly at Erra. "I never wanted to betray you, but you have to listen to Elan, the binding of the Well—"

"Enough!" Erra finally found her voice, and the word echoed above the noise of someone putting out the patch of flame. "Take her in chains."

"No!" Andra screamed. "Erra, listen to me, listen—"

A guard grabbed her, but she whirled, and the guard—

The guard caught fire. Andra backed up two steps, bumped into someone else, pressed a hand to that guard's shoulder, and there it was again, flame, and the guard shouted and jumped back in surprise.

Flame.

Andra was—Andra could—

"Erra, I'm sorry!" Andra shouted. "Stay back! Everyone stay back. I don't want to hurt anyone! I *never* wanted to!"

"You're a mage," Erra realized, even as fire lapped at the crowd, driving people back and away. Erra followed Andra, not caring about the flames that licked at her robe. She shed it as she moved. Andra glanced back, saw her, and stopped, pivoting to face her. A wall of fire sprang up around them, cutting off the rest of the guards and the other Highest. The searing heat was only hand spans away, but the flames stayed steady under Andra's control. People shouted from beyond it, but Erra didn't care what they were yelling. "You're a mage, you're one of them!"

"I didn't want to be!" Andra backed up another few steps, the fire moving back with her, sending up another round of shrieking. The gulf between the two of them widened, and some of the flames behind Erra dwindled. A group of guards sprang into action, pouring sand onto the fire to put it out, but she ignored them to focus on Andra. "I love you—but—but the Order found me. They told me what the Highest do to mages and what you'd do to me if you found out. I had no choice!"

What the Highest did to mages—they killed them. They had to. Magic was a danger to the world, and those who wielded it had to be stopped. That was why the brand existed. Erra reached for it now.

"I didn't want this—all I wanted was to be an artist, to make jewelry—I never wanted to be part of any of this! But everyone will *die* if you won't listen!"

Something struck Andra, coming through the fire that separated her from the crowd—an arrow. It hit her robe and tangled there but hadn't caught her flesh. She shrieked anyway, and everything went up in flames.

Erra screamed and hit the ground as the fire closed in, scrambling backward to where it had been contained. Smoke stung her eyes and she coughed, barely able to get a breath even when she was flat against the ground. She had to crawl as low as she could, trying to avoid the spreading flame, her skin blistering against the blazing sands.

Finally she reached the edge of it, emerging from the heart of the chaos. She didn't dare stand—there was too much smoke in the air, even here—but she wrapped her hand around the brand again and reached, tried to sense Andra and direct the awful visions toward her. But it was too late. She couldn't feel Andra the way she'd felt the mage at Danardae.

Andra was gone.

The fire had caught and spread. Erra finally got to her feet, fleeing back farther. A mass of people were swarming around her, trying to douse it with more sand and jugs of water. Tarrir was yelling orders, organizing them—only a few tents were beyond saving, and most of the camp could be protected if they moved quickly enough. Erra didn't know what else to do, so she grabbed an open jug, scooped up as much sand as she could, and joined the fray.

Slowly, the blaze was contained and put out. It hadn't spread too far, but there was a clear path of smoking ruins out past the edge of the camp, into the desert. Andra had escaped, setting fires as she ran.

Andra had been the very last person left who Erra had trusted fully, and she'd done all this. She'd never been trustworthy at all, had always kept a secret from Erra, had consorted with her enemies, and now . . .

"Highest!" Desinn pushed his way to her side. "The others have gathered. You should join them."

Erra followed him farther away from the fire and the mass of people working to put it out. She tried to breathe deeply despite the thick, too-hot air. They headed for Lady Callad's tent. Callad and Gesra were already inside, and Tarrir joined them a moment later. His robe was covered in soot, but he seemed otherwise unharmed.

"Your lover escaped," Gesra said with no preamble. "You could have stopped her, but now she's gone."

Erra shook her head. "I tried, but the fire . . . I couldn't breathe."

"So you claim." Gesra's voice was like a stone, and Erra knew that tone too well. It sounded so much like her father—his harsh judgments of anything he deemed a failure. Erra shook her head again, trying to clear it a little, and wondered if Gesra was right. Erra had been furious, she *had* tried, but it was *Andra*. She should have tried harder, gone for the brand first thing, no matter how difficult it was. Now there was another mage out in the world, and even though Erra hadn't let her escape intentionally, people might think she had. Because her lover, like her brother, was a traitor.

"Curse her," Erra said, voice shaking. She turned to one of the Avowed stewards who was hovering at the tent's entrance. "Get Elan. We need to question him."

The steward scrambled to obey. A few minutes later, Elan was dragged in, barely able to get his feet under him, still coughing. The tent he'd been chained in had been at the heart of the chaos—either he was very lucky, or Andra had been careful to spare him. He collapsed in a heap almost at Erra's feet, but a moment later he pushed himself to his hands and knees. He moved to get up and a guard shoved him back down. He glared up at her instead.

"You did this," she accused. "You turned her against me."

"No, you did that yourself," Elan said. "The Highest slaughter mages, and they always have. She never wanted to betray you, but when she found that out, she had no choice."

Erra choked on her instinctive answer, that she would never have hurt Andra. Because Andra was a mage. That meant killing Andra was her duty.

Elan actually laughed at her silence, an awful, choked noise, nothing of humor in it. "It didn't have to be like this. I tried to help you. I tried to show you the truth—"

Tarrir stepped forward and hit him, the back of his hand colliding with Elan's jaw and knocking him to the ground. But Elan didn't stop laughing, an edge of mania to it. "You see," he said, and spat. Blood landed in the sand. "You see, truth is the one thing the Highest fear. You could have just *listened* to me. But you decided to be like Father."

"Don't you dare talk about him," Erra hissed, and knew they had to silence him. The more he yelled about truth, the more the Twill in the army would start to doubt the Highest.

Before she could order the guard to gag him he clawed his way up to his knees. "Andra loved you and you drove her to this. *I* loved you, and now I don't even want to look at you. You think I'm the traitor, but you sicken me. You won't listen to anyone, even if it would save all your people's lives, and yours, too."

Tarrir hit him again. This time he didn't laugh, and could only rise to his hands and knees before collapsing again, one of his arms giving out. He gasped in pain and looked up at Erra, looking more like a stranger than ever. Before she could do anything—before Tarrir could, either, though another blow would probably knock him out—Gesra stepped forward, holding a slightly singed satchel. She wrenched it open and pulled out a few yellowed pages. "The mage dropped this. What is it?"

Elan looked up. "It's the truth—what little bit your ancestors never managed to destroy."

Gesra held one of the pages up and Erra could see the lines on it, but they didn't say anything at all. "It's gibberish."

"I can read it," Elan said.

Gesra glowered at him for a moment, then handed the bag and papers to the guard. "Burn it."

"You're that afraid of it?" Elan mocked. "You're that scared of even learning what your ancestors' crimes were?"

Erra grabbed the bag from the guard's hand and threw it

down in front of Elan. She pitched her voice loud enough for anyone listening from outside the tent to hear, because people *were* listening, and they *would* gossip. So let them gossip about this. "I'm not afraid of anything. Go ahead and read it all. There's nothing in our history I fear, and *history* can't change anything. You're still going to be executed—and if I ever see Andra again, so will she."

She turned to stare at the other Highest, saw them watching her just as warily. She knew exactly how this would look to them, what they'd think. That her father had cost them everything at Aredann, that her brother had betrayed them, that her lover had manipulated and spied on her. That Erra had failed to bring her to justice for it. That the Danardaes might be the family that cost the Highest everything and let chaos consume the world.

She was the only one who could stop that from happening now. She had to keep the world's trust in her. So she squared her shoulders and said to the other Highest, "You don't need to ask me anything else. I didn't know about Andra, and I never told her anything about our plans. And there's no one else in my life who was close enough to betray me. Not even Halann."

Gesra didn't look at all mollified, and Tarrir gave a very brief nod. Callad even looked a little mournful, but Erra didn't want that, either—she wanted their respect, not their pity. After everything this war had cost her, she deserved at least that.

But she'd never have it. Not until this cursed war was done, and the people who'd betrayed her were dead, and the world was back the way it was supposed to be.

Chapter 26

"Jae!"

Jae stood abruptly, jolted out of her morning attempt to coax the fields and the orchard to produce more. Gali was running toward her frantically. She blinked the glows of other-vision away and hurried to meet her.

"Jae." Gali started to speak, and paused to catch her breath. "Someone came up to the gate. She says she knows Elan, and that she has word from the army—from him. We didn't let her in, none of us know who she is, but she says she has to talk to you. Her name is Andra."

Jae jolted with surprise. Andra—Elan *had* told her about Andra. A member of the Order, if grudgingly, and Erra's mistress. But someone in the Order had betrayed them and given information to the Highest. Andra hadn't been at their enclave outside the cities, though, so she couldn't have known their plan. Unless it had been somehow passed to her.

But if she had word from Elan, if Elan was alive . . .

"Let her in. Bring her to the study. I'll get Lenni and meet her there."

Gali nodded, shooting the below-the-waist wave that meant *goodbye and good luck* as she went, and they parted ways. Jae hurried inside, wiping her hands on her robe. She ignored the dirty footprints she tracked into the house, the lifetime of habit that made her feel like it was her responsibility to stop and clean, and hurried to find Lenni and Karr. They made it to the study only a few minutes before Gali escorted Andra in.

Andra looked wild, her clothing ragged, her hair a frizzy mess of curls that had escaped whatever style it was meant to be in. She also looked *exhausted.* Jae stood to pour her a mug of water, which she downed gratefully before collapsing onto a cushion.

"Gali said you had word of Elan."

"And a lot more than that," Andra said, and looked at Lenni. "Erra found out."

Jae frowned, not sure what that meant, but from Lenni's gasp it had to be important.

Andra cleared her throat and said, "I'm a mage. That's how Lenni convinced me to join the Order. I hoped Erra would understand, I really think she might have, before all this, before Elan . . ."

A mage. *Andra* was the other mage Lenni had mentioned so many weeks ago, and she'd been hidden right in front of the Highest's faces.

"Osann is a traitor to the Order," Andra continued.

"Osann," Lenni repeated.

Andra nodded. "He was trapped in the city after the Break, but when Elan came in to look for me, he found Osann instead—and Osann took whatever information he was given directly to the Highest. I didn't know it was him until—until he told Erra about *me*. . . ." She shook a little as she spoke, and reached up to wipe at her eyes. "Everyone knows, now."

Jae had a million questions for her, about magic and what she could do with it. About what it might mean for the upcoming battle. But there was one other thing, first: "Gali said you have word from Elan. I didn't know if he was alive."

"He is," Andra said. "He was wounded and infected but Erra insisted they try to help him survive. But only so . . . She wants to execute him. They want to use him to hurt you."

Jae's world went cold and dark, as if enveloped in a sudden storm cloud. But it was just her mind, dark and stormy at the thought that Elan had survived, only to be killed now.

She shut her eyes and sagged, an ache building behind her ribs. If it was only her life in danger, she would trade it for Elan's without pause, beg the Highest to take her instead and spare him. But the world was so much larger than her desires, and she was responsible for so many other lives. All the Closest depended on her. They would die for her, and she had to live for them. As long as there was even a chance of ending this war alive, she had to.

Even if it meant that the Highest would kill Elan.

"I'm so sorry," Gali murmured.

Jae finally opened her eyes, nodded, and said to Andra, "Thank you. For telling me that he's . . . for the warning."

"But he did have a message for you," Andra continued. "We were trying to do more translation, but it's all lost now. But . . . but . . ." She sniffed and wiped at her eyes. "He found out how the Highest have killed so many mages. They have a brand. It's magic, I guess. One of them can always wield it to siphon away a mage's powers. It's bound with fire, so to unbind it . . ."

"I can't use fire," Jae said. "I'd like to know what elements you can use."

It took Andra a moment to understand, but she said, "Fire. Yes. But I'm not a very strong mage, I can't do the things you can. It's just . . . it isn't . . ." She trailed off for a moment. "Erra is probably the only one who can wield it. If she falls . . ."

"Then the brand can't be used," Lenni said. "So to protect your magic, Lady Mage, we have to kill Erra."

Andra crumbled, finally reduced to exhausted tears. She shook her head. "Couldn't you just disable her? Or separate her from it?"

Jae considered it, but Karr spoke up first. "Maybe we could, but she'll still be surrounded by the army, like at Danardae. I don't know how much control we'll have. They'll throw as many Avowed around her as they can, do anything to get her close enough to neutralize your magic. When we attack, we'll need to find her—target her immediately." He paused and nodded to Andra. "However we can."

"That could cost hundreds of lives," Jae said. "If they really use their whole army that way . . . once the fighting starts, I won't be much use. Hundreds could die just so we can kill one person."

"Yes, but if it protects your magic, it will be worth it," Karr said, and his voice rang with finality.

Andra sniffled and wiped her eyes on the ragged remains of her robe. Jae studied Karr for a moment. His open, unafraid posture. The scar on his throat. He'd come so close to death, but here he was, ready to risk his life for hers—hers, and the rest of the Closests'. Because if they could remove the brand's power, then one battle would be worth it, even if it was costly. If her magic held, Jae could defeat an entire army.

It was almost exactly a week later that Jae could sense the army, though it took another full day for them to be near enough for other people to see. The whole walled-in estate seemed to go still for the first time, as if admitting that all their preparation was over. Now, it was real. They simply waited while they were surrounded, because there wasn't anything they could do to stop it.

They were out of time. Everyone was as prepared as they could be, braced to fight. A large group had volunteered to try to force their way toward Erra to save Jae's magic, but even if they failed—even if Jae lost her power again entirely—the Closest were ready. All their fury would be focused into the battle, and they'd either win or die, but if they died, it would be fighting.

"Lady Mage," Karr said, grabbing her attention as she paced. "They've sent an envoy to the gate."

Jae fell into step with him, heading out to see what had happened. Lenni joined them, though she said, "I hope you don't plan to go out there. Jae, if they can get you with an arrow that easily . . ."

"They won't," Jae said. "I'll be able to tell if anyone is close enough for that, and if they are, I just . . . won't go. But if I can, I have to."

"I thought you'd say that," Lenni said. "There are four of them. Karr and Shirrad and I will accompany you."

Jae nodded, and they headed for the gate. They pushed the great door open, and she peered out. No, no one else from the army was close enough to harm her, and she didn't sense the strange magical gap that meant the brand was nearby, either. So she stepped out, leading the way.

She recognized the man in the embroidered robe who stood at the front of the envoy. Desinn Loerdan, formerly Elthis's favorite lackey. He looked older than she remembered, gray shooting through his dark hair, and he actually fell back a step when he saw her. Then he gathered himself and stood up straight.

She smiled a little. He was scared. That was something.

"Jae Aredann, I've come to demand your surrender," he said, his voice loud and steady, despite the fact that he looked like he might bolt at any moment. "We have Elan Danardae as our prisoner, and will trade his life for yours. If you will give yourself up, and your followers will surrender, the Highest have agreed to have mercy."

She hated herself for it, but she couldn't budge. Elan was gone, and no amount of begging and wishing would bring him back.

"I don't think the Highest even know what mercy is," she said, rejecting the Highest's terms. "They've watched generations of Closest live and die under the Curse. Where was their mercy then?"

"It was merciful that they didn't slaughter your ancestors, when they should have," Desinn said.

"No, it was not mercy. It was necessary for *your* survival. They knew, back then, that the Well was tied to the Closest, and would dry up if we all died. That is still the case. Remind your masters of that. If they kill us, they kill themselves. And tell them *my* terms: that they abdicate their power, each and every one of them. That they release their followers from all vows. That they and their army throw down their arms, and surrender to us. If they will do that, *we* will be merciful."

When Jae had first broken free of the Curse and realized her magic was unfettered, she'd felt unstoppable, sure that she could rearrange the whole world. She hadn't understood the consequences of her power yet, or how to use it responsibly. That had all come later, been harder lessons to learn, and they tempered her outlook now. But she could still summon the memory of that *feeling*, and she tried to put that into her voice as she continued.

"If the Highest do not surrender, then we will fight. If we win, they lose, and the Highest will die at our hands. And if they win, they still lose, because there is not a single Closest who hasn't vowed to die rather than return to a life of slavery.

Without us, the Well will dry, and what remains of the world will turn to dust."

"They said you'd say something like that," Desinn said, but his voice was quaking. "They say that's a lie."

"*They* are the liars. They'd rather risk your life—everyone's lives—than admit it," Jae said.

Desinn flinched but continued, "If you refuse their offer, they *will* execute Elan. Right in sight of this wall."

Jae stared him down and squared her shoulders. And though she hated herself for it, she said, "Then so be it."

Chapter 27

ERRA KNEW FROM DESINN'S EXPRESSION AS HE APPROACHED THEIR camp what the answer had been. Not that it was a surprise. None of them—not the Highest, who were sitting in their enormous tent, or Elan, who was in chains but kept within their sight, or any of their Avowed advisors or guards—had expected a surrender. It was only a formality, so they could remind their followers, after, that they had had wanted to be compassionate. It was more than the Closest deserved, and now they had earned the upcoming slaughter.

"Your terms were rejected, Highest," he said, addressing the whole group. "It was as you said, she made claims about the future of the Well, but offered no proof. But she . . ." He shuffled a little, not meeting anyone's gaze. "She didn't seem desperate. Just prepared."

"Do you hear that, traitor?" Gesra asked, looking at Elan. Who couldn't answer—he was gagged. "Your execution has been ordered. I suppose she didn't care about you very much, after all."

Elan couldn't speak, but his expression said plenty. The disgust he had for Gesra was evident.

"Are we prepared?" Callad asked, looking at one of her Avowed stewards. They had been moving their people into position all day. The wall had no exits but the single gate, as far as they could see, but that didn't mean they knew everything. So the whole estate was now surrounded, with Avowed guards overseeing the Twill they'd recruited. There were enough pockets of them placed around to engage anyone who might exit from anywhere along the wall, but the majority were here, with the Highest, outside the gate.

"Yes, Highest," the steward said. "Everyone is ready to fight—ready for this to end."

"Good," Callad said, and looked at Erra. "Are *you* ready?"

"Yes." Erra stood and glanced down at Elan. "Bring him. It's time."

She strode out, only pausing to accept the set of blades she'd need in the upcoming battle, a sword and a knife. The brand still hung from its tie at her waist and would be most important of all, but she might need to defend herself, too. She had only basic skills with the weapons—she'd been trained when she was younger and had worked to make sure she never fell out of practice, but she was no master. No one had ever thought she'd need to be, or that any of the Highest would. Their Avowed were loyal, and the world had been peaceful since the Curse had first been cast. Now, for the first time in generations, the Highest themselves would have to fight.

The Twill recruits swept out of her way as she walked forward, toward the wall and the gate. Far enough back to be safe, or at least as safe as anyone could be with a mage behind that wall. Though if the mage got close enough to strike at her, she'd have the brand and be able to strike back. Maybe it would be best if the mage tried—it might end this all even quicker.

Elan was dragged forward, barely able to walk with the thick chains around him. Mere manacles weren't enough anymore, since Andra had fled. He was pushed onto his knees, his wrists chained behind his back. Guards held him in place, but Erra was the one with the knife.

A slit throat was how Closest were executed. They were ordered to do it by their own hands, so no Avowed had to dirty their own with traitor's blood. But Elan wasn't cursed, so Erra would do it. She'd *volunteered* to do this, to prove once and for all that she was one of the Highest, and like the rest of them, she had no mercy for traitors—not for Elan, not for Andra, not for anyone who crossed her caste.

Knife in hand, she stepped close to Elan and looked down at him, and then up at the guard. "Take the gag out. He may have his last words. But it doesn't matter what you say"—she turned to him—"because we're beyond a chance for mercy."

The guard did as she instructed. Elan clenched and un-clenched his jaw, then said, "I wouldn't have asked for it. I *am* a traitor, Erra. Because I believe, I *know*, that you are wrong. That all this is wrong. I'd rather die than pretend otherwise. And I don't regret anything I've done."

"You should," she said.

"No. I only wish . . ." He looked up at the wall. There were people standing atop it, looking down. Jae, no doubt. Maybe Andra was one of the others with her, if this was where she'd fled. Erra braced herself, but there was no explosion of flame, no earthquake. Elan dragged his gaze back to Erra. "I only wish you were the person I thought you were. But I was wrong about you. You were only ever one of them."

"Enough," Erra said, swallowing shame like bile. She didn't care about a traitor's opinion. She didn't care about *any* traitor's opinion, Elan's *or* Andra's. She was Erra Danardae, she was her father's daughter, and she *would* protect the world as he had. This whole cursed revolt had to end now, no matter what that took, so order could be restored.

Which it would be. Things would be different, without the Closest to do so much labor, but the Twill would have to handle it. In exchange, the Highest would give them water from the reservoirs—for free, the way they did for the Avowed.

At least, for as long as the reservoirs lasted without the Closest. Erra still hoped that everything Elan had told her about the Well's binding was a lie, but knowing that the Closest really had crafted the Well left her a little worried. But she didn't dwell on it—she couldn't afford to. The drought was over, anyway.

She drew the knife and adjusted her grip on it. Elan didn't flinch. He didn't cower or even look away. Just gazed up at her, and suddenly it *wasn't* with the eyes of a stranger.

As she stood over him, ready to strike as he even tipped his head back, waiting, making it easier for her, she could only see him as her younger brother. She'd practically raised him.

But look where he'd ended up.

"Erra, it's time," Gesra said, stepping up nearby. "Everyone is watching."

She looked up, letting her gaze sweep from the figures on the wall out to the Twill who surrounded them, prepared for battle, to the line of Highest who were watching her. Gesra, Tarrir, and Callad.

She looked back at Elan, her brother, and her hand shook.

Tears pricked her eyes and she made herself step forward. Elan flinched finally, but only for a moment before he went statue-still again. Waiting, just waiting, for her to do it. To decide, once and for all, that she was like their father—would do what he would have—and that she *wasn't* the person Elan had thought. That she wasn't the one who would embrace the truth and seek justice, the one who believed that the lives of mages and the Closest mattered.

But her brother believed those things, those people, *did* matter, and he was willing to die for them. Erra stole a glance out at the army, up at the wall, and remembered the Closest woman who'd slid under the water silently. Who'd only survived because Erra had spoken up. Elan would have been proud if he'd seen that—

That was who Elan thought she was. Not like their father, but like him, willing to protect people. Not the world, but the people in it. Someone who would never condemn her own lover, the woman she cared about most in the world, just because mages held their own kind of power. Someone who wouldn't, couldn't, execute her own brother, just for wanting to save people. Someone willing to die for what she believed in.

Erra understood why those things were necessary. She *was* like her father. But as she looked at Elan's unflinching expression, she didn't want to be anymore. And she believed in *him*.

"Jae Aredann gave us terms, and I accept them," Erra said, and threw the knife down into the sand. Pain erupted in her chest, the brand she'd taken when she said her vows burning. She gasped, staggered, but made herself bear the pain. She straightened up, hand going to the bloody spot on her chest, and stood as near to Elan as she could. She'd just condemned herself to die with him, but so be it.

"I accept her terms, and I abdicate. I release my followers from their vows. And you would all be wise to do the same," she said, her voice shaking, but getting stronger as she spoke. She raised it, trying to be heard not just by the Highest who she didn't think would ever really listen, but by the others behind them. Their followers, Avowed and Twill alike, who needed to know.

"The Closest crafted the Well, and everything we all know is a lie," she continued, getting louder, shouting even as Tarrir opened his mouth. She had to make sure this was heard, and somehow, it was—her voice was louder than seemed possible, carrying above everything, unnaturally amplified. Her whole body tingled—magic. It was magic. Jae Aredann was doing this.

"It's all been lies," Erra said, echoing what Elan had tried to tell the world at the Break. "All of it! The War was a lie, the

Closest were never traitors. They were cursed to protect the lies my ancestors told, the lies we all believed! Everything the Highest have told you is wrong, and I won't be silent about it, and I will not punish my brother for telling the truth. Because the truth is that if we kill the Closest, we doom the Well and we curse ourselves, and I won't help with that. I won't."

Elan stared up at her in shock, but before anyone else could react, Gesra Caenn slammed into her. Gesra was old, and tiny, but the sudden jolt caught her off guard. Gesra slammed an elbow into Erra's stomach, driving her breath out, and as Erra tried to disentangle herself, she fell. Gesra was right on top of her, struggling, desperate, reaching for the knife. She was going to kill Elan—

No.

The brand.

Erra realized it and tried to roll out from under her, but it was too late. Gesra had grabbed the brand and pulled with all her strength, and small though she was, it was more than the loose tie around it could handle. It came free, the brand clutched in Gesra's hand.

Gesra rolled away from her, and Tarrir shouted, "Everyone loyal—to us, now! *Now!*"

Erra shoved her way back to her feet, trying to find Elan again as people began moving, shouting and shoving among themselves, fighting one another. Those who believed her against those who followed the Highest.

She grabbed her sword and dodged toward Elan as bodies pelted her, people screaming and frothing, with no way to even tell who was on which side. It was all she could do to reach Elan, who was still immobile in the midst of it, no longer the focus as Tarrir tried to create a formation from the chaos.

Erra towered over her brother, prepared to defend him with her life, swiveling to take on any threat that approached them.

Behind her, the gate came down. The Closest attacked.

✦✦✦

The moment Jae was told that Elan had been pulled up to within sight of the wall, she forced herself to climb up on top of it to watch. She owed him that. She couldn't save him, even though her very being ached with a want to. There was nothing she could do. If she dared raise magic to try to help, she'd be targeted by the brand—and she needed her magic to assist the Closest for as long as possible.

Magic aside, even if they opened the gate and sent a squad of Closest out to try to help, the group would have little chance of even reaching him, let alone getting to him in time, and they'd likely all be killed in the process. Her army would lose enough people trying to take out Erra; they couldn't throw away lives now, too.

So Jae watched, Andra at one side and Lenni at her other, and summoned the energy of the air to her. It would let her listen from a distance, as if Erra spoke to the air at Jae's ears instead of only to the people around her.

She heard Elan's final words, heard Erra's "Enough," saw Erra raise the knife.

Saw Erra hesitate. Then drop it.

"Jae, what's . . . ," Lenni started to say as Erra's words

reached Jae's ears. Jae stared into the roiling, confused crowd below and sent the air's energy careening outward, carrying Erra's words not just to her, but to the entire gathered army. Her speech echoed above everything, so clear that even the tremble in Erra's voice carried.

"It's all been lies, all of it! The War was a lie, the Closest were never traitors."

Jae was nearly dizzy, hearing the truth like that, from Erra's own lips, even though she'd known it. The crowd fell hushed for a moment.

"Everything the Highest have told you is a lie, and I won't be silent about it, and I will not punish my brother for telling the truth. Because the truth is that if we kill the Closest, we doom the Well and we curse ourselves, and I won't help with that. I won't."

"Jae!" Lenni grabbed her arm, demanding her attention. "They're about to start fighting themselves, look!"

Lenni was right: the Twill who'd been so terrified of the Closest and the threat they represented were shouting now, their shock fallen away, demanding answers from the other Highest. Who had none. But the Highest were all there, that was clear from the way the crowd swirled around them—Erra and Elan trapped in the midst of it, but the other Highest, too.

"We can take advantage of the chaos," Lenni said. "Some Twill will follow Erra, if we can get her out alive—and if she won't use the brand, then—"

"Go!" Jae didn't need to hear the rest. "I'll protect you from here!"

Lenni took off down the stairs, already yelling orders.

One of the Highest went mad and tackled Erra. That set off even more chaos, the storm of anger and fear that the Twill had carried with them breaking. The fighting was a deluge now, so many bodies crushed together, so frantic and violent that Jae couldn't track anyone with her true vision.

She slid into other-vision as easily as breathing, reaching out for a familiar feeling, and recognized Elan even in the midst of everything. Erra was standing over him, a few others at her side now, but they were surrounded by loyal Avowed. They were outnumbered, and would be more so soon—the closest throngs of the army that had been sent to ring Aredann in were running toward the fray.

Jae couldn't do much for Erra and Elan from where she was, beyond one small thing. She reached out, as if reaching for Elan, grasped the energy of the earth within the chains that bound him, and turned them to dust.

The gate came crashing down and Lenni led a charge into the fray. Somewhere in the crowd, the Closest's charge was answered, a group finally coming together, led by more of the Highest and their guards, with reinforcements coming from around Aredann.

She had to stop them. Lenni's force was outnumbered enough as it was. Summoning as much of the earth's energy as she could sense, she threw her arms outward, reshaping the world around her. The noise was like thunder from the ground as two chasms rumbled open, cutting off the main fighting—

But then they stopped.

Just like at Danardae, her magic hit a null area, large and expanding, moving closer. She gasped, knocked out of other-vision, and stared down at the chaos.

"You said only Erra could use the brand!" she shouted at Andra, as Lenni's forces were swallowed up in the fighting.

"That's what Elan said!" Andra stared out over the crowd, too, squinting. "It's—there, someone has it, someone else must be able to . . . oh *no*. They'll be slaughtered!"

Their strike force hadn't gotten anywhere near Erra in the chaos. And Andra was right: if the null area got any closer, she and Andra would both lose their magic—probably for good. Because without them to protect the wall, the Highest would eventually break in. The Closest inside would fight, but . . .

"It's bound with fire," Jae said, pushing back into other-vision. She could sense that much, but when she tried to throw any of her own energy at it, the null area ate it. "You might be able to get through."

Andra tried. Jae could sense it next to her as she gathered magic, the air heating up, and then released it. For just a moment, the null area sparked—yes, fire energy *could* get to the brand. But its magic was so enormous it swallowed Andra's easily.

"It's not enough," Andra said, though Jae could feel the air heating up around them again for another attempt. "I'm not powerful enough."

She loosed the magic again, but again, the null area lit and then faded.

Jae spared a glance at the rest of the battle. Lenni's force had been separated into two, her half throwing themselves between the Highest and the wall, trying to stop their approach. Karr led the other half toward Elan and Erra. Split like that, there just weren't enough people, Lenni gaining only inches of progress at a time.

If only there was some way to get everyone coordinated, attacking the Highest who had the brand, to link all their efforts together . . .

Jae grabbed Andra's hand. Mages *could* link their power. Janna Eshara had done it to bind the Well, and Taesann had, too, when he'd taken all the Closest's combined power and hidden it away. Jae held all that power now, and if she could link together with Andra . . .

"We need a blade, something sharp. It'll hurt, but we need . . ." She didn't have time to explain. Andra didn't ask her to. She produced a small knife, one probably better used for prying up mosaic tiles to use in her art than for battle. Jae accepted it and cut her arm, said, "You too," and Andra winced and followed the command.

Jae pressed their bleeding arms together, and as their blood mingled, Andra was pulled into the Closest's binding. Jae could sense her suddenly, sharply, as well as sensing her magic. Andra gasped.

"I'm going to try to see through your eyes," Jae said, though she had no idea if it would work. She blinked into other-vision and could see the link between them, followed it. Andra seemed to reach out for her, extending her mind as if she were extending a hand to hold, and Jae clasped it. Their energies meshed together more fully and Jae's senses went blindingly bright for a moment as she could feel things she never had before.

The world in front of her shined with strange clarity, now that she could sense all the elements. There was no true difference between other-vision and real vision, except where the brand dulled everything. But even that was different. Jae could *see* it now, the hot, angry, flickering light of the fire that had bound it and burned within it.

She reached for the well of power that belonged to the Closest, and with Andra still holding tight to her bloody palm, she called forth as much of that burning power as she could. And it *did* burn, searing her, but the agony didn't matter. Down on the battlefield, Elan and Erra were overwhelmed, cut off from the gate, other pockets of Twill fighting Twill too far away to help them, and the brand came ever nearer.

Jae accepted the burning pain, breathed into it, and threw the whole painful bundle of energy at the brand. The brand flickered, trying to absorb it all, but ancient and powerful as it was, Jae's magic was, too. The brand brightened, surging with power as it worked, but as it did, Jae could feel the fire inside it for the first time.

She reached for it, clenched her mental fingers around it, and pulled. It was like tug-of-war with a burning rope; her whole body ached with the effort, so hot she might collapse, but she kept her grip and pulled and pulled against it. The brand tried to tug back, struggling to stay bound, and a fire burst onto the battlefield, right in the group of Avowed. People screamed and whoever was holding the brand lost their grip. The brand's power flickered now that it was no longer channeled through a person. Jae gave one final yank and the brand erupted into sparks and flames, its binding snapped.

The threat to her magic was gone.

Jae sagged in place, exhausted and dizzy. She tried to hold herself up but crumpled, Andra barely managing to catch her and guide her down to her hands and knees on top of the wall. Jae looked out at the chaos below—the giant, jagged chasms, the fire, the knots of fighting and the bodies on the ground—and realized nothing had changed.

Though she was exhausted, she still had her magic and could still use it to save her people—except for those who had gone to try to save Erra and Elan. She wouldn't let the Highest's forces breach the wall, and the army outside was fighting itself. If enough of the Twill turned on the Highest, they might give the Closest an advantage in numbers, but even with numbers and magic and truth on their side, there was still so much fighting. Nothing she could do would settle this; there was no other power to link to that would ever bring about peace—

Except, wait, the link, the binding, the Well. Jae's head was spinning but she pushed back up to her feet. She looked through her exhausted other-vision, needing to stop the chaos to ensure that everyone would hear, to save as many lives as she could. She'd only done this once before, on a much smaller scale. It was imperfect at best, but she had no choice.

She needed more mud, and for that, water. She reached for the power of air and water, mingled together in the ever-present clouds overhead, and pulled. The rain hit hard and suddenly, dousing the flames that still lapped at the battle-field, turning the bloodied ground into a mudpit. She did the rest on her own, deepening it, then raising it, until it gripped everyone she could sense up almost to the knee. People screamed but stilled, not able to drag their limbs free, and thunder rumbled overhead.

Jae took a breath to steady herself, then another, gathered herself up, and used the same trick she had to project Erra's voice to project her own. "This ends now. There is no magic powerful enough to stop me, and I will not take any more lives than I'm forced to. I will have peace, and so I will offer you new terms. Throw down your arms, and I will give you the Well."

Chapter 28

A HUSH DESCENDED OVER THE BATTLEFIELD, AND FOR A MOMENT there was only the sound of the rain. Elan stared up at the wall in shock, but he couldn't do anything else. He'd barely been able to move, even before the mud had surged upward and wrapped itself around his legs, miring him, and everyone else, in place. He was still leaning against Erra, as he had been, but now they were trapped side by side, Karr only a few hand spans away.

Jae's voice continued, echoing above the rain splatters and muted groans from the injured people who were now lying in mud, half covered and in pain.

"The Highest will surrender, and free their followers from their vows," Jae repeated. "They will abdicate all the power they hold, and they—and their Avowed—will acknowledge that they will never rule over the Closest again.

"In return, I offer this. The Well is bound to the Closest's blood, to our bloodlines. As we die, it weakens. It is weaker now than ever, and another drought would surely end the world. But we can stop that weakening. I will allow any who wish to, to join us. Twill, Avowed, even Highest, should you choose to. When you join the binding, you become one of us; any evil done to the Closest will affect you. But you will share power over the Well, and responsibility for it, too. It will belong to any of us who choose it.

"Surrender now, and you may choose to join us. We will seek only justice for the crimes committed against us—not vengeance. We will have mercy. If you surrender. *Now.*"

Elan wiped mud and rain from his face, his heart racing. He'd thought it was madness, only moments ago, but now that Jae had announced her whole plan, it was nothing short of brilliant.

The first war had been fought over the Well, over who had the right to possess it. Every lie and cruelty since then had been for the same reason. The Highest had used their supposed control over the Well to maintain control over the world. And as long as only a select group had power over the Well, there would always be fear, and jealousy, and fighting to control it. But to turn that into a shared burden, to make the Well something that truly belonged to everyone, and that everyone together had to protect . . .

It wouldn't heal the wound in the world immediately. It didn't even mean there would never be war again. But it would bind the people on this battlefield together with those behind the walls, and begin to give them a way forward, a chance for peace.

Erra dropped her sword and raised her hands, her palms open. Elan doubted she knew the Closest signal of safety, but it was a strikingly similar gesture.

"I have already given my surrender and abdication," she said, voice pitched loud. It didn't carry as it had before, but enough people could hear it to make a difference. "I will join you."

Elan twisted, staring at the stuck, drenched, confused crowd. Finally he could make out a figure that had to be Lady Callad, toward the back of the crowd that had been fighting its way to the gate. Her voice, too, carried far enough: "Yes, yes, curse you. I surrender, and I abdicate."

There was a long pause and finally someone shouted, "Lord Tarrir is barely conscious—he surrenders. And ..." A longer pause, then, "Gesra Caenn is fallen. Her daughter isn't among the army. We surrender."

It must have been one of Gesra's closest advisors who was shouting, or else whoever it was just didn't care. Either way, the crowd seemed to accept it—accept the fact that with another Highest gone, and the rest surrendered, the war was over.

Elan was shaking where he stood, overwhelmed, barely able to comprehend it. All around him, Avowed were dropping their weapons and raising their arms, following the Highest into surrender. But those nearest to him had already chosen their side before Jae's decree—many of them, like Erra, had bleeding wounds on their chests, where they'd once been branded. Broken vows meant the brand would turn fresh and raw and bloody, as his had. All the Avowed now seemed willing to bow to Jae, but these ones had decided before her decree. They had come to their senses in the midst of battle, and done what was right.

Erra was trembling, too, still stuck in the mud, bleeding not just at the brand but from other battle wounds. There were tears streaming down her face, though it was hard to tell them from the rain that still fell.

As Elan looked up at Jae, she raised her hand, and the wind with it. The clouds that had been overhead were swept away, the storm moving off with them, revealing the sun above. It was hard to believe it had been there all along, but there it was, still shining, warming them all, as Jae looked down at them and they all stood, waiting, ready.

Finally someone behind Elan, well out of sight, started to cheer. It was one of the Closest who'd fought, but the noise was picked up by others on both sides of the wall, a ridiculous cheer of joy and relief in the midst of the mud that still trapped them. Elan felt a laugh bubble up inside him, reached out to clasp Karr's shoulder, and said, "We won."

It took a full day to dig everyone out of the mud. Jae joined the Closest work groups that had agreed to help and used her power to loosen the mud, which had practically turned to rock as it had dried around people. They started with the wounded, moving through the whole army to find those who were hurt the worst and rescue them, tend to them as much as they could, before they started the long, difficult work of freeing the others.

The army's camp was in chaos. Most of its supplies had been rendered unusable by the mud or the storm; tents had been blown away or ripped apart, wagons of supplies overturned and lost. Aredann was already flooded with people, thousands more than the small estate town could support, and this nearly doubled that number again.

They'd make do.

It was a dangerous decision, but Jae brought the wall back down. Both sides were nervous about it, the peace so tentative that it would only take a few angry words or a single person's rogue action to start the battle again. It might have been wiser to keep the two groups apart, with the Closest safe in the town and the army outside.

But when Jae had offered her enemies a chance to join her people, she'd meant it, and she knew she'd have to prove it—immediately. With the wall lowered, they could share resources more easily. Closest handed out food and water and clothes to those who needed them. They helped mend tents and erect shelters for those that didn't have any.

No one was happy about it, no one enjoyed it or developed a sudden feeling of camaraderie. But no one fought against it, either, and she accepted that this was all she could do. The rest would take time, and trust, and couldn't be rushed.

Every day for a week, they shared supplies and resources, the former Highest and Avowed sending messengers back with news to the rest of the world. Jae spent every waking moment trying to ensure that everyone had food and clothes and shelter, meeting with the impromptu council that was meant to represent everyone, and working. She barely had time to eat or sleep, let alone speak to anyone about anything other than how the peace would work.

Not even Elan, though she saw him in the council room every day. He always sat with Erra, and he always smiled when Jae came in, but they hadn't had a moment alone, and Jae hadn't tried to find one. Not that she didn't want to—she did, badly. But maintaining the tentative truce required her full focus, and besides, she had no idea what she'd say.

Yes, Elan had survived the battle—thanks more to Erra than to her. When it had been a choice between his life or risking thousands of her people, she'd known what was right. But now, seeing his smile and lifted spirits as he rebuilt his relationship with his sister, she didn't know how to tell him that. How she'd make him believe that even though she'd been willing to sacrifice his life, it had been like sacrificing her own heart. That she knew now that she cared for him, the way he said he cared for her.

If he still did, knowing she'd been prepared to watch him die.

Instead, she worked and slept and only remembered to eat when Karr or Gali pushed her into a seat in the kitchen and put food in front of her. She spoke with anyone who asked for her ear, she heard the news from messengers as they arrived from across the world, carrying word back and forth from Aredann to every other estate.

Jae let the work of maintaining the peace consume her, and realized it would be her work for the rest of her life. She'd spend the remainder of her days trying to sew together the worlds of the Closest and the former Avowed and Highest, carefully elevating the Closest's status while not letting anyone else's resentment bring back the discord and war. Even though it meant smiling when she didn't want to, and being lenient and merciful with those who'd once held power over her, because she needed their help. The Highest had given up their power, officially; but in truth, it would be years, maybe generations, before the ingrained obedience of separate castes faded away.

Jae doubted she'd live to see a time when no one really thought of the four Highest families as rulers anymore. But she could at least lay down stones that would begin that path, and hope that those who followed her continued to build it.

A week after the surrender, she realized what her next step would have to be, and fell in with Karr to meet the others in the larger study—the small one wouldn't fit the whole group. As they walked, she said, "I have a question, if you'll forgive it."

"Of course, Lady Mage," he said.

"Are you . . . are other Closest angry with me?" She hated that she had to ask it, but she knew even her own people stood in awe of her and weren't likely to seek her out with dissent.

Karr considered it as they walked, and finally said, "Some are. Some of us wanted to see the Avowed dead for their cruelty. I did—I *thought* I did. But you promised mercy in exchange for peace, so we accept it."

"They will work off their crimes," Jae said, a promise she'd made her people and intended to keep. It was only a scant idea now, one she still had to figure out fully and follow through on. Every Avowed was guilty, in a way; they'd all prospered thanks to the Curse. But not every Avowed had been actively cruel to the Closest, and—with the Council's agreement—she would sort out those, the worst of the lot.

There were lost estates out in the desert, long abandoned. There was a map to find them at the Well, in the same strange room as the mosaic memorial to Janna Eshara. Jae would send the worst of the lot out to find them, and to begin the hard work of restoring them. Most were so ancient there would be almost nothing left, she suspected; the work of rebuilding would require a lifetime. They wouldn't be left to do it on their own, but it would keep them mostly separate from the people they'd once tormented, and the labor would keep them busy.

She'd only mentioned the idea in passing, knowing it wasn't a perfect solution, but to her surprise Palma of all people had volunteered to lead the first group—as soon as those who'd chosen to do so had joined in the Well's binding. She was working to convince other Avowed to go with her by choice, since the first estate restored would be her own. Only a few Avowed seemed interested, but Jae would select the others who'd join them eventually—the ones she wanted out of the way. Sadly, that group couldn't contain the former Highest—even though she wished it could. On bad days, she considered it a kinder fate than they deserved.

But it would keep her promise to Tal. And compromises, as much as they rankled, still let her take step after step forward.

They reached the study and she looked around it, taking in the sight of so many different people who'd all come together. There were Elan and Erra, of course, together, with Shirrad and a few others who'd come to refer to themselves as the Burned Avowed—their brands had burned when they'd broken their vows, switching sides rather than following the Highest once they knew the truth. It was a point of pride for them.

There were the other former Highest, still looking far too wealthy and powerful. Tarrir was recovering slowly from burn wounds, and Gesra Caenn's daughter had arrived at last to surrender officially. All the former Highest except Erra were constantly surrounded by toadies from the former Avowed. There were also members of the Order, Twill and Avowed alike—Lenni, of course, who had picked the young Casinn as her right hand, replacing Palma.

Osann had fled, too, more dramatically, almost the moment he'd been freed from the mud. He was wanted, reviled by both sides. He'd betrayed the Highest by joining the Order in the first place, and then betrayed the Order, too. No one trusted him, and when Jae found him, he would be placed among the exiles.

There were other Twill among the council—Andra and a handful more who'd been pushed to lead by their fellows. And, of course, there were the Closest. Gali and Karr were the ones Jae knew best, but several others who'd come from enclaves scattered around the world had joined. Some had been with Jae almost since the Break, but others were newer, had joined them as they'd retreated. One, an elderly woman named Sanna, had arrived only after the peace, bringing with her what was almost another small army. The Closest she'd gathered, on the other side of the cities, hadn't managed to find their way to Jae's group during the retreat to Aredann, but had followed as soon as they'd heard.

Jae sat on one of the empty cushions in the room, knowing there would be the usual onslaught of questions and concerns, so she held up her hands to ward them off. "Sorry I'm late. I was thinking, and I've come to an important decision—for all of us."

Already the former Highest were frowning. Jae hadn't made many edicts since they'd surrendered, and she was loath to make declarations now. She knew the Closest would follow her, but if the former Highest and their followers didn't, it could erupt back into fighting. She didn't want that, so she consulted them whenever possible, tried to enlist their aid. Even when she didn't want to. But this was her decision alone.

"According to the texts Elan translated, the brand that sealed your vows also sealed your magic away," Jae said. "With it gone, and your vows dissolved, you all must realize that there will be mages in the world again, among those who used to be Avowed.

"The Twill have always had mages. The difference is that now they'll be able to live without fearing for their lives." She glanced at Andra. "And as for the Closest—our magic was taken from us for generations, too, hidden away and preserved. I hold it now, all of it. More of it than is fair.

"I'm going to release my power back to the Closest. I will still hold some—I don't know how much is really mine, but I know that most of it isn't. Which means I will still be a mage, but I won't be capable of great works anymore—at least, not alone. No more walls or earthquakes. There will be other Closest mages, and I will no longer have that kind of power."

It took a moment for everyone to understand, and it was Shirrad who said, "I don't know if that's wise. With the peace as tenuous as it is . . ." She cast a glance at the former Highest. "Your magic may be needed to enforce it."

Jae had already considered that. The fact of the matter was, Shirrad was correct. It was the threat of Jae's magic that had really scared the Highest into accepting her terms, with the offer of the Well to soften that blow. But that was why Jae had to do this.

"If my magic is all that keeps this peace alive, then it will die with me, someday," Jae said. "We need it to last beyond our own lives. And in the end, the world will be safer if more people hold power, not fewer."

"And you aren't worried about . . ." Shirrad looked around again. "About the short term?"

"Of course I am," Jae said. "But I have to believe that we'll get through it as best as we can, and build for the future. Not just tomorrow, but the day after, the year after, ten years after. You all need to know that I believe that's what we're doing. That's why I offered to bring you into the Well's binding. I will do anything to make this peace stronger."

That got murmurs of agreement, first from the former Highest and their supporters—Jae had known they'd agree with anything that would weaken her—and finally from her own allies.

From there, the meeting turned to more practical matters: the resources it would take to move so many people safely through the desert to the Well, where they would conduct a series of ceremonies to bring more people into the binding. Jae listened and gave advice and let others begin most of the preparations.

That night, she stood alone in the overgrown courtyard garden, her hands placed on the rim of the fountain Janna Eshara had built. She could still feel the flicker of Janna's power in it, still binding it, and wondered what Janna would think of the work she'd done. Of the ways the Well had been abused, and the changes that would happen now.

She shut her eyes, pulled herself into other-vision, and could sense the Closest clearly through the binding. She looked inward, saw her own vast well of power, and with a breath, she released it. It dwindled like an untended fire in the night, from a full blaze to a few embers. But she could see glowing embers throughout the Closest, too; could see people who'd been born with the potential to be mages but had never been able to access their power, who would rise tomorrow with new senses.

She reached out in other-vision and found she was now limited. She could sense the earth under her, the water in the reservoir, still bright and easily reached. She could even touch the air, feel its familiar, jarring buzz, though it was harder to command it. Fire once again escaped her. And none of the elements were as strong as they once had been.

No, she wouldn't be able to shake the ground ever again. But she gripped the fountain, and concentrated, and when she opened her eyes, flowers had come to bloom in a ring around it.

She smiled and went inside to rest. Tomorrow, they would finally start the trek to the Well.

Chapter 29

Erra had thought the orchard that grew above the Well was impressive, until she'd seen the Well itself. *Nothing* looked impressive next to that. All that water, a glittering, vast oasis, and as she'd stared at it, she'd thought of the thousands upon thousands of people who'd died for it—during the War *and* under the Curse. All the unforgivable acts her ancestors had committed over this incredible, beautiful sight.

She'd raised her hand to the healing brand on her chest, and made herself look away from the Well's splendor. There was work to be done.

Aredann hadn't been able to sustain so many people, even with magic encouraging the crops and reservoir, but the Well could. Its orchard was so vast that no one among the hundreds and hundreds who'd crossed the desert would go hungry.

The first days after they arrived had been spent working to erect shelters, gather food, and organize people. Erra had never realized just how much of her stewards' time had gone into logistics, when all she'd had to do was give orders and let others obey them. Now, she worked every day; she refused to ask anyone to do work she herself wouldn't.

It was hard. But it was, slowly, earning her the respect of the Twill, and even some grudging Closest. Elan was the one who'd gently suggested she set an example of willingness to work, reinforcing the decision she'd made on the battlefield. He was right, of course. He had been right about everything.

But, as she gathered fruit and roots into a giant basket that she'd bring back for others to cook, she couldn't mind too much that it was her little brother who always knew what to do. Because, even though she wasn't sure she deserved it, Elan had forgiven her. And now she could see him as he was, not just as the younger brother she'd spent their youth trying to protect.

Elan was strong, and brave, and more than anything, Elan was compassionate. He'd always wanted to help everyone he met; now, he always seemed to know how. She'd seen Closest children come to him with skinned knees, she'd seen terrified former Avowed confide fears in him, she'd seen members of the Order of the Elements talk to him about strategy and peace. Elan had found a place, and a purpose, and he thrived.

Erra had lost so much of her own purpose, but she was still proud of him.

"Erra?"

She dropped the fruit she'd plucked into her basket and turned. Andra had stepped into view. She had on a deep blue robe, and a delicate silver band twined around her forearm. She'd probably made it—maybe just out of a scrap she'd found somewhere. In the midst of everything, Andra had confessed that she'd only ever used her magic to make jewelry, heating the strands of silver and gold she spun together with more delicacy than any forge could ever manage.

No wonder everything she made had always been so splendid. She could do things that, literally, no other jeweler could. Erra's breath caught at the sight as she remembered, unbidden, a dozen moments when Andra had placed a necklace around her throat, so gentle and careful, so close and intimate. It all felt like so long ago, and Erra could barely bring herself to look up at Andra.

But she did, and cleared her throat, and said, "I thought you'd be with the mages. Training."

"I was," Andra said. Mages had started appearing among the Closest, just as Jae said they would—but they'd also appeared among the Avowed, and even one other Twill, who had always seen strange things but had never known why until now. "But using magic is exhausting. I've never done it so often before. So we're done for the day."

"Ah." It was hard to tell through the orchard's canopy, but it was late in the afternoon.

"So I wanted to come find you, and heard you were gathering food." She stepped closer, reached past Erra to pluck a yellow fruit from the tree, and dropped it into the basket. "I wanted to talk to you."

Erra swallowed, and confessed, "I wanted to talk to you, too, but . . . I was also avoiding it."

"I know," Andra said, with something almost like a smile. "I do know you pretty well. I just wanted to . . . to say that the secrets I kept—"

"I know," Erra interrupted. "You had to. I wouldn't have understood, and the poison the other Highest believed . . . if they'd found out, or my father had . . ."

It had been hard to admit to herself, but if her father had found out Andra was a mage, he would have had her killed. Erra would have protested—but now she had to wonder if she'd have been successful, or if she'd have gone silent when threatened with disavowal. If she'd have let herself believe her father's lies about mages being too dangerous to live. If, without having been pushed to the point where she had a blade at her own brother's throat, she would have changed at all.

She wished she knew. Now she'd never be sure.

"I hated every moment I lied to you. But I had no choice, and I really did think the Order was going to help. That we'd find a way to show you the truth and bring you to our side," Andra said. "That was the only reason I ever really helped them, told them *anything*. Because I wanted you to reach a point where you could know and it wouldn't matter."

"Because you had faith that it could happen," Erra said. "You and Elan both. But I didn't deserve it."

"You made the right choice in the end."

"It was nearly too late," Erra said. She'd come so close to killing her own brother.

"But it *wasn't* too late." Andra met Erra's gaze. "You

can . . . you can ask me anything you want to know, now, and I won't lie."

Because they both knew there was one question left. Erra dreaded finding out the truth, but made herself ask, "Did you really love me? Or were you only ever a spy?"

"I really loved you," Andra said immediately, and Erra felt a rush of relief that left her knees weak. "I begged to be allowed to make deliveries to you, when I was an apprentice. Just so I could see you."

Erra smiled. "I really only kept buying things from your shop so you'd come deliver them."

Andra gave a quiet laugh at that, but continued, "I used to have headaches, see strange things, but no one knew why. It wasn't until after we were together that Lenni found me and explained what it all meant. She helped me learn what I could do. It was exhilarating, but terrifying, and when I found out what the Highest did to mages . . ."

Erra looked away. "I truly didn't know. I didn't know mages existed at all, but . . . the other Highest did. I'd have been told when my father got a little older, when I was closer to inheriting. And they'd have tested me with the brand and . . . and made it my duty to kill any mages they found."

Andra looked away from her, and Erra hated herself. Because a dark, terrible part of her thought that she would have accepted that burden, and turned against Andra. Elan didn't think she would have—he'd always believed in her—but she really *was* too much like her father. She'd have to spend the rest of her life working against those instincts. Trying to be the woman Elan saw her as, not the one her father had raised.

"I was so scared," Andra said. "So I did the best I could,

I let Lenni force me to spy. I . . . I never wanted to hurt you. I'm sorry."

They worked in silence for a few minutes, plucking fruit, standing so close that Andra's shoulder jostled Erra's with every movement. Erra wanted to beg her for forgiveness—forgiveness and more—but she didn't know how to ask. She could order and command, but asking . . .

She cleared her throat. "I don't hold any power anymore."

"You have influence," Andra said.

"Yes, but . . . but Halann didn't marry me for mere influence," Erra said. Halann hadn't joined the army that had marched to Aredann. He'd stayed in Danardae with their children. Like most of the former Avowed, he wanted to join the Well's binding and secure his place in power—but he couldn't leave Danardae until Erra returned to be with their children. "My title was the only reason he agreed to marry me, and the reason I had to agree to marry him. And now that reason is gone. I think it's safe to say that if I ask him to put me aside, he will. And I certainly will for him."

"Oh." Andra blinked, and turned to face Erra. They were very close together now. "That's . . ."

"I never loved him. The children, yes, but . . . Halann and I weren't even friends. I never trusted him. But I always trusted you." Erra danced around the question, hoping Andra would answer it without her having to come out and plead.

"And I lied to you."

"You had reason," Erra said. "So the blame is mine, and . . ." Andra still didn't volunteer anything. Which meant that even though Erra wasn't sure she was worthy, she made herself keep talking. "And I miss you. I'd like to be with you again, if you'd like that. And I'd like to think we can learn to trust each other—entirely, this time. That if Jae can rebuild the whole world, we can at least rebuild . . . rebuild this. If you want to."

Andra was silent and still for a heartbeat, and then another. Erra's cheeks went hot. She had once thought she understood everything about Andra, but now knew she had no idea. Maybe she never really had.

But then Andra smiled, and it was the familiar, beautiful smile Erra had always known, and Erra trusted it, trusted her, and leaned in to kiss Andra gently and take her hand. She'd lost plenty in the Break, but she'd gained this, and that was worth plenty, too.

Chapter 30

JAE TREASURED HER FEW STOLEN MOMENTS ALONE MORE THAN water. She'd somehow grown accustomed to having people always seek her out in a crowd, having eyes on her all the time. She'd gotten used to not just speaking up, but doing it loudly, sometimes shouting down a whole room of people. None of it came naturally, and she was sure she disappointed everyone who sought her out, looking for someone brave or noble to follow.

She did the best she could. She accepted that she needed to always be visible, accessible, that she belonged to the whole world now. Somehow, giving her power back to the Closest— or more precisely, giving the Closest's own power back to them—had made her *more* of a symbol of the peace. Her presence alone could quell fights, soothe egos. Even among the former Avowed.

So the moments she did manage to steal away from the rest of the world and spend by herself were precious. Today was the first day she'd claimed more than a few minutes for that cause.

They'd been camped up by the orchard for weeks, living off the food her ancestors had so wisely planted. They'd cut into it quite a bit, though, not just eating it away but actually felling trees and using them to build up shelters. There was a full town now, with stone buildings she'd worked with the fledgling mages to raise, a few wooden structures, and a whole vast dune of tents.

Tomorrow, they'd begin the process of adding people to the binding of the Well. Because the binding was already in place, it wouldn't require a life to be sacrificed, as it had when she, Tal, and Elan had first come here, alone. When she'd lost Tal. But it *would* require a lot of magic, a lot of energy, a lot of time.

So today she had decided to take some time for herself to prepare. Disentangling herself had taken the whole morning, but finally she'd fled to the slippery, weathered staircase that wound downward to the Well itself.

She hadn't climbed all the way down, though, just stopped on a slightly widened landing and sat. She could look down at the Well from here, or up at the cliffside. She was alone, and she could finally breathe.

There was peace. It was real. It was still difficult, as if

she was the fulcrum balancing a dozen different weights, and a single shift would send the whole thing askew again. But there *was* peace and her people were free.

As she stared out at the waves, she thought of Tal. She'd promised him she'd have mercy, and, she thought, she had. She hadn't given in to the anger that still often thrummed inside her. She hadn't let the Closest loose that anger, either, though she wondered if she should have. If they deserved their vengeance.

But vengeance wouldn't move anyone forward. It wouldn't help the peace last.

Footfalls echoed down the steps and she braced herself, waiting, but it was only Elan. He stood still on the stairs, and then took a tentative step toward her. He held up one hand, open, because he was alone and it was safe to talk.

Not that she knew what to say.

"I'd like to sit, if you don't mind," he said, pointing to the rocky outcrop she'd perched on. She nodded and shifted over so he could join her. "I'm impressed you finally managed to get away from everyone for a little bit."

"Me too. Tomorrow will be tiring, though. I needed . . ."

"I know," he said. "It must be exhausting for you, having all these people who need you."

She nodded.

"You're doing an incredible job," he said. "You're exactly what they all need. What *we* all need."

"I'm trying," she said.

"He'd be proud, you know," Elan said. "Tal, I mean."

She glanced over at him. She'd known who he meant. It was impossible to sit like this, watching the Well, and not think of him. He'd sacrificed his life to make this possible—the Break and the peace both.

"I've been trying to find a moment to talk to you for days," Elan continued. "Because I finally translated the last of those pages. Good thing Erra didn't toss them in the fire after all. I've passed them off to the mages now, to learn to read—if you're sure you don't want to join them. . . ."

"I don't have time to learn anything like that," Jae said, an edge of bitterness in her voice. Maybe someday she'd be able to, but for now, when people wrote out and signed promises, she could only scribble something she'd been told was her name. She never felt more like an ignorant, barefoot Closest than when that happened.

"Of course," Elan said. "I'm sorry." He cleared his throat. "I think I pieced it all together, finally. What that Rise was, why everyone was so afraid to use magic."

She glanced at him, surprised, but asking still wasn't an instinct for her. He continued anyway, as if she had.

"From what I can tell . . . when our ancestors' ancestors first found this land, it was a paradise. Not a desert. There was war after war to control it, because it was fertile and beautiful, and to control it was to hold power."

"That sounds familiar," Jae said, staring at the sun's rays glistening across the Well.

"Eventually one group—ancestors to the Closest and Highest both, and everyone else—decided to take control by keeping everyone else out. A bunch of mages worked together, concentrated all their power, and raised a chain of mountains that were impassable. That was the Rise."

Jae stared sharply into the distance. With her other-vision

weakened, she couldn't feel the horrible pull of the jagged peaks she knew were out there. The last time she'd been at the Well she'd been able to sense them, and they'd terrified her. They had been so dark and wrong and twisted. The memory tugged at her mind.

Elan started to continue, but she shook her head, and he fell silent. She shuddered at the memory of the mountains' power, bizarre and twisted as it was, and then, yes, she knew where else she'd felt it.

"The knife," Jae said. "It was so powerful because it was made of stone from the mountains. That's why it was so hard for me to destroy, too."

"Oh." Elan sounded a little surprised. "That's . . . I wonder why they did that, why Janna would have carried a knife like that."

Jae shrugged. All she knew was that it was ceremonial, and it had been passed down through Janna's family for generations.

Elan continued, "The Rise turned out to be a huge mistake. It interrupted the energy of the elements all around, but there was no way to fix it. And worse, the whole world began to change. Whatever the mountains did to the magical world, they did to the physical world, too. Because what had been a paradise died, and over generations it became . . . this." He gestured at the world around them. The desert.

"So when Janna Eshara suggested creating the Well to preserve what little water they had left, to ensure that they wouldn't all die of drought, people were scared. They knew they needed to do something, but the idea of such a huge work of magic was terrifying, too. Because what if it went wrong?"

"Ah." Jae nodded.

"The Highest were mages who'd sworn never to let magic ruin their world again. That was why they didn't join the Wellspring Bloodlines. And why, after the War, they decided to seal all magic away forever—at least, as much as they could. They thought the Curse and the Well would last forever, so there was nothing else they needed it for, and it was dangerous."

Jae nodded again. So the Highest had turned away from magic, killed any remaining mages they could find—they'd slaughtered the Order, and done the same to every Twill mage they'd run across since.

"I'm sure there's more to it. Lenni says there are still other documents we can translate, now that it's safe to bring them out of hiding. Letters and journals and more," Elan concluded.

"That's good," Jae said.

They fell silent, watching the Well together for a while. It was nice to just sit quietly with Elan. It hadn't happened in so long. Not since before . . .

"I thought you were dead," Jae said at last, forcing out the truth. "And once I knew you weren't, I still thought you were lost."

"You saved my life," Elan said. "You got me out of those chains. I'd have been trampled, even after Erra . . ."

"But I hadn't planned to." Jae swallowed her shame and made herself speak. "I thought saving your life would cost the Closest their best chance at freedom, so I wasn't going to, until Erra surrendered and Lenni thought our best chance was to save her."

"I see," Elan said, and turned to look at Jae. "Forgive the question, but is that why you've been avoiding me?"

"Yes," Jae said. The Curse was gone, she was free, she could lie now. But not to Elan.

Elan was quiet for a long moment, then placed his hand over hers. "Thank you for telling me the truth. I understand why you made that choice. I . . . sort of suspected it, actually, and I was at peace with it. I would have died to save the Closest's freedom. I'm glad I didn't have to, but I would have."

"I wish you hadn't . . . hadn't come so close to needing to."

"That wasn't your fault," Elan said. "And the fact that you told me the truth just now, that you would have sacrificed me to save your people . . . that's why I followed you in the first place. Out here the first time, and everywhere since. Because you're honest and devoted, and you always do what's right. Even when it's hard. Jae, that's why I . . . I still . . ."

He trailed off, and she stared at him. He looked uncomfortable and didn't say anything else.

"I care for you quite a bit," she said at last, remembering what he'd said to her so many weeks ago. She couldn't stand to look at him as she spoke, so she stared up at the cliff face instead, tracing the jagged cracks and the way the colors in it were layered and stacked.

"Yeah, that's what I was trying to say," he agreed. "That's why I still care for you so much."

"No, I meant . . ." She *made* herself look at him this time.

"I meant, *I* care about *you*. I . . . I feel . . . I'd have given anything—almost—to save you. I *wanted* to. I did."

He smiled slowly, like he truly hadn't expected it. Her heartbeat sped up as he raised her hand to his lips and kissed it. She swallowed heavily, feeling a little shaken and unsure, as he lowered her hand again.

"I know you've survived awful things," he said. "Rannith, I mean. And I don't want to . . . It's all right if it . . . if you don't want to . . ."

"I don't want to think about Rannith," she said, though she wasn't sure how not to. Because no one had ever kissed her but Rannith, who had raped her, and then Elan, when she'd panicked. Even now, the thought of Elan kissing her again . . . She didn't know what she felt, but her stomach churned with anxiety. She didn't want to disappoint him, but she didn't know how not to.

"I just meant, if it takes you a long time," Elan said. "I'll wait until you're ready. I'll help you however I can. That's all."

She had to look away and made herself breathe slowly, deeply. Their hands were still joined, and this time she was the one who brought his to her lips. Who kissed his hand gently, and realized it was shaking because her own hand was shaking.

Elan gave it a gentle squeeze, and they sat quietly for a long time, as the sun began to sink. She'd watched the sun set over the Well before, several times since the whole of the world had come out here—and once before that, with Elan and Tal. So long ago, now.

She tore her gaze from it, up to the cliff face, and thought that the cracks and lines of the cliff were almost like Closest art. So subtle no one would even know there was a pattern or picture to it. Except Closest art was meant to be remade over and over again, and something like a cliff was forever. Or so close it didn't make a difference.

She gazed in other-vision. She was weaker now, but earth was still her strongest element, and she could sense the cliff easily enough. She stared at it, willed the lines and the colors to shift. Elan gasped next to her, watching it all change.

Jae wasn't much of an artist, but she knew Tal's face by heart, even now, months later. The lines of the cliff came together, swirling into place to show him as she remembered him: smiling, kind, protective. Here, watching over the Well he'd given his life to.

She didn't know if anyone else would even notice the change, unless they happened to sit here on the landing and look up at it. But that was all right, too. Tal was gone, and all that was left were her memories and his legacy, and that was enough.

As the sun set, she leaned against Elan, surprisingly comfortable with her head on his shoulder, with their fingers tangled together, sitting in silence. Until, at last, she had the energy to stand. "They're probably missing us up in the camp."

"Mostly missing you," he said, smiling, and stood to lead the way. "And dinner would be nice."

She nodded and followed him up, but just for a few steps. Then she stopped.

She looked back once, at the image of Tal hidden in the cliff face, at the Well, at the sky, where a few stars were barely visible on the horizon. Elan waited for her while she took it all in. Then she turned to walk up the steps, to return to the people who needed her and to whom she'd given her life, almost as surely as Tal had given his.

And, for the first time since he'd died, she felt at peace.

Acknowledgments

So you know how conventional wisdom says that writing a book under contract for the first time is the hardest thing ever? It turns out that's totally true, and there are so many people I need to thank for getting me through this.

First, my amazing agent, Hannah Bowman, whose vision for this book was much bigger than mine and who pushed me to get it done. And of course, my fantastic editor, Kate Sullivan, whose encouragement, wisdom, and patience helped me turn this mess into a story. Major thanks to the whole team at Delacorte Press. My experience with these two books has been so wonderful, and I'm eternally grateful.

I have an incredible group of first readers who talked me through multiple drafts and more freak-outs than I can count: Rachel, Jess, and Maddy, thank you for everything. Enormous thanks to Brittney for her vital insight on sensitivity issues. Thanks also to Margot, Jen, and Nicole for the endless cheerleading.

Thank you to my extended family and friends for all the lovely messages and support. Thanks to the amazing YA book blogging community, who are so welcoming to new writers, especially Nori for her incredible enthusiasm and positivity. Finally, a huge thanks to my work family: everyone at Remedy, but especially folks at The Body (past and present) and most especially Myles, Olivia, and Aryeh.

I feel like the orchestra is about to play me off, but seriously: thank you to everyone who read Jae's story, everyone who encouraged me to write it, everyone who emailed or tweeted or otherwise messaged me about their excitement. You are all awesome, and I owe you some serious high fives. Like I said, writing and sharing these two books has been an incredible experience for me. Thank you for being part of it.

Did you miss the beginning of Jae's story?

Turn the page for a special look at
Bound by Blood and Sand.

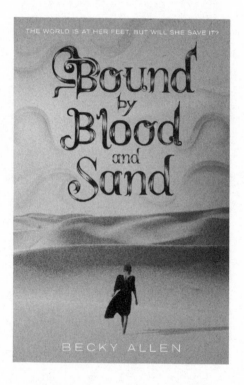

Chapter 1

SOMETIMES, WHEN THE SUN MADE HER DIZZY AND HER SKIN BURNED and peeled and there was no water to spare, Jae thought about revenge. She was in charge of the estate's grounds, and here in the garden, a cactus loomed over her work. Decades old, it overshadowed everything but the fountain. Back when it still rained, the cactus had grown enormous red flowers. Now there was no rain, there were no flowers, but the spines still grew, some of them as long as Jae's hand and as thick as her finger.

She tossed weeds into a sack so she could drag them out back, but she eyed the cactus for a long moment before turning away. She'd never be able to get her hands on a real weapon, but if she ever had a few minutes of freedom from the Curse, she could do damage with one of those spines.

"Jae? *Jae!* There you are! Don't move!"

Jae's body went stone still at the unexpected order, which locked her in place where she knelt. She could only shift her gaze to look up. Lady Shirrad was already moving away from the window she'd yelled from, leaving the faded gold curtains swaying in her wake. So Jae waited, using the moment to catch her breath. As orders went, just waiting wasn't so bad. Not yet, anyway. Though if Lady Shirrad was looking for her, it was to give Jae yet another task.

The Lady strode into the courtyard a minute later, the scent of noxious perfume accompanying her. That meant bad news. Lady Shirrad only covered herself in perfume when there wasn't enough water to bathe. That meant there would be even less water for Jae to use in the garden this evening—and less for Jae and the other Closest to drink.

The sneer on Lady Shirrad's face made her look older than seventeen. She and Jae had been born within a day of each other, but that was all they had in common. Lady Shirrad's features were softer, her skin a lighter brown, and she wore an embroidered red robe with sandals, where Jae had only a stained, shapeless tan dress and bare feet.

Hand on her hip, Lady Shirrad declared, "This garden looks horrible—like it's dead."

Jae just waited, still kneeling. The Curse didn't allow her to speak in front of anyone Avowed unless it was to answer a direct question. Lady Shirrad was right, though. The courtyard garden wasn't much to look at anymore—an open, square space in the middle of the building, with red and orange rocks ringing the cactus and a few scraggly bushes. The bushes' leaves were brown now, dying, just like the few tufts of grass that had fought their way up through the stones and sand.

Jae could just remember the way grass had covered the whole courtyard when she'd been a child, and that there had been real flowers. Those had died off years ago. Years before *that*, according to her mother, the fountain set back in one corner of the courtyard had actually worked, with fresh water flowing down into its trough, free for anyone to drink—even the Closest. Now the fountain was just an oddly shaped sculpture of four columns overlapping one another and linked together in the middle, representing the four elements that mages had once called upon for magic.

"I have guests coming, and it can't look like this when they arrive. What can you do about it?" Lady Shirrad continued.

Jae braced herself as she answered. The Curse forced all of the Closest to tell the truth as well as they knew it, but the truth didn't always make Lady Shirrad happy. This certainly wouldn't: "Without more water, I can't do anything at all, Lady."

Lady Shirrad narrowed her eyes, an expression that was usually accompanied by a sharp slap. But thankfully, she only said, "Then use what you need to, but don't you dare waste a single drop."

The weight of the order gripped Jae like stone sandals, so heavy that she'd barely be able to trudge forward until the order was completed or lifted.

"I can't have Aredann looking like this when they arrive. I don't even want to *think* about it. Do you understand?" Lady Shirrad demanded.

"Yes, Lady," Jae said, understanding what mattered: the order she'd been given, and that Lady Shirrad would be even more frantic and impossible than usual until her guests had come and gone again. Lady Shirrad had been Aredann's Avowed guardian—its absolute ruler—since her father had passed away when she was thirteen, and she hadn't had many visitors since. No one seemed to want to travel as far as Aredann, especially during the drought.

"Good. Now get to it." Lady Shirrad started back to the arched entryway, but then paused, her hand on her hip and her sandal tapping against the floor. "Do you know where your brother is?"

A bone weariness, worse than any day under the sun, wrapped itself around Jae's shoulders at the thought of Tal and Lady Shirrad. At least this truth came easily. "No, Lady."

Lady Shirrad gave her one last scowl at the negative response, then swept out, her swirling robe kicking up dust. Jae finally straightened up, her body protesting the change in position. She took a moment to stretch as she decided how she'd go about her work. The Curse would give her that much freedom, at least. As long as she was working, obeying Lady Shirrad's orders, she could do what she wished.

She stooped to pick up the last few weeds that had escaped her, annoyed at how those could grow even ages after the last proper plants had died. She'd want them all gone before she claimed one of the clay water jugs from the basement to use on the bushes and grass. There was no point in watering weeds.

At least Lady Shirrad had allowed her the water she needed. After a year of giving Jae only smaller jugs or water skins, barely enough to keep the garden alive, Jae could now use whatever she required. But rather than being a relief, that tiny bit of freedom left Jae dry, brittle. More water for the garden meant less for the livestock and the fields, less for cooking, less for bathing and cleaning. Less to drink. There simply wasn't enough to go around, and Lady Shirrad's order meant she cared more about impressing her guests than she did about keeping the Closest slaves from getting sunsick as they worked.

The garden's life was more important than Jae's own. Jae glanced at the overgrown cactus again as she hauled the sack of weeds out, stooping under the weight of her orders, and under the weight of the Curse of obedience that compelled all Closest.

The sinking sun stained the garden bright orange, and Jae shielded her eyes. Even her dark skin practically glowed under the intense light as she set about watering the garden, trying to save the dying grass.

In a landscape of unbroken browns and tans, under a sky that was endless blue all day and star-speckled black at night, green was the color of wealth. Green meant thriving plants, which meant thriving people.

The grass was brown. Jae frowned at it, dizzy for a moment, and sagged against the fountain until the spinning sensation passed. She heaved a deep breath, willing herself to move, to just get back to work. She had to return the rest of the water, the little bit that sloshed at the bottom of the massive jug. But the water was so tempting. . . .

A shadow flickered at the arched entryway into the courtyard. She reached for the jug, willing whoever it was to go about their business and not bother her. But the person stepped into the garden silently—barefoot, not causing the pebbles to grind. Jae's gaze flicked sideways, and she was relieved to see it was only Tal, her brother.

He caught her glancing, and smiled, then waved with an open hand, which signaled that no Avowed were near enough to see or hear him. It would be safe for them to talk. Even so, he walked toward her silently, and then stopped next to her on the path, brushing his hand against her elbow in a silent greeting.

They were twins, but he moved through the world with an ease she'd never mastered. It was in the way he glided from the doorway to join her; it was how he sat near her, light and relaxed, as if the Curse didn't weigh him down at all.

He nudged her elbow again, and when she glanced down at his hand, he opened his palm to reveal a date. He pressed it into her hand and murmured, "You look exhausted."

She had to lean in to hear him, and she chewed the fruit for a second before answering, "I've been outside all day. Be careful. Lady Shirrad was looking for you."

"I know, but she just keeps missing me." He gave Jae a sideways smirk. Lady Shirrad adored Tal, treated him with kindness she never bothered to show anyone else. He was the only one of the Closest who ever ate or drank his fill, a privilege he earned by smiling to Lady Shirrad's face and saving his scorn for when her back was turned. But he used her favor to get away with scrounging up the few scraps he could, and he shared these first with Jae and then with the other Closest. Sometimes Jae thought his position as the most favored of the

Closest was the only thing that had saved her from dying of exhaustion or sunsickness.

"Lucky you," she said. She didn't know how he managed it. The Curse would never allow them to lie with words, so Tal used his body instead, acting for all the world as if he adored Lady Shirrad. His smile was his only weapon, but he wielded it ruthlessly.

She didn't have Tal's advantages. They looked similar enough, but the sharp features that were handsome on him were awkward and boyish on her. Tal was gorgeous and knew it; Jae was a mess of scraped hands and gangly limbs. Where he wore his hair in long curls, bound at the nape of his neck, she kept hers cropped almost to her scalp. Considering that she was nearly as flat and curveless as he was, only the fact that she had a dirt-stained dress instead of loose pants made it clear from a distance that one of them was a girl.

She stood and took a step toward the jug, but the dizziness hit again. She paused, waiting for the sensation to pass, but Tal was at her side this time. He guided her back to the fountain carefully, his hand gentle on her arm. While she waited for the world to stop spinning, he grabbed the smaller water skin she'd been using for the plants and held it out to her. He pressed it into her hands, urging her to drink.

She tried to push it back, turned away, as if not seeing it would suppress the longing. "Not allowed," she said, mouthing the words because her throat was too dry to do much else.

He understood anyway, frowned, and didn't let her release her grip on the skin. "Tell me if the Lady actually said that."

She didn't have to obey an order from him, another

Closest, but if she didn't answer, he'd ask it as a question. The Curse *would* force her to answer that. No matter who asked, the Closest were compelled to answer all questions. So, to spare herself, she said: "She ordered me not to waste any. Tal, I have to work."

"I know, I know," he said. "Traitor's blood means a lifetime of toil. But you *can't* toil if you die of sunsickness. So you have to drink. She might as well have ordered you to."

Jae shook her head. If Tal explained that to Lady Shirrad, the Lady would laugh and let him drink what he wanted. If Jae tried to explain it, the best she could hope for was that Lady Shirrad would roll her eyes and tell her to get back to work. Jae knew full well what the lady had meant by her order.

But Tal was right. Lady Shirrad hadn't actually ordered her not to drink, and Jae couldn't work like this. If she got dizzy again, she'd probably spill all the water she had left, and that really would be a waste.

Hands shaking, she brought the skin up to her lips, telling herself that Tal was right. If drinking allowed her to obey, then drinking *was* obedience.

The Curse allowed her to drink. When it didn't immediately punish her, she swallowed greedily, nearly draining the whole thing before she stopped. It was like breathing for the first time all day.

When she was done, Tal pulled the skin closed and set it aside for her. She shot him a grateful look but said, "I still have work to do. The front path is a mess."

"I'll help."

"The Lady will see you out there," Jae said.

"She'll find me eventually anyway," he said, his head so

close, it nearly touched hers. "I might as well help you in the meantime."

Jae hesitated, torn. She wanted the help, anything to make the work go faster. Anything that would keep Lady Shirrad from deciding that Jae hadn't done a good enough job. But at the same time, she knew what Lady Shirrad wanted Tal for. The same looks and charm that won him relative freedom came at the price of him having to hold his smile when she brushed her fingers over his cheek.

Tal caught her gaze, gold-flecked eyes sincere. "Don't worry about me. I can handle the Lady," Tal said, then stood and offered Jae a hand up.

She ignored it and stood on her own, guilt warring with anxiety in her gut. Accepting Tal's help would practically offer him up to Lady Shirrad for the evening, but without his help she'd be working all night. All she wanted in the world was to rest. But Tal was her brother.

"Jae," Tal finally said, barely audible. He wasn't smiling at her, pretending things were fine. He was as tired as she was, but he was still waiting for her. "Ask me if I mind helping you."

She shook her head. She didn't have to ask; he wouldn't have offered to answer if he didn't mean it. And while he might find ways to twist the words of his answers when Lady Shirrad asked him questions, he wouldn't do that to Jae, so she nodded, trusting him.

Tal helped her for as long as he could, until Lady Shirrad came out to find him and lead him away. He brushed a hand against Jae's shoulder as he left, a silent goodbye. That left her on her own, working until the moon rose and the temperature dropped, and finally there was nothing else that had to be done immediately and the Curse would allow her to rest.

The Closest's quarters were dark and quiet. They were tucked away in a corner of the house, rooms with low ceilings and few windows, where the Closest ate, slept, and gathered in their few free moments. The rooms had housed paid Twill servants once, but as the drought had gotten worse, fewer Twill had been willing to stay at Aredann. Jae had occasionally overheard some of the Avowed complaining that it was disgusting to allow traitorous bloodlines to live under the same roof they did, yet somehow, she'd never heard them complain about having Closest slaves to replace their servants.

The Closest's main room had ancient, stained squares of carpet covering most of the floor, layered over one another so that no one would have to sit on the bare stones. There was a small fire pit where they could cook, and a stone cistern that sat empty. People gathered near enough to the fire to see each other, close enough to hold murmured conversations.

Tal was kneeling in front of an old woman named Asra, her hands in his—Jae had to walk close before she could see he was applying a salve to burned skin on her hands. Jae had no idea how he'd gotten it, when he couldn't even speak to ask Lady Shirrad for it, and she didn't dare ask him. She didn't know whether he was really stealing, and as long as she didn't find out for certain, that was the truth she'd be able to tell if she was ever asked.

Tal saw her and mouthed "Hello" then stood. "You might as well keep the rest of that, in case you need it," he said to

Asra, and then joined Jae. "I'm assuming you haven't eaten yet. Come sit with me and Gali while you do."

Jae helped herself to a small portion of the stew that had been left near the fire, then sat with Tal and Gali, another of their friends. Tal was cross-legged, but Gali knelt facing the wall, her fingers brushing across it, painting it with ash and charcoal. The walls in here were plain tan bricks and had been covered in designs for years and years now, drawn over each other, blending together to cover the bricks almost all the way up to the ceiling. It wasn't like the brightly colored Avowed art that adorned most of the halls and rooms in Aredann. Avowed art was always a celebration, eye-catching and beautiful, meant to be kept forever. Closest drawings were subtle, nothing but grays and black, nearly impossible to make out. It would be washed away if they ever had water, and drawn over again and again in the meantime.

Jae sat with her brother and Gali and reached out to lightly touch Gali's elbow. She looked over at Jae and nodded tiredly before getting back to her drawing. This close, Jae could see it was a person in profile—Tal, probably, judging from the hair.

"I was going to go looking for you soon," Tal said. He wasn't loud, but he didn't whisper, either, and a few people glanced over at them. "I was starting to worry you'd never be done."

"So was I." Now that Jae was sitting, her feet throbbed. The idea of standing up again, even just to walk to the smaller room where her sleeping mat waited, was unbearable.

Gali added a detail to the wall. When Jae studied it, she could make out the sharp lines of Tal's nose and jaw. "Today was long," Gali said.

Jae gave her a concerned look, not daring to hint that she'd like to know more. Gali had been selected to join the household because she was pretty, and when her days ran long, it was usually because she'd been called to someone's sleeping chamber, another order the Curse wouldn't let her disobey, another punishment for crimes that had been committed generations ago. It happened to all of the Closest who worked in the household.

When Lord Rannith had summoned Jae, it had been the only time she'd fought to disobey an order, struggled against the Curse's grip—not that struggling had done any good. If she ever had even a heartbeat free from the Curse, Rannith was the person she'd seek out with her cactus spine. But Gali caught her glance and shook her head.

"I'm fine," Gali said. "The Lady wanted everyone's sleeping mats cleaned, and all of their blankets. It's the first time in weeks. And there's no water."

"It's the same everywhere, even the garden, I think," Tal said.

Jae nodded. "I was told to use whatever I need. But I don't know where she thinks the water will come from."

"The Well will provide, as long as the Highest rule," Gali intoned, rolling her eyes as she mimicked the serious tones Lady Shirrad's advisors used when they said that. And they always said that. Even now, in the midst of a drought and with their reservoir dropping lower and lower.

The Highest still ruled, but the Well barely seemed to provide anything. Maybe that was what the Highest intended, at least for the Closest, but the rest of Aredann wasn't descended from traitors. Jae couldn't believe that an Avowed guardian like Lady Shirrad would be left to suffer.

"Listen."

The word all but echoed in the room. There was no compulsion behind it from the Curse, but the entire room went silent. Jae scowled as she turned to look at Firran, the Closest who'd spoken and who was now standing by the fire pit. Years ago, Lady Shirrad's father had appointed Firran their leader, so that the Lord would only have to speak directly to one Closest. Firran had snapped up that scrap of power like one of the dogs Lady Shirrad's family used to keep. When he spoke, it was always loud and demanding—orders like most Closest would never give one another.

Even aside from the order, he wasn't exactly polite. Closest always shared what they knew with one another; it made all of their lives easier. But they didn't go demanding and interrupting, or speaking in the loud tones of the Avowed.

Still, the rest of the Closest now gathered around Firran, knees touching, sweaty shoulders brushing, as closely as they could. Firran didn't mind raising his voice, but the rest of the Closest preferred the quiet.

Except Tal.

"What is it?" he asked, smirking a little, meeting Firran rudeness for rudeness. Closest didn't order each other around, and they *never* asked each other questions.

Firran glared at him as he was compelled to answer, "I know who Lady Shirrad's visitor is." He waited a moment, and when no one else interrupted him, he continued in that same booming, pompous tone. "He is the son of one of the

Highest, the grand warden of all reservoirs—Elan Danardae. His father sent him to tour Aredann to see our plight."

"They already know our plight," Gali muttered, not quite loud enough for Firran to hear—but Tal stifled a laugh. Jae stayed silent but had to agree. The Highest were the ones who'd cursed them, generations ago, when the Closest's ancestors had rebelled. If they were sending someone to visit Aredann, it definitely didn't have anything to do with the Closest's desperation.

"No wonder the Lady was in such a tizzy today," one of the others said. "But it's good news, if the Highest are finally coming to our aid."

"But they aren't," Firran said, some of the bluster dropping from his voice. "Lord Hannim told Lady Shirrad that there are other estates like Aredann, where the reservoirs are going dry. There's not enough water, not even in the whole Well, so some estates are being cut off."

"But there's *always* been enough," Asra said, voice creaky and unsure, as someone else said, "They can't just cut off whole estates," and someone else snapped, "I don't understand; talk sense!"

Firran held up his hands, waiting for the commotion to work itself out. "They say there are too many people in the world now, more than ever before, and that's why there's not enough water anymore. All of the wardens agree, the Well can't sustain everyone. So some estates . . . The Highest have decided to leave some estates entirely, take their Avowed and even the Twill and leave the rest of us here to die in the drought."

This time, no one seemed to know what to say. It made a

sickening, twisted kind of sense. If there were too many people in the world, then of course the Closest would be the ones left to die, to bring that number back down. Their ancestors had been spared all those years ago, allowed to live as slaves, so long as they were cursed so they could never rebel again — but the Highest would never hesitate to trade Closest lives for the rest of the world.

"That can't be," Tal said finally, standing, but even he sounded shaken. "Lady Shirrad would never leave Aredann to be abandoned."

"You mean Lady Shirrad would never leave *you*," Firran said. "They certainly won't take the rest of us Closest."

"She would never leave *Aredann*," Tal repeated. "And the Well will provide. It has to. The Highest will make it."

Firran shook his head. "Believe what you will, but I know what I heard. If the Highest order it, Lady Shirrad will have to obey. They'll send the water somewhere else, Aredann will turn to dust without it, and we'll all die here."

Tal shook his head, but he didn't argue. There was no point. Firran was telling the truth as well as he knew it. He spent more time with Lady Shirrad than any of the rest of them, even Tal, and he overheard all of the Avowed's business. Jae didn't like him, but she also didn't doubt him. And if what he'd heard was true, then soon — maybe only days from now — all of the Closest at Aredann would be left alone, without the protection of the Well, and with no water, in the middle of a drought.

"Come to bed," Gali murmured, wiping her sooty hand on her dress and leaving a smudged handprint, a new stain on a garment that hadn't been cleaned in months. She offered that same hand to Tal, who accepted it but looked at Jae. He nodded toward the chamber they shared with a few others.

Jae followed them slowly, stiff and sore in a hundred different places, still thirsty and too warm after her day in the sun. Tomorrow would be just as bad, or worse. And so would every day after—somehow, it always seemed as if things got worse. Every day was hotter, drier, and longer, and the Curse had no mercy.

She thought about that as she lay down on her sleeping mat, a few hand spans from where Tal and Gali were now intertwined, exchanging comforting words so low that Jae couldn't make out what they were saying.

Without the Well's protection, the Closest would die in days, of sunsickness if not thirst. But if the Avowed all left Aredann, then there would be no one to give the Closest any orders. For those few, precious days, it would be almost like they were free. And maybe a few days of freedom would be better than a lifetime spent as a slave.

About the Author

Becky Allen grew up in a tiny town outside Ithaca, New York. She works at TheBody.com, an online HIV educational resource, where she is the website director. She lives in Manhattan with her sister, Rachel, and their cat, Lily. It was a conversation with her sister about irrigation that inspired Becky to wonder about a fantasy world where irrigation was fueled by magic and what that would mean. Their discussion became *Bound by Blood and Sand* and its sequel, *Freed by Flame and Storm*.